Tremauré Reborn

Tey Kins

This is another great story to come from Tey Kins. This is my third story and first novel to date. I have many more stories to come, some just like this one and others that have my own flair for story telling. I all hope that you enjoyed reading The Last Day of and The Swampmire Inn, if not then grab you a copy today.

Cover by: Taracu_art

ISBN 979-8-89269-649-4

This book is dedicated to
Mrs. Silver, thank you for believing in this book
and me from the day I started it.

and

Carol, thank you for enjoying my stories. I
wish you could have read this one before you
left us.

Table of Contents

Chapter 1 …………..…...……...……….. Page 1

Chapter 2 …………….…...…………..… Page 19

Chapter 3 …….....……..……...….……… Page 35

Chapter 4 …………….…...………....…… Page 56

Chapter 5 …….....……..………...….…… Page 71

Chapter 6 ……………..…...………...…… Page 93

Chapter 7 …….....……..…...……...…….. Page 106

Chapter 8 …....……..…....……..……… Page 121

Chapter 9 …....……..…....……..……… Page 134

Chapter 10 …………….…...…………… Page 149

Chapter 11 …………….…...……...…… Page 171

Chapter 12 ……….....……..…………....... Page 182

Chapter 13 ……………….....…...……… Page 199

Chapter 14 …………………………..…… Page 217

Chapter 15 …………………..……….. Page 240

Chapter 16 …………………....……….. Page 260

Chapter 17 …………………..………... Page 281

Chapter 18 ………………………….… Page 305

Chapter 19 …………………..……….. Page 326

Chapter 20 ………………………….. Page 343

Chapter 21 …………………………. Page 358

Prologue

What is control?
Is it something that can simply be done or is it something that has to be learned? Those who have it tend to live long healthy lives,but also have something deeper lurking inside.There is such a thing as too much control to the point where there's nothing but an empty void. The concept of control is to suppress one's animalistic or true tendencies.
What if the beast inside was real?
The beast inside has to be controlled because if it's not, it will always win and you'll ultimately lose your humanity.

I've spent years suppressing the wolf inside of me until it was necessary.
When is it necessary, is the real question.

Chapter 1

No matter how a person attempts to plan for their life, it doesn't always go to plan. I thought I was supposed to be like everyone else, go to college, get a degree, a good job, and then get married before having a few kids. That's...*normal,* in my opinion. I thought my life was going to be like every other person's, however, I have a not so normal secret.

I awake to the sounds of birds chirping and the sun glimmering through the blinds of my bedroom. I check my phone and see a few messages from my girlfriend Catalina and my friend Jakobe. Her message states that she's excited to see me. While Jakobe's message reminds me he'll be coming over in a few hours. I sit up on my bed before getting dressed for the day. A few hours later, I hear a knock at my door. I walk over to check the door and see it's Jakobe.

After I open the door, he speaks to me, "Damn bro, you look rough," he says walking through the door and picking his hair.

"Yea I know, I didn't get much sleep last night," I respond.

"You weren't online last night, I thought Catalina sunk her claws into you," he laughs.

"Nah, that's tonight," I laugh back.

He and I sit on my couch reminiscing about the next few months. He's going to the military, while I'm going to college. A few hours go by and we've been talking while playing video games. Somehow, the topic of our childhood comes up and Jakobe mentions what happened when we were kids.

"Remember how freaked my dad and your mom got?" Jakobe asks, laughing.

"How could I forget?" I answer. "It damn near took an entire chunk out of me."

"Yea, but it didn't. We were sure you were going to turn into a werewolf," Jakobe says, snickering.

"If only, then my life would have something interesting happen. Besides a black werewolf where do they do that at?" I ask. "Two things wrong with your theory, one I would have bit you already and we'd be two black werewolves and two, isn't it already too late? That was so long ago. If I was, we'd see something by now."

"Yea, I guess you're right," Jakobe laughs as he's looking at the clock. It's almost 7. "Oh shoot, I gotta get home. I promised my parents I'd watch my lil bros so they can go out tonight."

"Ight man, I'll see you later," I say back. "Don't forget you're covering for me, right?" I ask, walking him to the door.

"Yea, yea, I know. I'll tell your mom that you're spending the weekend with me, so you can have some *alone time* with Catalina," he responds before closing the door behind him.

I can't help but think about the night Jakobe mentioned as I walk to my bedroom. I look into my mirror, "If only I could tell him," I say to myself as my eyes begin to glow golden yellow.

Seeing the light reflect off the mirror and slightly illuminate my brown skin is always interesting. When my eyes glow it always feels more natural than just seeing my natural brown. I thought I'd hate seeing myself this way, but I don't. That attack changed my life and after my first change, I thought my life was ruined, but that's not entirely true. My name is Damien Nichols, and I am a werewolf.

I don't like lying to my friends like Jakobe, my mom, and my girlfriend, but I don't think they'll understand. They'll worry about me and possibly make things worse. Jakobe is one of my best friends and has been since we were kids. However, I don't want to get him or anyone else involved. My eyes go back to normal as I start packing for the weekend with Catalina.

Before I can tell any of them what I've become, I want to see if there is a way to control this. I stop for a moment, looking at all of my notebooks, full of data I've gathered. I've gained some control in the last few years, but I'm still having trouble. I can't seem to find out who bit me, but I'm left wondering why they did so in the first place. What I do know is that I am a danger to myself and others if I can't control the wolf.

I open my laptop to look at the video of last month's change. There's nothing different about last month or the month before. I know I can't stop looking for the werewolf that bit me, if I want a cure. I haven't met many other werewolves, so I'm at a total loss. Most of the time, I stay to myself out of fear, though I've longed for more.

I used to wish I could find the one who bit me and ask them why and, if possible, punish them for ruining my life. I didn't want this curse, I wanted them to take it back or tell me the cure. So far, nothing I've found can tell me how to get rid of lycanthropy. Why did they do this to me? Why did they want to turn me into a killer?

So many questions, but not enough answers. I stand up from my desk, close my laptop, and put away my notes, so my mom wouldn't find them. I then go back to packing, gathering my toothbrush and deodorant. That's the way I used to feel, now, the only thing I want to do is to thank them. My life has changed for the better since I turned for the first time two years ago. I'm stronger, smarter, faster, and more confident than I have ever been before. It would take all day to list all the things that were wrong with me, but to name a few, I was uncoordinated, clumsy, I'd get panic attacks, and I'd get sick like every other week if I went outside.

I walk over to the night stand that holds many unopened, prescription bottles, "I don't know why I even refill these," I say, slightly agitated. "I haven't used any of them in years." I take them out of the drawer and take them out front to happily empty each bottle in the trash can.

I walk back into the kitchen for a bottle of water where I see a note from my mom on the fridge, telling me she'll see me when she gets back. My Mom works a lot of nights, so I can hide this from her. I've never met my father, so he wouldn't care either way. I know it's not the best idea to suffer in silence, but honestly who can I tell? And if I do, who's going to believe me?

As I head back to my bedroom, I'm wondering if I can learn to control this on my own. In trying to do so I've become an introvert, so I won't hurt anyone. So far I've somewhat learned how not to change on a full moon, so I figure that tonight I can visit Catalina and I can be a normal boyfriend for once. I zip up my suitcase and go back down the stairs, locking the front door as I leave before getting into my car.

On the way to Catalina's house, I keep thinking about the first time I changed. I often thought about ending myself due to the amount of pain I'd go through during each shift. However, as time passed, the pain also subsided. I realized that I can't bring myself to do it. Something inside told me to endure it.

My fingers grip the steering wheel tightly as flashes of memories of my first change run through my head. During those first two changes, I wanted someone to kill me. It felt like my body was on fire. Hair growing and protruding from my skin that feels like red-hot needles coming from the inside. My bones

5

break and reshape themselves. A pain I can only attribute to being mauled, but from the inside. It was so bad that I was sent groveling into the ground every time.

I typically get fragments of memories, of either running through a field or hunting, never more than a short flash of info. I always remember the wind rustling through my fur and the feeling of wanting to hunt for food. I don't like hurting animals, I love them, except for cats, they hated me before I became a werewolf.

The memories come to the forefront of my mind. The feeling of my paws hitting the ground with the raw power I'm granted under the full moon makes me feel like the apex predator.

The wolf's presence becomes very prominent, I look into the rearview mirror and see my eyes flashing yellow. I quickly shut them after pulling over to the side of the road. My heart is pounding in my chest. It feels like I'm about to shift right here in the car. I take a few deep breaths to calm myself down. I sit up in the driver's seat, before pulling down the visor for a second look. My eyes are back to normal.

"Is this really the best time to see Catalina with the full moon being tomorrow night?" I ask myself. "I'm fine, I was okay with the last full moon, so this one shouldn't be any different."

I look up ahead, and see a dead deer on the highway. It reminds me of the first time I woke up next to the animal carcass. I couldn't believe my eyes.

There was blood all over my hands, mouth and chest. Even after I got home and washed it off, I could still smell the blood for a few days afterward. It honestly seems to never wash off. My senses are heightened whether I'm turned or not. They're always amped, I can smell a squirrel fart a mile away.

A few months later, after realizing that my life wasn't ruined, I decided to try to learn to control the change or at least try to. This is my life and my body. Is what I thought. So I began taking the necessary steps to try controlling the wolf. I had no idea that I could, but what else could I do?

The first step was to see what I looked like when I transformed, so I found an abandoned den in the woods and set up a camera. When I wolf out, I turn into a hulking wolf, with wolf legs, human hands, arms and torso, and human head with a wolf's snout. I looked like the werewolf from Van Helsing. The first thing I noticed were my eyes. They were glowing an amazing golden yellow color that lit up the room. The light reflected off of them is just like you'd see on any other animal.

It was painful to watch myself transform for the first time. I heard my screams morph into howls, my bones breaking and reshaping, turning me into an unrecognizable entity. I shivered thinking about it, but that's not enough to stop me from doing what needed to be done.

I got back onto the road and for the remainder of the drive to Catalina's I remember how much I've prepared for this. All the time I've spent nerding out, studying to understand the wolf before and after I turn. I seriously doubted that I could learn to control it in the beginning, but I wanted to control it and so far my track record is pretty good.

"I can do this," I acknowledge as I look at a picture of Catalina and me on my phone. "I can have one normal weekend with my girlfriend and nothing will go wrong. You got this."

I watch the surrounding cars. These people know nothing about the monster that lurks within me. I desperately want to tell Catalina because I feel that I can trust her. We've been together a little over a year now so she should be one of the few people who know, Right? I figure that when I'm finally able to control this I'll tell her.

"Should I tell Catalina this weekend while I'm over?" I ask myself as I'm entering her neighborhood." "I have no idea how she's going to react. If I do, we could take the time to go over everything," I contemplate.

I'm filled with the anticipation of just having the weekend alone, just me and her. Unfortunately, the full moon is tomorrow and I still don't have full control yet, but I'm very close. After all I've learned about not changing under a full moon I'm confident that I'll be fine. Sometimes, I have trouble keeping my mind at the forefront during a change, and my consciousness takes a second to take control.

I text Catalina that I'm around the corner. 30 seconds later, I hear her front door open and her stepping outside. There's a slight breeze allowing me to smell her perfume, even though I'm two blocks away. I love being a werewolf sometimes. These heightened senses are amazing. If and when I do learn to control this fully, I'll never have to worry about anything ever again.

When her house comes into view, I see her standing there in her favorite dress, smiling. A smile that can warm anyone's heart. The tenderness of her presence exudes everywhere. I love seeing her caramel skin and thick curly hair that lay on her shoulders. It doesn't matter if I'm man, beast or something in between. I know that I want to be with her no matter what the cost.

"Hey there stranger," Catalina giggles as I park in the driveway.

"Hey yourself," I reply. "I was wondering if you can help me. I'm looking for the best place in town where a guy can rest his weary head."

Catalina bites her lip, "I think I know just the place. Come right on in and I'll see what I can find for you."

"Well thank you for your kindness ma'am, I think I'll take you up on that," I say, in a southern drawl.

Catalina's attempts to hold in her laughter falters, "I can't with you. Get in here," I nod and we head inside. "Put your bag in my room. I'm making dinner, it should be ready soon."

Everything is going so smoothly and that makes me feel all the more guilty for not telling her that I'm a werewolf. An hour later, we're sitting at the table for dinner laughing and joking about school, friends and talking about our relationship. We've been together for a year so I guess it was time for the talk right? After dinner, we sit on the couch and turn on a movie. After fifteen minutes or so, I put my arm around Catalina who straddles me, smiling innocently.

"Oh we're starting already?" I chuckle.

"Did you really think we were just gonna watch the movie?" she puts my hands on her butt.

"No, but I thought we'd get further into the movie," I laugh.

"Well, I could just get off and we could continue watching if that's what you want."

I grin and stand up, holding her in the air, "I got a better idea."

"Ooh my strong man," she moans excitedly.

I carry her to her room, and on the way is when I realize that she isn't wearing anything under her dress. She isn't the only one planning for tonight. I get excited, as a huge smile appears on my face.

Once we were in her room, she drops her dress, where I can see her beautiful body. I step closer as I slowly caress her forearm. We kiss for a few minutes and in less than that we're going at it like rabbits. A little while after, we take a shower to clean up and head back downstairs where we notice the movie is still playing.

10

I laugh, "You wanna go back to the beginning?" I pause the movie and look at Catalina, "It's about an hour and a half in."

"Yea, we probably should," Catalina responds.

It's getting late at this point and instead of watching the movie in the living room, we decide to go back up to her room. We're going to watch a few episodes of a show we've been binging with a few snacks. Because of our extracurricular activities, we start to fall asleep right around the first episode. I hear Catalina snoring, and I smile as I look at her before kissing her forehead. Then I turn off the TV and go to sleep.

The next morning when I awake, I reach for her, but she's not there. I check my phone and see that it's 10 A.M. I then smell eggs and pancakes. Catalina is downstairs humming as she's cooking breakfast.

"Damn, she beat me to it," I say to myself.

I get up to put on a pair of shorts before I walk downstairs. Suddenly, my phone goes off. When I grab it, I see a notification that the full moon is tonight.

"I should be fine, I've been fine for the last few months so far, but I should still tell her," I say to myself. "I will soon enough, just let me get past this full moon, please."

I proceed to walk downstairs and into the kitchen. I see Catalina cooking in one of my shirts, "Well, well, well, what do we have here?" I ask, smiling.

"What?" she turns smiling. "I just wanted to do something nice for you."

"Nice for me? You cooked dinner last night," I declared. "I should make you breakfast."

"You're lucky you're cute, remember the last time you tried to cook something?" she mocks.

"Th...that was different," I stammer. "I may have started a lil fire, but I've been practicing since then."

Catalina laughs, "Your mom let you back into the kitchen?"

"It's not that bad," I say, looking at the floor.

"Awwe don't pout Miel, mama's gonna take good care of you," she says while lifting my head, putting my hands on her hips and gyrating them.

I instantly perked up, "I like this."

"That's my strong man, now you can help, but you have to do exactly what I say."

I nod as Catalina tells me everything I can do. She isn't just making pancakes like I thought, she was making breakfast burritos, wrapping in pancakes. They smell so good, I can never figure out how she makes them, but I know I'm happy when they're done and in my belly.

After we eat breakfast, Catalina tells me she's been looking into some things for us to do today and wants my input. Truthfully, I want to just stay in, but I know that isn't an option for the entire weekend.

First, she suggests we head to the mall, then afterward go to lunch. I knew she was going to propose that, but I expect her to propose we go to Macy's or some other place like it. She instead insists that we get some new gear for us to go paintballing after lunch. Then she recommends we go Go Karting before going back home to finish the movie. I smile and kiss her, she's always thinking of me and willing to do some of the things I like.

After breakfast, we go upstairs to get ready for the day, even bringing an extra set of clothes for paintballing. When we get to the mall, Catalina still wanted to look at and buy some clothes. Rather than argue it, I go along because it's more important the time we're spending together.

Eventually, we leave the mall and go paintballing. It's cute to see her shoot the paintballs. I'm surprised when I see her hitting the targets dead on. I smile because she's been practicing and wants to show me. While there, we meet another couple that's looking for a challenge, couple vs. couple. We end up winning because neither of them have the aim that they thought they have. After the game the guy comments on my reflexes and how I always seem to know where he was without trying. He asks if I was in the military, I told him I wasn't, I just got lucky. Thank you werewolf senses and speed.

Afterward, we go to lunch at a nearby ramen restaurant. The food is so good. We've never been there before and never had authentic ramen, so now is as good as any to try the place.

"Wow, that was so good," Catalina says, as we walk from the restaurant.

"Yea it was, I'm full," I say, rubbing my stomach.

"Should we just head over to the racetrack?" she ponders.

"Honestly, I don't know. I'm good with just going back and possibly going tomorrow," I say.

"You sure Abucheo?" she asks in a cute voice.

"Yea I'm sure," I respond. "Yea let's go back. We can go to the track tomorrow and then whatever you want to do."

"Aww Abucheo, ok let's go," Catalina kisses me and we got into the car to drive back to her house.

When we got back, we settle in first before watching a movie. Soon after, we start to prepare dinner. I tell her I'll fix dinner this time since she made dinner last night and breakfast this morning. Even though I'm not the best of cooks, I tell her that I won't burn down the house.

"Mmm, it's smelling good in here, you might know what you're doing after all," Catalina says, as she walks in the kitchen.

"Maybe, but don't distract me," I reply. "I want to get this right for you."

"I'm sure it will be just fine. I can't wait to try it," Catalina encourages.

Twenty minutes later, we're sitting at the table with a glass of wine. When I sit the plate in front of her, Catalina's eyes widen. "You, you really made this?" Catalina asks.

"Yes, I did, don't look so surprised," I snicker.

"Well *sorry.*" she giggles.

We eat dinner, with a piece of chocolate cake for dessert. I clean the dishes and we settle down to finish the movie from last night. I queue up the movie while Catalina makes some popcorn. Everything is going so well. I'm having the normal life I want. I can trust her, can't I? There's no reason I can't. I have to tell her tomorrow for sure. Catalina comes back with the popcorn and we start watching the movie for the third time.

"We're watching the movie this time right?" she asks, smiling.

"Oh yea, for sure no worries," I say smirking, "Though I should be asking you that question."

Since it was still early enough, we were able to watch and finish the movie. By the time it was over, she's lying on my chest, in my arms on the couch watching and that always feels good. Catalina got up to get some more popcorn, I look at the time and the moon should be rising at this point. I don't feel anything wrong, so I lower my guard. The large grandfather clock in the foyer strikes eleven. As the sound rings in my ear, an intense pain strikes me in my right side.

I'm changing, "No, not right now. Ugh," I groan in pain under my breath.

When Catalina comes back into the room, I turn away from her, as my vision starts shifting and my fingers starts to shake. I take a few short breaths trying to reign it in. Somehow I manage to calm myself down and hold back against the change.

"What's wrong?" she asks, concerned.

"Everything is fine. Just an upset stomach," I say with a nervous chuckle.

"Are you sure?" she asks worriedly.

"Yes I'm sure." I slightly groan.

When the pain finally subsides, thinking I suppressed the wolf. I think I'm going to be fine. Before I know it, the clock strikes midnight. This time when the pain returns, it's stronger than before. I'm not sure why, so I stand up and hurry to the bathroom attempting everything I can to hold it back. I hope that there's something else I can do to stop myself. Usually, I can hold the wolf back, no problem, but this time it feels…different…stronger.

"Abucheo, is everything ok?" Catalina asks from outside the bathroom.

"Yea just give me a second," I reply.

"Okay I just wanted to check," she says, as I hear her walk away from the bathroom and back downstairs.

I look in the mirror and my wolf-eyes are showing with their golden yellow glow. I try to bring back my human ones, but that didn't help. I pause to take a few sharp breaths and focus on my breathing. A few minutes go by and I do everything I can to stop me from changing, nothing is helping. It's like the wolf is forcing itself out. The pain only grows instead of subsiding. My teeth start growing in my jaw as they open my mouth. Then my nails start to change into claws.

16

"C'mon, c'mon," I say, concentrating as hard as I can, trying to stop the change, so I can keep myself human. I'm able to stop it for now, but it won't last. I can't stay here. I run out of the bathroom and down the stairs, "Babe, I'm sorry I have to go," I head toward the door.

"Go? Why? What's wrong?" Catalina asks, as she comes over to me concerned.

I hold out my arm, keeping her at a distance. "N... ugh...nothing's wrong, but I have to go."

"Do you want me to come with you? I can help," she asks.

"N...no. I'll be fine, I'll be back soon I promise," I groan.

Before she can say anything else, I grab my jacket and run out the door as fast as I can. When I got outside, I thought of using the car, but I don't want her following me. Instead, I use my wolf speed to run as fast as I can into the woods. I try to stay in the shadows of the night as I pass the cars in traffic. I have to stay focused and not reveal myself. There has to be a safe place so I could change, that's as far from anyone as possible.

I run for twenty minutes, hoping it's far enough. When I got to my spot in the woods, I start to frantically take off my clothes. Before I can get my pants completely off, the pain makes me drop to my knees. The pain is so intense that it's worse than I've ever felt before.

"What is wrong with me?!" I scream. Why is the wolf fighting so hard to get out? It's never done this before. "I thought, I'd gotten used to this, what is going on?!" I ask as I screamed in pain.

Then I hear footsteps behind me. The sound of those steps, that smell...Catalina followed me. I turn around to see her staring at me with a frightened look on her face. I try to keep from facing her.

"Abucheo, what's wrong you're scaring me," she says in a scared tone.

"Catalina, get away from me now!!" I scream in an altered monstrous voice. The sound of my voice makes her take a step back. I can't hold it back any longer. "I didn't want you to find out like this... I'm sorry."

The next thing I know, I'm roaring in the pain of shifting into a werewolf. The hair that grew on my body felt like tiny fiery needles all over. My nose changes into a snout, turning me into the 9ft monster, hunter and killer. The last thing I hear is Catalina screaming.

Chapter 2

The next morning, I wake up in a different part of the woods. The sun shines brightly through the overhead trees. My head is foggy as I sit up trying to focus. Suddenly, the memories of last night come flooding back into my mind. Catalina was there when I changed and I have no idea what happened after. My heart skips a beat. I'm unable to move since I'm frozen in place.

My pulse starts racing as I try to remember what happened to her, but I can't. I'm too afraid to look at my hands or my body in fear that I'll find her blood on me. I know I have to, but I'm hesitant. I love her so much. The last thing I wanted was for her to get wrapped up in this. I've never killed anyone. I don't want to look at myself seeing that I hurt her.

My eyes start tearing up, "Why couldn't you just run when I asked you to? Catalina, what did I do to you?!" I cry out.

"Hmm? Why are you screaming?" I hear her mumble. "It's too early."

Catalina is right next to me and I didn't notice. A huge grin appears on my face, "Baby you're alright!"

I wrap my arms around her and immediately realize that I'm naked and thought to cover myself.

But she's already seen me naked, so there's no reason to worry. I lay next to her in relief and kiss her forehead.

Catalina sits up rubbing her eyes and yawns, "Why are you naked in the woods?"

"Because I don't want my clothes to rip when I turn. You've seen what I turn into. The wolf is a 9-foot monster. I'd rather be naked, then burst out of them."

"Aren't you cold?" she asks.

"Not really. I tend to run a lil warmer than most," I smile.

"Yea I've noticed, how come you never told me?" she questions.

"I didn't want to scare you, do you think it would be that easy to say, '*Hey, Baby by the way I'm a werewolf*'?" I ask.

"Yea, I guess not," Catalina admits.

"Wait a minute…" I puzzle. "Why ain't you dead?"

Catalina stops for a moment, becoming very silent, "I'm not sure…to be honest. When you left last night, and took off running, I had to follow you. I was seriously worried about you. Then when I saw you running faster than cars on the highway and I didn't know what to think. And when I saw turning, you looked like you were in so much pain… I wanted to help…but I wasn't sure how. So when you told me to run, I tried to back away slowly. Then you noticed me after I hit against a tree. You turned and snarled before jumping toward me. I started running away in fear, but you were too fast and caught up to me and

20

tackled me to the ground. You were about to kill me, but I…I don't know… it… it just stopped."

"What? Just stopped" I ask, puzzled.

"Yea, it was about to kill me and I remember screaming your name. It paused for a second, looked in my eyes and I guess a part of you was still inside… and…recognized me. I kept calling your name and you sort of changed. You were still a werewolf…but I could see you in its eyes. The wolf then helped me up, put me on your back and took me around the woods."

"Ok…" I say, a little confused. "I've heard on a few forums that if you call a werewolf by its given name you can help bring it back to its senses, but I thought that was just a rumor. I'm so glad you're ok and I'm sorry I didn't tell you," I hug her. "I wanted to tell you so many times and I was going to today, but surprise…I guess. I still don't have full control yet and sometimes I can hold it back, but other times, not so much."

"This wasn't one of those times was it?" she asks quietly.

"Unfortunately, no. I'm gaining control, but it's still hard. I'm able to use a lot of its strength and speed whenever I want to. Eventually, I do hope to be able to control it indefinitely."

"How do you know you'll be able to?" Catalina asks concerned.

"To be honest, I don't, I've seen it done in movies and they say the longer I fight for control, the more I'll have. I hope I will be able to soon," I explain.

"I hope so too," Catalina tried to sound hopeful, but I can hear the fear in her voice.

"One other question… How'd you catch up to me?" I question.

"When I saw you running, I got in the car and drove after you,"

"You got a lead foot just like your dad," I laugh.

"You know it," she says, smiling.

As we walk back to her car and drive back home, Catalina asks me how I became a werewolf. I tell her the story of how I was bitten and how I didn't turn for the first time until our junior year of high school.

Nine years ago, when I was about ten, I was attacked by an animal. My mom told me it was a timber wolf by how she described it, but I now know it was a werewolf.

I was set to go camping with my friend Jakobe, his father Mr. Jefferson and my friends, Davion, Jamal, and Terrance that summer.

The day before we left I was so excited, we talked about it all school year long. We made sure to pack everything that was needed. Water, extra clothes, food, our tent and sleeping bags. The three of us were so happy to finally see what camping was all about. Though the three of us thought we were helping, Davion's dad. Mr. Jefferson was the one to make sure we actually packed everything. Since we only packed snacks and hugs for the trip.

That night we started everything off right by sleeping over at Davion's. The three of us were too excited to sleep. Going to bed at 9 P.M. probably didn't help either. We had to wake up at 2 the next morning and leave for the campgrounds. Mr. Jefferson commented that leaving early was so we could get a good spot for our tents.

We helped pack everything in the car and then we all slept while he drove. We drove for three hours and just as he predicted, there were already people there. Though it was only two other families. Since there weren't that many people yet, we were able to set up in a good enough spot. Mr. Jefferson saw us getting restless and allowed us to go play with other kids, while he finished setting up the tents.

We went to play at the nearby lake. It was so cool to be in nature. The trees were so big and vibrant. The water in the lake was so clear that I could see all the rocks, the fish, beneath it. Everything was so amazing near the river, I couldn't believe my eyes. Soon after I noticed a small plant. It was different from anything I'd seen before. I bent down to touch it and pick it up.

"Don't!" Mr. Jefferson screamed, stopping me before I could touch it. "Don't you know that you shouldn't touch things especially when you don't know what they are?!"

"Yea, but I just wanted to see what it was," I said.

"It doesn't matter, if you want to touch something out here you ask me first. That's a poisonous flower. I don't want you getting sick on my watch. Leave it alone."

"Okay I will," I said, a little afraid.

He went back to the other adults, while I went back to play with everyone else. A while later, we walked back to the campsite. On the way there, I saw more of those strange plants,

"Look, look there's more of them over there," I said.

Davion and Terrance saw them all over, they told me that they already knew not to touch them. They laughed at me because I got in trouble. I stuck my tongue out at them and told them that they were punks.

We played by the lake for a few more hours and even went fishing. I only caught two, but everyone else caught three or more. Later on, Davion, Jakobe, Terrance, Jamal and I all watched as Mr. Jefferson skinned the fish and cooked them for us to eat. I'd never seen anyone do that before and I was captivated by his skill with a knife. Soon after we ate the fish we made s'mores for dessert.

Once we were full, we played a little with sparklers, and told ghost stories around the fire. Soon enough we were off to bed. Later that night I woke up to use the bathroom. I was a little restless so I thought this might help me sleep. I went to a nearby tree that I thought was just outside the tent to relieve myself. I hadn't realized in my foggy young mind that I wandered off farther than just a tree outside my tent. When I turned around, I saw nothing but the dark woods. I walked for a few minutes and soon reached the lake that we were playing around in. Davion, Terrance and I laid some sticks pointing back to the campsite, in case any of us got lost.

With only the light of the moon and sticks guiding me, I started walking the 5 minutes back. As I made my way back, I heard a crunching behind me. Rather than turning around, I stopped for a moment out of fear. When I didn't hear anything further, I started walking again, but faster. I got the feeling that something was following me, when I heard the sound of growling, so I began to run. I was sure that something was following me. I just didn't know what it was.

I was running for what felt like forever. When I turned back to see what was chasing me. All I saw was big red eyes. Finally, I saw the tents in my sights. It was just past the next few trees. Before I could reach it, I tripped and fell over a root. I tried to get up and run again, but I couldn't because my pant leg was caught on a tree branch. Then I hear a loud snarl. It sounded like it came from all around me.

I looked around, attempting to find out where it was coming from. "Help me!" I cried out as I got my leg free and began to run.

No one was around to hear me when it jumped on me and pinned me down. It snarled before biting me at my side.

"AHHH, somebody save me!!" I screamed.

I looked down and saw blood coming from the wound and its mouth. I soon began to lose consciousness, my vision started to blur. I could barely make it out, but I saw Mr. Jefferson running towards me and shooting at the animal biting me.

"Get away from him, now!" he shouted.

One of the shots struck the monster. It roared in pain and then ran off into the woods.

I then heard Mr. Jefferson firing another shot before rushing towards me, "OH MY GOD, ARE YOU OK? We have to get you to the hospital."

The pain in my side was so unbearable. It sank its teeth so deeply in my side. He picked me up just as I lost consciousness. When I opened my eyes, I had a splitting headache and an intense pain on my side. It was impossible for me to even attempt to sit up. I was in a hospital bed, surrounded by my mom, Mr. Jefferson, Davion, Terrance, Jamal and Jakobe. They were all standing around my bed waiting for me to wake up. When my mom saw me open my eyes, she went to get the doctor, who soon came to see me a few minutes later.

"Well, I'm glad to see you're awake, you gave us all a scare there," he says. "From our recent tests it looks like you're going to make a full recovery."

"Isn't that great?" My mom asked gleefully.

"Mrs. Nichols, your son has such a strong heart that it helped him through the last few nights," he explained.

"What do you mean?" I asked. "How long was I sleep?"

"A few days, we kept you sedated while we were trying to make sure there wasn't any internal bleeding or infection." The doctor walked over to me. "Let me check your bandages and we'll see where we are." He lifted my bandages and had this look on his face. I didn't know what it meant but he didn't look too happy. He grew very silent.

"What is it, doctor?" My mom asked.

"The bite mark seems to have almost completely healed."

"Isn't that a good thing?" asked Jakobe.

"O...of course it is KB," answered Mr. Jefferson.

I still can't figure out why Mr. Jefferson replied to Jakobe the way he did. At the time I thought he'd be happy that I was getting better. Maybe there was something I was missing. The doctor asked for my mom and Mr. Jefferson to talk with him in the hallway. Davion Jamal and Jakobe and Terrance all stayed behind in the room. We ended up watching cartoons while they talked.

After a little while, the three of them came back and I could tell something was off. I couldn't explain it, but I know they were holding onto something that they didn't want to tell me.

The doctor then smiled and said, "Young man there is nothing you have to worry about.

"What's going to happen to me?" I asked. "Am I

going to get rabies?"

"No, no nothing like that," The doctor chuckled. "We're going to give you some vitamins and antibiotics to make sure that you won't get any infections.

Even though my Mom and Mr. Jefferson were smiling, I felt like whatever they talked about was distressing. The doctor then told my mom that they'd need to hold me for another few more days so they could monitor me. I felt like I had ruined the trip and everyone's fun. Mom told me not to worry about it, but that still didn't stop me from feeling responsible.

Mr. Jefferson saw the look of disappointment on my face and told me not to worry about it. He then said we'd try again next year with more traps so nothing like that would happen again.

A week following the attack, I was sent home and I thought everything was going fine. My side wasn't hurting anymore and I was taking all the vitamins that the doctor prescribed. A little while after the wolf bite, I noticed that I no longer required my inhaler or any of my medications. I felt stronger, healthier and overall better than I had ever had in my life.

My coordination was better and I wanted to be outside and enjoy myself. I felt better than ever. I asked my mom about going to the park but she insisted that I stay inside for a little while longer. I liked this feeling and I wasn't sure why she wouldn't let me outside. I was able to smell and hear better than ever before.

When the other kids in the neighborhood found out about my accident they started calling me Wolf Boy. It wasn't the best nickname, but I supposed it was better than them mocking me for being weak right? Some of them avoided me, because they thought I had rabies while others thought I'd become a werewolf. For a little while, it was fun to be getting attention from the other kids.

One morning, I was awoken by the sound of a car horn. It made me jump out of bed, because it sounded like it was right in front of me. I looked outside, but I couldn't see anything. Which was weird, because I could have sworn that the car was out front. Then I heard the sound of a truck backing up BEEP, BEEP, BEEP. It rang in my ears, like it was out front of me.

I covered my ears attempting to muffle the sound and looked outside. Again there was nothing there or down the street. I tried to ignore it, but I couldn't. After the sound of the truck, I heard people talking. It was so loud that it was hard to focus. No matter how hard I tried, I couldn't ignore the sound. I had to find out where it was coming from.

I got dressed, put on my glasses and went to brush my teeth. Just after I finished brushing my teeth and spit out the last sip of water, I noticed my K9s were slightly elongated. Highly tempted, I touched the tips of each one and they felt like the end of a knife. I looked at my finger and saw a small amount of blood. I had pricked my finger on my own teeth.

Shocked, I looked back at my teeth and they were

back to normal. I wiped my hand with toilet paper and continued. I thought about telling my mom, but I didn't think she would believe me since there wasn't any more blood coming from my finger. Afterward, I went outside to find out where the sound was coming from. I didn't know it at the time, but this was the first and last time my werewolf hearing was at 100%, before I had my first change. I walked around attempting to find the source of the sounds.

Before I knew it, I walked about three blocks trying to find what I was looking for. I was hearing people move into their new house, something that was happening three blocks away, I heard like it was right in front of me. I saw a man and a woman guiding the movers on where to put all the boxes and furniture.

I didn't know why I could hear them moving in and I still questioned it up until my first change. The only answer I've been able to come up with is that my body was preparing for the change and it delayed it. That's when I felt a small breeze and I caught wind of something. I wasn't sure if it was the smell of lotion, shampoo, or even the flowers being planted, but I was excited to find out.

I pursued the smell and it led me even closer to the house of the people moving in. The scent led me directly in front of the house, since it had just rained the night before and the grass was still pretty wet, great for planting flowers into the ground. The combination of rain water and the flowers that were in front of the house were amazing. The wonderful smell was coming from the front yard. This house used to belong to Mr. Cooper and now it belongs to these people.

That's when I saw Catalina for the first time. Whenever I'm around Catalina, this is what I smell. It's such a pleasant one. Her mom loves to grow these flowers. and it always follows her. Catalina noticed me while she was playing with her dog when she looked in my direction. She tried to get her dog to come over to me, but he was afraid of me. It refused to move from that spot. I wasn't sure of why then, but now I know it's more likely due to me being a werewolf.

"Hi my name is Catalina, and I just moved here from Boston," she says with a smile. "What's your name?"

At first, I was astounded at just the sound of her voice. I'll never forget it, she sounded so kind. Nothing has changed about her since then. I immediately developed my crush on her from that point on. It took a few seconds, but I was able to muster up the courage to introduce myself.

"My name is Damien Nichols, I live down the street," I blurted out. "I live a few blocks from here."

"Is there any cool places to play? Like…any parks?"

"Yea!" I say excitedly. "There's a park and there's a playground at the school I go to,"

"Cool! Could you show me?" her eyes lit up.

"Y… Yea I guess I can," I muttered.

Suddenly her mom came up to us, "Hey Cat, who's

your little friend?" she asked.

"His name's Damien." she responds, "He says he lives down the street."

"Hi Damien, nice to meet you. I'm sure you two will be close friends," her mom says smiling.

Her mom told me that Catalina would be starting school with me in the fall and hoped I could show her around. She was almost right. We started out as friends, but after a few years we somewhat drifted apart. She got really popular where I didn't. Though I was involved in some school activities, I wasn't as much as she was. I never stopped liking her. I just waited until I felt I could ask her out and when the time came, I did and she says yes.

Catalina's mom went back to assist with the movers and her gardening, leaving us to talk for a little while longer. She asked for us to stay in the front yard where she could see us. We were only able to play for a short amount of time because my senses were still in overdrive and other things started to happen.

First it started with my vision. I was seeing things weirdly and I'd rub my eyes trying to get it back, but it would shift back and forth. When my vision went back to normal we would play some more. I'd get distracted soon because my hearing would go in and out and I'd hear buzzing and I would swap away bugs that weren't there. It happened so much that Catalina made weird faces at me.

I could smell car exhaust, trash and so many more

things that weren't even near us. I couldn't take it anymore. I told Catalina that I was feeling sick so I wouldn't make her feel like it was something she was doing when I covered my nose. I used to like the smells of my neighborhood, but started to hate it. I sprinted home and locked the door. Spending the rest of the day in my room.

Later on in the night I started to feel sick and I started to get a headache. I told my mom and she gave me something for it. I put the covers over my head and went to sleep. I ended up sleeping for the rest of the day and didn't even eat dinner that night.

Following that day, my senses went back to somewhat normal. They were still stronger than most people's, but they weren't that strong until I had my first turn. My eyes did get better, instead of wearing glasses and my eyesight getting worse, it got better. I noticed that since that day I didn't need my inhaler anymore either. I could run as long as I wanted to without seriously getting tired compared to my classmates. That also didn't stop them from calling me Wolf Boy either.

I figured that the wolf basically changed everything about me and I'm much happier now that I don't get sick anymore. When I looked online, I thought I was going to turn into a werewolf, but when my first full moon came, nothing happened. Everything was going well until I had my first change. That's when I was able to use my true werewolf strength.

After my first change, I learned that I can lift 2 tons,

and up to 10 tons while transformed. I always thought I couldn't tell anyone and I'm so glad that Catalina found out. I feel a huge weight has been lifted off my shoulders. Now I don't have any secrets from her. I can be myself with her 100%. That's all I need. I love that she doesn't see me any differently. She says it's cute that I had a crush on her since that day in her yard. It wasn't the same for her, but she did admit to starting to have a crush on me sophomore year. I smiled saying I was happy to have a chance at all.

When I finish telling her everything that happened to me up to this point she tells me she's sorry and promises to not tell anyone. We get back to her home and I take a much-needed shower. Afterward we sit on the couch relaxing.

"I love you," Catalina says in a warm voice. "You don't have to worry, you can talk to me anytime you need to."

"I love you too," I say with a smile.

Chapter 3

Three months later, just like any other night after every full moon, I find myself miles from home, having no real way of getting back. I'm hopeful that I can locate a nice enough person that would be willing to take me home. I'll have to make up a good enough excuse this time. Maybe I can say I got lost while camping and I've been pranked by my friends after drinking last night. I smell a farm not too far from here. I look at the ground and see a fresh kill. Is it a deer or cow? I can't tell, it's too mauled for me to make out. It could be a horse, pig, or moose? The wolf will eat anything it gets its claws into.

I struggle to my feet, realizing that I'm not too far from my usual spot in the woods. I gather my belongings, such as my camera and spare change of clothes. I use the spare water with soap and a washcloth to wipe the blood from my face and mouth before drying off with the towel. My body aches as I stretch to clean my body. I just want to get home and sleep.

Now that I'm dressed, I text Catalina that I'm alright and trudge in the direction of the farm, to try to hitch a ride. After leaving the clearing, I spot Mr.

Jacobson tending to chickens. I'm a lot closer to home than I thought.

"Hey Damien, another all-nighter in the woods?" he asks, as I approach.

"Yea, you could say that," I laugh.

"I don't know how you do it. There have been reports of wolves in the woods, but no one has been able to find anything."

"I haven't seen anything so far, but I'll keep a lookout. Do you think you could give me a ride back?"

"Sure, let me just check with the Mrs," he responds

"Appreciate it, let me know if there is anything I can do."

After ten minutes, Mr. Jacobson asks me to help him with his outside work. I am happy to and a few hours later, he takes me home. I thank him for the ride and walk into my house. I'm so exhausted that I just walk to my bedroom, not saying anything to my mom. Another change and barely any steps forward. I drop my bag and lay on my bed before drifting to sleep.

I've met a lot of interesting people since becoming a werewolf. Mr. Jacobson is one of them. He and his family are so nice to me that I help them whenever I can. When I wake up I watch last night's tapes. I see myself transforming as usual, however I spot something different afterward. In the video, I see another werewolf in the background of the video. They seem friendly towards each other, but I can't make out anything. Who is this new person? The wolf didn't attack them, so has it met them before?

I watch the video a few more times and I see the same thing. The wolf made a friend, but I can't remember anything about them. Later that night, I show Catalina the video and she's just as curious as I am. Maybe next month they'll reveal themselves. Unfortunately, I was wrong. For the next three months after every turn, I see the same wolf video. They are interacting with me, but I can't recall any of it. I'll have to see if there's any way I can keep them around.

That's what I do, on the next full moon I'll bring an extra set of meat to keep the other wolf around. There's a piece of me that's a little afraid of who they might be, but maybe they can help me. The night before the moon rises, I set up all the food and my cameras to capture everything. To my surprise, when I awake the next morning, I see him laying across from me. Unsure of what to say, I offer him a towel and some water.

Once we were cleaned and dressed, I introduce myself. "Hey, my name is Damien," I say, holding out my hand.

He's silent the entire time until he sees my hand, "Braheem Howard," he says in a low voice.

Braheem is taller than I am, a slightly muscular build with dark brown skin and a quiet demeanor. Upon seeing him, he's the type of guy I'd normally avoid, but I can't write him off just based on how he looks. With all the excitement, I start asking him questions about being a werewolf as we stagger through the woods. I talk about how our wolves have been running together. He's reluctant to say anything. Just proceeds forward After a few minutes he tells me to leave him alone and walks off on his own. In the days that follow I run into him a few more times. I try to talk to him about it, but he still pushes away.

Then on the next full moon, the same thing happens. I invite him to grab a bite to eat at a nearby diner and offer once more to work together. It takes some convincing but, I finally get him to talk to me. We talk and he agrees to work together. He tells me he's had trouble turning as well, but is willing to work with me since I revealed I've had some luck in learning control.

I was happy to finally have another person going through the same thing as me. We spend the next few months sharing all the information we've collectively gathered. I could tell that even though he agreed to work with me, he's hiding something. Rather than press him on a past he may not want to talk about, I'm just glad to have someone to talk to. Catalina warns me to not get too close to him since I don't know much about him, but the wolf would know if he was bad right?

Braheem asks to change with me on the next full moon. I was taken aback when he came to me with it, but I know it took a lot to ask me. This time I remembered us running together and the wolf feeling excited to have a friend. Things have been going great. We've learned and grown so much together that for the first time I think I have a real chance of controlling the wolf.

It's been a few months since I've met him and Braheem still doesn't share much about his past, but I figure he'll come around. He usually keeps to himself. Whatever he's gone through before has left some trauma and I wonder about it since he carries it on his shoulders. I haven't really seen him relax or enjoy himself.

Today, when I woke up, I see a text from him, asking to meet him in the woods. I get myself ready, telling him I'll be there shortly. I tell Catalina where I'm going so she knows and head out. When I find Braheem, he's sitting on a log with a serious look on his face. I've never seen that expression on him before. I walk up, give him a dap and ask what's going on.

"Hey Bro, how you feelin?" he asks in a strong tone.

"I'm good, wassup?" I question.

"I been thinking about it a lot and the only way we're going to do this is if I tell you everything about me," he says in a low voice.

"B, you don't have to, I get it," I say sincerely.

"Nah, it's all good I have to. We should trust each other right?"

"Yea, you're right," I say as I nod.

"A…are you the werewolf that bit me?" I ask.

"What?! No, it's nothing like that," he responds.

"I was just asking, I was curious."

"Again, no. I want to tell you that I ran away from home after almost killing my family during my first full moon five years ago," he reveals. "I tried to talk to my parents about it, but they put me out. Since I didn't have a place to stay afterward, I've been hoping to and from cheap motels doing odd jobs to get money for food and clothes. That was until I met you."

I didn't notice it before, but Braheem was a few years older than me. "Damn man, I'm sorry," I say sympathetically.

"It's all good," he responds. "It's just good to finally talk to somebody about this," Braheem admits. "I know you think I can teach you a few things, but I'm more afraid of myself than anything. Like you, I choose to stay to myself, trying to stay off the radar, But there's always those who will find you."

"What do you mean?' I inquire.

"The reason I was so stand-offish towards you, is because the first werewolves I met call themselves pure breeds," There's vindictiveness in his words. "They offered to help me and I thought I found a kinship with them, but they only bullied and messed with me. It wasn't until six months in that I learned that those of us who are bitten are at the bottom of the food chain compared to them. They call us mutts."

"Damn that's rough, I'm sorry," I say somberly.

"That's not the worst part, they put me in a cage on the full moon and watch me turn and laugh at me that I didn't know how to stop the change. They made it a joke watching me struggle month after month,"

40

Braheem's voice is shaky. "When they were tired of me, they let me go like I was some dog."

At first, I was a little skeptical, but the seriousness of his tone and the intensity in his eyes tell me he's saying nothing short of the truth. Braheem further explains to me that when he got away from them, he was hunted by werewolf hunters who call themselves Tailors. They track down werewolves young, or old and kill them indiscriminately. He's been lucky so far, but is always looking over his shoulder. He says his father raised him to be a strong man, but a strong man can only get so far on his own. A man needs at least one other person he can rely on and he's choosing me. That's why he decided to tell me everything.

I'm humbled by his decision to trust me. I dap him one more time and we talk about how he and I would be in some serious trouble if we were to ever get caught by the Tailors or the purebreds. Braheem expresses that he barely escaped them the two encounters he's had with Tailors. He informs me they use a plant called wolfsbane and silver against us. When I asked what wolfsbane was, he showed me a picture. I then remember the plant from the camping trip.

I look it up on my phone and see that it's one of the most poisonous plants to ever exist. Not just for werewolves, but also for humans. I thought that silver was a myth, but it's not. Wolfsbane to werewolves is what garlic is to vampires. Humans should never pick this plant up without the proper gloves.

The gravity of our situation dawns on me. It's been three years, how did I go all this time without seeing any of this? We need to look out for one another, it's the only way to keep each other safe. I never thought we'd need to do so from our own kind, but if we don't, we could end up being killed. I stand up and suggest we go back to my house so we can go over what I've learned through my research and videos. Hesitantly, Braheem agrees.

In the coming weeks, our mission for control seems to be almost complete. It's been great having another wolf to go over all of this with. Day by day, the goal of learning to control the wolf at all times is becoming achievable. We are doing pretty well on our own, but there's something still missing. One small thing that's stopping us from getting the results we need.

One day as I'm walking through the campus and going over my notes, I see one of my classmates Darius Chambers. Darius went to high school with me and now we go to the same college. When he first walked past, I saw he had a few bruises on his face. When I try to ask him about it, he brushes me off and continues on his way. A few days later, I see the bruises are gone, almost like nothing happened to him at all. I thought that was weird, since his face was semi-swollen and he had a black eye.

Darius is the shy and quiet type of guy, but whatever is going on is changing him. He's been acting strange, sometimes lashing out at others. I take out my phone and call Jakobe to see if he knows anything about what's happening to him, but he doesn't. I call Davion and he suggests I leave him be since it's not my problem. Something in me is telling me to help him. Maybe he's going through something at home and isn't sure how to talk about it.

The following week after class, I notice he's being bullied by some other classmates. Two guys who used to bully him in High School are going after him again. They're asking for money they don't need. All the onlookers in the crowd do nothing to stop them, so I will.

Suddenly, my ear twitches, I hear Darius growling. Even though he's looking down, I can see his eyes changing color. His light brown eyes turn the same golden yellow that mine do. I rush over to stop him from doing something he'll regret. He can't do this here because the hunters will be after him.

"Was that a growl?" one of the bullies asks.

"Hey, break it up," I order.

"Aw look at Wolf Boy here to save his little cub," says the other bully.

"Call me whatever you want, leave him alone before I kick both of your asses."

"Try it," the first bully says, stepping in my face.

He then jumps at me and I push him hard enough that fell over, "Leave Darius alone from now on," I say sternly.

"Ard whatever you freak," he says standing back to his feet. Everyone around records us all. "Be careful, they won't always be around."

"I don't need them to be, you do," I threaten.

They leave and I ask Darius if he's ok. He tells me I should have left him alone. That he could have handled it. I try to talk to him about what I saw, but he tells me I didn't see anything. I try once more, but there are too many people around for me to say what I want to. I was prepared to out myself to make him feel comfortable.

After school, I tell Braheem about it and he tells me that I should leave Darius alone. I can't do that, I know Darius and he wouldn't do anything like that unprovoked. I can feel it from him. Since Braheem and I were able to help each other, I doubt that we won't be able to help him. Since joining together, Braheem and I have gotten stronger, adding another would improve our odds.

It takes a lot more convincing, but I was able to get Darius to speak with me and Braheem. Darius just needed someone to talk to. He was the kid who was always at the guidance counselor's office. They did what they could, but he still could go down the wrong path. I remember hearing that his problems stem from his parents being alcoholics, so he had to fend for himself a lot of the time.

We met at our spot in the woods, "How'd you get turned?" I question.

"I got in a bad way with some bad people." Darius began to say. "This guy Andre was offering cash to be runners for him, so I applied. I just didn't know the runners needed to be werewolves. After my first job, he paid me and it was easy money. Then he told me he was a werewolf and bit me. And that's all she wrote. My first full moon, I turned in the house and trashed everything. I told my parents we were robbed. Though they were pissed, they didn't come at me. I didn't know what else to say to 'em."

"What would werewolves need with drugs?" I ask.

"I never asked, I just picked up the bag, and dropped it off. Andre wouldn't let us use cars, cuz we'd always get pulled over, so we hoofed it. It's easier to transport as a werewolf."

"Then what happened?" Braheem questions.

"I went back to Andre and he told me this was what I needed to be officially part of his pack. He told me he'd teach me how not to change under the full moon."

"Did he?" Braheem asks.

"Yea, and I was running for him for the last 8 months. Even though I was there something felt off."

"What do you mean?" I ask him.

"I'on know, everyone else was swearing their allegiance to him as their alpha, but it didn't feel right to me. So when I saw my chance, I got out and came to school and never looked back."

"I have one question, what's so special about an alpha?" I ask a little confused.

"I didn't tell you?" Braheem questions.

I shook my head, "No."

"Damn you've been a werewolf for three years and you don't know? My fault, I thought I told you."

Darius laughs at my inexperience, "Alphas are stronger than us, they are the leaders of the pack, you know, like in animal packs."

"Yea, okay," I nod.

"Unlike us," Darius began to say as he made his eyes glow. "Alpha's have red eyes to go with being stronger and faster."

I look at Braheem, who corroborated his story. I must look like a fool not knowing this information."

"Don't worry Dame, other than us, you haven't met any other werewolves, we don't blame you for not knowing," Braheem says with his hand on my shoulder.

I nodded my head, understandingly, "So did Andre teach how to control the change?" I ask Darius.

"Yea, why?"

"We've been trying for a while now and it's been hard," I answer. "We can't seem to get it just yet."

Darius then told us that the key to learning to control the wolf is similar to controlling your anger, just on a larger scale. Since he'd always had anger issues, especially as a child, he has somewhat of an advantage. It only took a few months and he had it down pact. Learning that we can change at any time, not just under the full moon. We ask him to teach us and he is happy to.

Over the next few months Braheem and I learn the techniques to fully control ourselves under the full moon and to trigger the change whenever we want. Darius asks me why I'm working so hard. I tell him that I almost killed Catalina and I never want to put her in that situation ever again. He understands and says If he had a girl he'd do the same thing.

Darius explains that the key is to stop fighting the wolf for control. The wolf is a part of us, at all times. He describes it as our primal instincts given the physical form of a wolf. The only way to get what we want is meditation, it's all spiritual. On occasion while meditating, I've seen the wolf in my mind. I had to understand it and it had to understand me. It's nothing like Dr. Jackal and Mr. Hyde, it's more like man and the beast inside.

Eventually Darius joins Braheem and I and we become a small pack of three. We've almost been caught by Tailors a few times, but can defend ourselves and get away. Darius has come to terms with being a werewolf and his past, after seeing two other black men just like himself. He's become self-confident and more outgoing. A lot of people at school also noticed shortly after.

It feels like I've been with these two a lot longer than I have. Sometimes I think that there's something that drew us together. We've become somewhat of an official pack, but we're missing an alpha, and the way they've described them, I don't want to. We talk about why an alpha has red eyes and we have yellow, but we haven't been able to find the answer. We have our speculations, but no real answers.

The three are now successfully able to control ourselves during our shift under the full moon or not. Catalina was ecstatic when I told her. I really have to thank Catalina, Braheem and Darius, because without them, I don't think I would have been able to get this far. I'm not fighting for just me anymore. I was fighting for them too. Though Catalina knows about Braheem and Darius and they know about her, I keep Catalina's involvement to a minimum, so she can't get hurt.

It's been about a year and a half since Catalina found out and things were going pretty well. Braheem, Darius and I are getting along well even transforming together under the full moon. We haven't encountered any Tailors or other werewolves. I thought everything was going well.

That was until today, as I'm walking out of a store, I feel malicious intent. I can't tell where it's coming from, but I know that it isn't good.

As a werewolf, we have a heightened sense of empathy, the ability to feel others emotions, both human and animal. It's like I know what their intentions are and I don't have to be in the same room as the person to feel it. I feel in the pit of my stomach that whoever they are, they're after me. Instead of making a scene, by looking for them, I get in my car to go somewhere else instead of driving home. I want to see if I really am being targeted. I make several turns to see if I'm being trailed. My hunch is correct, every turn I make, a car behind me makes the same one. I can't see who's in the car behind me, so I drive through the warehouse district to try to catch them off guard.

I get out of my car and go behind a nearby wall. The car parks right behind me and I hear someone getting out of the car to follow me. Without a second of hesitation, I yank the person and throw them to the ground and roar in his face.

"P…please don't kill me," he pleads.

"What do you mean don't kill you?" I ask. "You were following me, I sensed you back at the market."

"Then you should know that I'm not alone," he says, smirking.

Just as he says that another person comes up behind me and sticks their claws into my back. I screamed in pain as I tried to use my claws to swipe the person behind me, but I missed them. She picks me up and throws me aside and stands next to her partner.

"Who are you two?" I ask in pain.

"Don't worry about who we are. Just know that we were sent here for you," I hear her say.

Less than a second later, they both attack me simultaneously. I'm able to dodge their assault thanks to my self defense training, but they are better fighters than me. I have to wait for my opening and attempt to gather myself. They put me on the defensive, attacking at the same time, with no room for me to counter. Each punch is followed up with another or a kick. These two are used to fighting together. They're great at fighting, but seem new to being werewolves. That means they may not be able to control themselves as well as I can.

I don't want to hurt them, but they're not giving me a choice. They've backed me into a corner and I only see one way out. My eyes glow and my claws grow. They pause for a moment before attacking me once more. I catch their punches before throwing them back as far as I can. Why did they pause after seeing my eyes? It's like they were expecting something different. I use this moment to my advantage and scale the nearby building with my claws. Once I get to the roof, I jump off, get back into my car and drive away.

I look in the rearview mirror and to my surprise, they aren't following me. I immediately call Darius and Braheem to tell them everything. I Watch the mirrors the entire time, I'm on the phone with them. They ask me if everything is alright. I tell them that I'm fine, and I'm healing. I caution that we need to watch our backs moving forward. I don't know why they attacked me, but I don't think they are done.

It's wishful thinking that that was the end of it, hoping that I scared them off and they won't attack me again. It's been a week and nothing's happened. I go to our spot in the woods, we started calling the Den to meet Braheem and Darius, so we can turn under the full moon, but they're later than usual. Suddenly, I hear two people walking towards me and turn around thinking they're Braheem and Darius. That's when I smell those two again. They're trying to jump me on a full moon hoping to overpower me.

"Hey, member us?" the girl asks.

"Course I do," I respond. "What do you want?"

"We want to kill you," she answers, quickly.

"Why? I don't know either of you, nor do I have beef with either of you."

"It doesn't matter, you have to die," her companion says.

They both begin removing their clothes, no longer wanting to talk. These two are on black air force energy. I know where this was going, so I remove my clothes with them. Before I can utter another word, my attackers change and charge at me rapidly. I don't want to hurt them, I just want to understand what their motive is. But there's no time for second guessing, I have to protect myself.

It's a mistake to come at me on a full moon. In my werewolf form, I've noticed that I'm a little stronger than Darius and Braheem. Just like before, they attack me in unison. This time they use their claws to their advantage. There's no denying their skill and teamwork. I'm getting deep cuts from their claws all over my body. The pain is intense and I can feel my body healing, but the cuts are coming too fast. Some being deeper than others.

My strength being great is nothing compared to their speed. They eventually get me on my back and bleeding, eventually, I turn back to human gasping for air. This can't be the way I die. Why are they trying to kill me? I have to find out.

They turn back into their human forms and pin me down. I look deep into their eyes, as the woman is about to strike me down, but she hesitates. I can't waste this chance. I gather the strength I have left and force myself to turn back into a werewolf.

I grab them by the neck and choke-slam them as hard as I can. They each scream in pain and gasp for breath wildly after I use their bodies to dent the ground. I roar in their faces to show how serious I am and start to sink my claws into their necks.

"S...s...stop...don't kill us please!" The woman pleads in fear, while trying to breathe.

"Why the hell not?" I ask, after turning human. "You two just tried to kill me again."

"W...w...we didn't want to, we were told to kill you," the man coughs wildly.

"You think I'm going to believe that?" I ask fiercely.

"It's-cough-the truth," the man says, still struggling to breathe.

I look each of them in their eyes. I want to believe them, but can I? "I'm not sure if I should believe either of you, so I'm only going to ask you this one time." I say in a serious tone. "Who sent you to kill me?"

"Let us go and we'll tell you," the woman says, holding onto my hand at her throat, attempting to pull it away.

I'm reluctant to let them go, but something about this entire thing feels off and I want answers, so I release them from my grip. They sit up holding their necks. Soon after, I hear Braheem and Darius coming to join us.

"Yo D, you aight?" Braheem asks. "Who are they?"

"Yea I'm alright," I respond. "These are my two new friends I told you about. They were walking black air forces til a second ago." I say as I stand up inspecting my wounds, seeing them healing.

"We should kill them," Darius says sternly.

"No, no, no, no, no" she says frantically. "Someone told us to come kill him. "We aren't cold blooded killers," she expresses.

"But he's covered in blood," Braheem points out. "How do you explain that?

"Chill B, this isn't all mine, but they didn't act alone, I can feel it. She stopped just before she killed me. Let's get cleaned up then we're gonna talk this out," I turn my attention to them, "If I find out you're not telling me the truth, I'm going to rip out your throats with my teeth," My eyes glowing as I threaten them.

We walk to a nearby lake where we wash off all the blood. Even though I've healed, my insides still hurt. I think a few of my ribs were cracked, and some organs may have been hit, so I'll take it easy for a little while.

Now that we are all clean and clothed, I tell them to introduce themselves. We learn that their names are Omar and Chantelle Williams. They are siblings who were sent to kill me by their alpha, a man named Darnell. Darnell has been made aware of Braheem and Darius and me. Apparently, he thought I was an alpha trying to take over his territory. He didn't want me influencing any other werewolves in the area into joining me, so he tasked Omar and Chantelle to kill me. After they killed me, they were to bring him my head.

I listen to them tell their story, while also listening to their hearts. Paying attention to every word they say. Nothing about what they're telling me seems like a lie. As they saw, I'm not an alpha. I don't have red eyes, mine are the same color as theirs. Omar says they tried to tell Darnell that after our first fight, but he didn't listen. He told them that they must have followed the wrong person and to try again.

"Why do the two of you do what he says?" Darius asks.

"Cuz he's our alpha and that's the only chance we have at being human again," Chantelle responds.

"What do you mean?" I question.

"He's the one that bit us and because of that, he says he's the only one who can change my brother and I back to human. We just have to do what we're told."

I take a deep breath and against the judgment of Omar and Darius, I believe them. After hearing their words, I feel sorry for them. "I'm not sure if there really is a way for him to turn you back, but I want to see it for myself," I say.

"How?" Omar asks.

"Darnell said he'd turn you back after you brought my body in, right?" I look directly into Chantelle's eyes.

"Yea, this is supposed to be our last job and he's going to turn us back after we bring him your body," Chantelle's words are filled with hope.

"Ight, let's give the nigga what he wants and let's see what happens," I say confidently.

"Dame, no we don't know these niggas like that," Braheem warns. "We don't know if what they saying is true."

It's cool B, I want to see for myself," Darius interjects.

"Y'all curiosity is going to get us killed," Braheem urges. "It's just the three of us and y'all niggas want to go up against an alpha?"

"This is our lives we're talking about here!" Chantelle exclaims. "Why would we lie about this? We don't want to be these monsters, he turned us against our will, who would choose to live like this!?" Chantelle screams.

Braheem pauses before letting out a heavy sigh. "Ight, but I'm watching, y'all." Braheem points at Chantelle and Omar.

Chapter 4

Over the course of the next few days we plot out how we're going to set this up. The only way we figure this is going to work is if we stage it to make it look like they beat and tied me up before taking me to their hideout.

I warn Chantelle and Omar that there are many rumors on how to turn them back, however I don't think there is a way to make them human again. However, I'm willing to find out with them. Chantelle and Omar tell me that they understand, but if there is even a slim chance, they're willing to risk it because they don't want to be werewolves. They are fine being human.

We wait a few days, to make sure we can really sell it. Each day, they keep in contact with Darnell so he doesn't think anything is fishy. When the day finally comes, we cover me with deer blood and I rip my clothes to make it seem like I was badly beaten. When Chantelle and Omar walk me to their hideout, Omar carries me on his shoulder. After we enter the warehouse, he puts me at his alpha's feet, while I pretend to be unconscious, waiting for the right moment.

"Ight Darnell, here he is, now give us what you promised," Chantelle demands.

Darnell smiles before standing up from his chair and walking behind them, "You two have done great for me," he begins to say. "Everything I've asked of you and then some," he says, pointing to me. "Are you sure there's nothing I can do to convince you to stay with me?"

"NO!" We want to be human again," Chantelle screams. "He's my little brother and I have to protect him. We want to be human, not monsters."

"Monsters...?" Darnell Laughs. "Silly girl, we're not monsters, we're apex predators and we run this world. Do you want to be the rulers or sheep?"

"We *want* to be human dammit!" Omar exclaims.

Darnell immediately turns to Omar, grabbing him by the throat, "Lil nigga. I gave you power beyond your wildest dreams and you spit it back in my face? You better show me the respect I deserve or you'll never be human again."

"Please, we just want to get this over with," Chantelle pleads with tears in her eyes.

"Very well, your sweet voice has warmed my heart," Darnell says in a slightly nicer tone. "Now kneel down and I will give you what you want," he says, letting go of Omar.

Chantelle and Omar get down to their knees and close their eyes. Seconds later, Darnell starts snickering, "Y...you two are priceless, there is no cure for lycanthropy. There's one theory about killing the werewolf that bit you, but I don't intend on dying anytime soon," he says with a devilish smile.

"You lied to us, you bastard," Chantelle cries out. "How could you do such a thing?!?"

"And miss having unwilling parties do my bidding for me?" Darnell asks sarcastically. "Even if you did manage to kill me, it would only work for one of you. So, who's it gonna be? Big sis or lil bro?" Darnell points at them.

Chantelle and Omar look at each other in horror. Not knowing what to say to the other. They are defeated, realizing their wish to be human again will never come true. The one thing that gave them hope is now gone.

"I told you that there's no cure," I say, as I stand up undoing the ropes that bound me.

"You're alive, how?" Darnell asks, surprised.

"That's not important," I respond. "What is important is, even though they tried to kill me, I got the chance to talk to Chantelle and Omar. They told me how they were being forced to fight for a cure. A cure that's nothing more than a fairy tale you fed them. These two finally get the chance to see who you truly are, a manipulator."

"Who the hell do you think you are?!" Darnell asks ferociously. "I'm the alpha. The only way to become one is through strength. That's all that matters lil nigga!"

"Nah nigga, what matters is not using those beneath you, that's not a real leader. Leaders keep their word and I'm going to help you keep yours," I say, baring my claws, fangs and my eyes begin illuminating.

Darnell starts laughing, "They were right, you're not an alpha, you're just a beta. You think you can take me on? Well let's see."

Suddenly, I feel an immense wave of energy coming from him. I'm not sure why, but it feels like he's emitting his will towards me. The wolf inside of me is submitting to him. I feel it deep in my spirit. Is he using his status as an alpha to make me lose the will to fight? I try my hardest, but I can't resist it. Whatever this is, I'm being forced to my knees and neither of us has thrown a punch.

I look over at Chantelle and Omar, they're looking at me with such worry in their eyes. I came here to save them, yet I'm on the verge of losing a fight before it began. I have to help them break free from Darnell's grasp, not succumb to it. I take a few sharp breaths and begin to fight against my instincts. Can I go against the will of an alpha? The wolf inside isn't ready to give up and neither am I.

My body surges with a strength I've never had before and slowly I rise to my feet. These few seconds seem like I've been attempting to stand for hours. Eventually, I find it within myself to stand tall and stare Darnell in the eyes.

"That was tough lil wolf, this the first time I've seen a beta resist an alpha," Darnell says, slightly impressed. "You two, go see what he's got."

Two wolves charge toward me, and I sense that they aren't going to hesitate like Chantelle or Omar. An upside is they don't seem to be as good of fighters as they are either. I'm easily able to take them down. After knocking them out, I turn my attention back to Darnell.

"C'mon Darnell, why send the cubs after me? Too afraid to fight me yourself?" I say, provoking him.

This is going to be my first fight against an alpha. He already has a large imposing presence that's more than just physical. My legs start shaking, almost ready to kneel before him again. My will is struggling to resist his. I know he's better than me in every way that matters, but I have to try, if I we're going to walk out of here.

"What's wrong mutt?" Darnell mocks. "Afraid to cash the check you wrote?"

Suddenly the shakiness in my legs stop, "Not at all, I'm just trying to figure out what to break first, your nose or your arm." My heart is pounding with excitement.

I thought I was afraid, but that turned into anxiety, which is now flooding my body with adrenaline. I hope I have what it takes. Darnell sends a few more of his pack to attack me. They are tackled soon after by Braheem and Darius.

"We'll handle them, you take care of Darnell," Braheem says.

Darnell gets upset upon seeing Braheem and Darius. He roars before transforming. There was something strange because it's not a full transformation. He's baring his fangs and his claws, but his face and body has also changed. He still looks human, but his features have become more wolf-like. Is this because he's an alpha? He growls before charging at me with an intense fury.

He swings his claws at me, followed by a series of kicks. Through instinct I barely dodge him. I block many of his hits and hope to counter him. After dodging his first few strikes, I got cocky and act too early by throwing a punch.

He stops my punch and swipes his claws against my abdomen. His claws are as sharp as daggers. I take a few steps back due to the pain, almost paralyzed I watch as my own blood soaks my shirt over the animal's blood. I've been cut before, and usually I'm able to feel myself healing, but this is different. Darnell comes at me once more with relentless fury.

He catches me off guard by sweeping my legs and pinning me down, "Nigga did you really think that you could come into my house and expect anything else? Those two are *mine.* Betas respect their alphas and then they form a pack," he says getting closer to me. "An alpha can never tolerate weakness," Darnell begins to say. "A pack is only as strong as its alpha. You have no pack, you're an omega."

Darnell picks me up and puts me into a headlock, showing me Braheem and Darius have already been subdued. I didn't see that coming so quickly. He tells his pack to pin the three of us against a wall. I can't do anything, but struggle against them. Darnell punches me in the side before digging his claws into me. I immediately scream in pain.

"You three, make sure he watches," Darnell commands.

With me beaten and bleeding, I can't move, no matter how hard I try. Darnell turns his attention to Omar and Chantelle. All I can do is watch as he kicks them. There's no fight left in either of them. How could there be when everything they hoped for is gone? It hurts to watch the blood dripping from their faces and the hopelessness in their eyes. Neither is trying to fight back since there's nothing left for them to fight for. I think they want to die, their hope that death will be a better relief than being a werewolf.

I can't take watching this anymore, my anger slowly rises within me this, "*Leave them alone!*" I scream.

Darnell laughs, "Well, well looks like you do still have some fight left."

I want to desperately help them, but I'm still being pinned down. Darnell makes his way toward me, his pack members bring me up to my knees as he approaches.

He kicks me in my stomach before he leaning down to my face, "What you say lil nigga?"

I cough before trying to sit up. His pack members push against me, keeping me down. I start to feel stronger. The rage that built within me serves as a power boost, giving me the strength I need. If I give the wolf control I might be able to win this. I feel my heart racing as my ferocity burns like wildfire. I will prove to him that you can't just use people and discard them whenever you want to.

"Look this lil nigga has that dog in him," Darnell laughs.

He instructs his betas to let me go, saying he'll take care of me himself. When they let go of me, I stand and Darnell offers to let me have the first punch. He's strong and his arrogance knows no bounds, but I don't move. I want him to feel powerless. After waiting a few seconds, he throws a first punch and I catch his hand with barely a thought.

"LET.... THEM... GO," I say monstrously, squeezing his fist, looking into his eyes while mine glow intensely.

I look over at Chantelle and Omar who are still lying on the ground bleeding and pleading for help with their eyes. My rage continues to grow from their helplessness. Seeing him beating them and enjoying it plays on repeat in my mind. An even bigger surge flows through my body. Darnell pulls his hand from mine and gets ready to throw another punch. I use the weight from him pulling his arm away to spartan kick him in the chest, sending him across the room. Disbelief arises on his and everyone else's face.

"How could you do that to me?" he shouts. "You're a beta, an omega. You have no power. I'm the alpha! I have all the power!" Darnell exclaims.

"Do you think I care about that?! You're hurting my friends!" I scream.

"Wrong Darnell," Chantelle announces. "He may not be an alpha, but he has a pack," she says coughing and struggling to stand.

Omar, Darius and Braheem stand next to her. They're badly beaten, but they all stood tall, as all of Darnell's pack members lay unconscious around them. Seeing his pack defeated, Darnell grows angrier. He races at me before frantically throwing punches at me. He can't stand seeing Omar and Chantelle stand with me instead of with him. I don't know why, but all his strikes are moving in slower than before. I can anticipate his every move.

I manage to not only out maneuver him, but catch him off guard, by using his punch to throw him over my shoulder. I slam him so hard on his back that I knock the wind out of him. Before he can recover, I reach for his neck and pin him down. My hand clenches around his throat, as I dig my claws into his neck.

"Now if you didn't hear me before," I say angrily. Leave them alone and let them be. You've already ruined their lives and you *will* release them."

"Let go of me, Runt. I am the alpha and I have the power," Darnell asserts.

I want to hurt him, but can I kill him? The only thing running through my mind is how he hurt Omar and Chantelle. The wolf inside wants to kill him. I begin squeezing tighter, because he's the one who needs to feel powerless. With the slightest amount of extra pressure I can teach it to him. I raise my other hand preparing to slit his throat with my claws.

"Damien stop!" screams Chantelle. I pause from hearing her voice. I'm doing this for them, why did she stop me? I turn to her. "Look at what you're doing."

Listening to her words, I stare at Darnell.

"Why'd you stop?" Darnell asks.

"Because I'm nothing like you," I respond. "You kill and lead like a dictator with no regard for anyone else's life but your own."

"C'mon you have it in you, I saw it," Darnell contests. "You may not have the eyes of one, but you sure as hell have the power of one. You're an alpha kid, you should act like it. Kill me!" Darnell tries to convince me.

Even with the anger inside and my hand on his throat, I can't bring myself to do it. A piece of me wants to and I truly feel he deserves it, but I can't kill him. I should do what's best for Omar and Chantelle and killing him isn't the way. I slowly loosen my grip on Darnell's throat.

"C'mon lil bro, let me show you the ropes," he offers. "Be my second in command and when it's your time you'll take my place and become the new alpha of this pack."

I stare at Chantelle and Omar who are standing next to Braheem and Darius. I think about it for a few seconds. I know that there are things he can teach me. Things that I may not be able to learn on my own. I would be safe especially with him by my side.

"What are you looking at them for? All the power you'll need is between the both of us, not them. We can kill them or reign them in to build a stronger pack. Together we'll be stronger than any of those pompous purebloods or even the Council." Darnell smiles fiendishly.

"Nah Darnell, I ain't with any of that," I say, letting go of him. "I'm not an alpha, but I will become one because my pack members see and respect me as their leader, not because I killed you or anyone else. I won't use my power that way."

I stand up and start walking over to everyone else. Darnell's pack members come to and saw everything. A sea of confused faces as they're no longer sure of what to do after seeing their alpha losing. They back away as I get closer.

"It's time to go," I say, gesturing to the four of them.

"Don't turn your back to me!" Darnell screams, as he lunges at me.

"Behind you!" Darius warns.

I turn as Darnell tackles me to the ground and starts clawing at me violently. I can't break free. All I can do is cover my face. I tried to show him kindness in sparing his life and this is how he treats me?

"Why are you still fighting even when you lost?!" I scream desperately.

"Because I'm the alpha and I'm not going to let some lil no name nigga disrespect me and destroy what I built here," Darnell roars. "I am superior in every way!"

That is it, I can't take it anymore. It's either him or me and I want to live. This is a hard decision, but he made it easier. Since there was no other way, it's time for me to act.

I give into the wolf's rage and completely turn, overpowering him. I throw him against the wall on the other side of the warehouse and before he can react, I rush him and punch through his chest. I have hold of his heart and rip it out as fast as I can. Afterward, I take a step back and change back into my human form.

I look down at his heart as it beats in my hand for a few seconds, before it stops. I look back at his body and see it lying limp.

As he lays there dying, taking his last breaths, Darnell says to me, "See... I knew you had it in you to kill me. A....and now...you real...really are an alpha..."

With a grin, he exhales with his last breath and fades away. All at once, I feel a surge within myself. Nothing like I've ever felt before. What is going on with me? Everyone comes running to my side.

"Damien, are you ok?" Omar asks.

"T...that...was the first time I've killed anyone," I respond. I...I feel horrible. "I didn't want to kill him, I swear. I only wanted to help the two of you be free of him."

"We know you didn't," Chantelle says, solemnly.

"Damien…your eyes," Braheem says.

"What… what about them?" I ask, frantically.

"They're…red," Braheem responds.

"Red? Are you sure?" I ask confused.

"Yes, just as red as his was," Chantelle responds.

"So if you kill an alpha, then you become an alpha?" Darius asks.

"I guess so. It works that way in the wild doesn't it?," Omar adds.

"Guess that makes you the new top dog," Darius jokes.

None of us know what to do. I'm an alpha now, but what does that mean for us and Darnell's pack? Are they going to follow me now, or will they run off by themselves? Unfortunately no one has an answer. They're all looking at me for direction, but I'm not sure how to give them one.

I'm in no shape to stand up and leave, so we sit there for twenty minutes to rest. Those in Darnell's pack start leaving one by one, but are stopped by men in black suits. They're everywhere, rounding us all up before sternly asking everyone questions. Who are they and what do they want? I'm in no shape to fight if we need to.

Once they secure everyone they explain to us that they're a part of the werewolf Council's Defense and Secrecy force. I'm shocked to find out that there's a werewolf's Council. That's never in the movies.

The Council Defense and Secrecy Force questions everyone while tending to our wounds. Their job is to make sure that werewolves are kept a secret from humans. A few of the medics are werewolves, while others are human. We learn that there are hospitals all over the planet dedicated to treating werewolves, some of which are in our city. The person who helped us introduced himself as Tevin, who is human.

Tevin tells us that they've been looking for Darnell for years. Darnell has been rounding up runaway kids and turning them against their will. He killed his previous alpha and then everyone in his pack, becoming one of the most dangerous werewolves alive. Not only did I take his rank as an alpha, but also his title as one of the most dangerous werewolves.

"Why are you telling us all of this?" I ask.

"Because you went up against an alpha and won," he responds. "You didn't kill him for power or to take his place, you killed him to protect your friends and that's rare with your kind."

"What's going to happen to us?" Chantelle asks.

"They're going to take your names down and enter you into the official registry. There aren't many alphas like yours that don't belong to a purebred line. They're going to look into his history and watch all of you."

"They don't know about all werewolves already?" Omar asks.

"No, it would be impossible to know of every werewolf. There are some like Darnell who turn people indiscriminately, or get turned accidentally. Usually, before one learns to control themselves under the full moon, they either don't get found because they're killed or captured by the hunters, live in isolation or they join an alpha who also hasn't registered themselves. So when things like this come up we try to get as many names as possible so we can keep up with everyone."

"To keep the secret safe?" I ask.

"To keep all werewolves safe, the Council exists to keep the status quo," he responds.

Tevin finishes bandaging everyone and leaves with the rest of the medics and the defense force. Those that were still in Darnell's pack went with the Defense Force to figure out their place in the world. Since most of them were with Darnell for the same reasons as Chantelle and Omar, they have nowhere to go, they follow the defense force or disperse.

Some of them were runaways and only have been werewolves for a short amount of time. I'm hopeful that they are going to find better lives, but I can't be sure. Chantelle and Omar decide to join Darius, Braheem and I instead of going with the others, bringing our pack total to five.

I am not sure what we were going to do next, but I address everyone "Let's go home and get some sleep. We'll figure everything out once we've healed and rested."

Everyone nods and we head our separate ways. I go home, call Catalina and tell her everything that happened tonight. After a lengthy conversation with her, I go to sleep unsure of what would come in the future.

Chapter 5

Since that night, I've spent the next year training with my new alpha abilities. In human form I can now lift up to 6 tons whereas it was only 2. In wolf form I could lift 10 tons, now I can now lift 15. My top running speed while human was 75 MPH now it's increased to 95 MPH. That also extends to when I'm in wolf form. My top speed was 350 MPH, now it's 375 MPH.

I've also noticed that I've gotten a little more aggressive, meaning I have to keep my temper in check. The wolf and I didn't like everyone for a while. I had to apologize to Catalina almost every day when I'd get mad over small things. Usually I made up for it with gifts or taking her out shopping or for dinner.

Since the beginning, I noticed that I always feel stronger with Braheem and Darius alongside me. However, since becoming an alpha and having Chantelle and Omar with us, I feel even more powerful. They say a wolf is only as strong as its pack, but this is on a different level altogether. There are times that 15 tons might as well be 10, especially when we're together.

Everyone has also been treating me differently. Not badly in any way, but more like they're giving me more respect. It was subtle at first, but has increased over time. Chantelle, Omar, Braheem and Darius act like bodyguards whenever we're together. I guess they've accepted me as their alpha, but it's a little much at times. It's not like I wanted to be an alpha anyway. I only want to live in peace with everyone.

Even though it's only been a year, having Omar and Chantelle with us feels natural. My self-doubt has crept in on more than one occasion and I often asked how I'm supposed to be their alpha? What do they expect from me?

In my search for answers, I realize that we're seriously lacking in offense, so I ask Chantelle and Omar to train us and they're more than happy to help. They are two of the best fighters I've ever seen. Their technique is amazing and just what we need. We typically call them the dynamic duo because if they're attacking at the same time it doesn't go well for anyone and I would know. It's better for all of us to learn how to fight, especially in human form, rather than resorting to transforming. Their discipline has also helped us better understand ourselves.

While Chantelle and Omar are great fighters, they still had trouble with the changing, but Darius helped them. They're mission to protect themselves, became to protect the pack. With a few months of training, they eventually learned to control themselves like everyone else.

Today is our monthly meeting and Chantelle tells us about a weird encounter she had. She was approached by someone who asked her to join her group. I ask her if the person said group or pack. Chantelle says she asked and the woman told her group not pack.

"Wait how'd they know you are a wolf?" I ask.

"I don't know, they must've either been watching me or saw me change," Chantelle replies.

"Did you see them change too?" Darius asks.

"No, she just came up to me and gave me an offer," she answers. "I declined and walked away. Though that didn't stop her from asking me a few more times. Then, I came here and told y'all."

"We have to be careful, we don't know if they're Tailors or not. We shouldn't jump to conclusions," Omar adds. "She got a name?"

"Yea, Jay," Chantelle replies.

"Is she hot?" Omar asks, excitedly.

Chantelle, looks at him with annoyance, "Nigga, I don't know, I was too focused on how she found out I'm a werewolf."

Omar sucked his teeth, "I was *just askin, damn.*"

We laugh at the two of them. They stare at each other and laugh as well. Seeing them smile and mocking each other is great, because they were down for a while after Darnell's lies were revealed. I wonder why Jay asked Chantelle to join her crew? Is she a part of another pack that's trying to recruit other werewolves, or could it be a Tailor trap? I don't have the answer, but I tell Chantelle to be cautious moving forward.

A few days later, Catalina and I are on a date at a local café that just opened. We've been here for about an hour when I sense something wrong. I start surveying around us to see if anyone is watching us. I can't see anyone, so I start listening to everything around us. A few seconds later, I hear someone speaking suspiciously.

"Ok girls, we have exactly three minutes to get in, get the money and get out," a female voice says.

"Right, we get then we get out," a second female says.

"Don't worry, after we hit here we'll be set for a little while," the first female voice says.

I can't place where they are, but they sound close. I remember that there've been a number of thefts around town in the last few weeks. From the way they're talking, they could be the thieves. Listening to them a little longer, I hear them talking about robbing the bank a few blocks over. I can't believe what I'm hearing.

"Is the car parked far enough away?" the leader asks.

"Yea it is, but we'll have to run pretty fast and throw around anyone who gets in our way," says the second voice.

"Are you sure no one will get hurt?" a third female voice asks.

"Some might, but no one'll die. Make sure we get in, rip apart the teller stands, grab the cash and get out. There's nothing they can do about it."

From the way they're talking, it sounds like they're werewolves. If that's true, then they'll have a huge advantage over the security in the building. I can't let them get away with robbing the place and risk them revealing werewolves. I listen closely as the three of them enter the bank. I need to act before someone gets hurt. Even if the police get called, they can't handle this.

I look at Catalina, "Baby, there's a few werewolves up the street robbing the bank," I whisper.

"What do you mean?" she asks. "How could you know that?"

"I've been listening ever since I got this feeling, then I heard them talking about going in and robbing it."

"Are you sure?" she asks in disbelief.

"Yes I'm sure and I have to stop them before things get messy. They could get arrested and expose us all," I say concerned.

"Why does it have to be you?" she asks with worry in her eyes.

"It doesn't, but someone has to stop them before we all get in trouble. Remember the Council and Tailors I told you about? I still don't know that much about either of them, but I don't think they're going to let werewolves robbing a bank slide. Do you?"

Catalina sighs, "Ok, but be safe."

"I will, you take the car home, and I'll catch up later."

Catalina smiles and tries to put on a brave face for me, but I can tell she doesn't like the idea. I pay our bill before we leave and I kiss her on the forehead. Before Catalina drives off, I apologize to her for ruining our day out. Though I'm stronger than I was before. I still have doubts about whether I can stop them. As I walk closer, I feel a tightness in my chest. I may be an alpha now, but I don't feel like it. I have no Idea how they're going to react to me, or what I'm going to do about this.

I walk along the side of the building as I listen closely. So far everything is pretty normal on the inside. I put on my hood and pear into the window. I'm unable to spot the three of them because they're trying not to draw attention to themselves.

"You girls ready?" their leader asks.

"Whenever you are," says the other.

"Just give the signal," responds the third.

They don't seem to be using earpieces, they must speaking in low voices, and using their hearing. That way there can't be a record of any calls or transmission while they're robbing the bank. These girls are very smart. There's no time for thinking, I have to stop them now before she gives the signal.

"I don't think you three should be doing this," I speak softly.

The three of them pause for a moment from the sound of my voice. I watch the three women, stop like they're frozen in time,

"Wh...who are you?" asks the leader, I recognize her voice, she's Jay.

"Look outside the window," I say, standing there with my hood on.

Each of them turn their heads and see me standing just outside the bank's window. I gesture them to come outside and join me. As I walk away I hear them leaving one by one. I lead them a few blocks away, to a nearby alley.

When I'm sure no one can hear us, I turn around and ask, "What are the three of you doing and why?"

"It's none of your business what we're doing!" exclaims the leader.

"Yes it is, the three of you almost robbed a bank and were in danger of exposing yourselves if you got caught."

"We weren't going to get caught," says one of the other two.

"You don't know that, what were your plans for the cameras, the silent alarms or the cops if they showed up?" I question.

"We would have handled it!" Jay insists.

"With what? Being a werewolf, doesn't stop bullets."

They're taken aback for a moment. Unsure of what to say. After a brief moment, Jay asks me, "What is it to you anyway?"

"I don't want anyone to get hurt," I say softly.

"Look here captain save a hoe, we were doing fine before you showed up," she says, glaring at me while baring her fangs and her eyes begin glowing.

"You showed me yours, now I'll show you mine," I stare at them and blink one showing my eyes. Their bright crimson glow makes each of them flinch and they almost take a step back.

"He's...an alpha Jay, we have to get out of here," one of them squeals.

"You idiot, we're not supposed to say our names," Jay snarls. "So what if he's an alpha? I can take him."

Without hesitation, Jay begins attacking me, throwing her claws wildly. Thanks to Chantelle, Omar, I easily evade all of her attacks.

"Stay still dammit, are you too afraid to fight?" Jay asks angrily.

"No, I don't want to fight either of you. I just want to talk, that's it," I reply.

"Sure that's what the last guy said, before he turned the three of us into werewolves and ruined our lives!" Jay screams in pain.

I stop for a moment and look at the two girls who each have sad looks in their eyes. They're just Like Braheem, Darius, Chantelle, Omar and myself. They were turned against their will. Jay uses her claws to cut my face through my distractions. I turn away from the force of her swing.

"We should go before things get worse," one of the girls says.

When I look back, the three of them are gone. I search, but find no trace of them. I hurry out of the alley before someone can notice me. I call Catalina and tell her that I'm coming back. Luckily, I'm not far, so I'm able to run home in less than 20 minutes. After I get back, Catalina is waiting for me out front.

Once she sees me, she rushes toward me, "I was so worried is everything ok?"

"Yea everything is fine," I answer.

"What about your face?" she asks worriedly.

"Don't worry about it, I was just caught off guard," I say, wiping the slight remnant of blood from my cheek and showing her that there's nothing to worry about.

The cut is already healing, barely anything more than a paper cut. I reassure her that there's nothing to worry about. Catalina settles down and we go into the house, attempting to enjoy the rest of our day together. I can tell that she's still concerned, but I tell her I'm fine.

Over the course of the next few days, I go out with Braheem, Darius, Omar and Chantelle, to search for Jay and her two friends. They're very elusive, perfectly timing their previous robberies. Robbing places within minutes, barely any witnesses and perfect precision. Though they haven't tried to rob a bank since then, I know they'll resurface soon. While tracking them on their last robbery, we lose their scent within a few blocks. These girls know how to cover their tracks.

It takes a few more weeks, but we manage to find them. I track them using their scent and catch them walking down a street. After spotting them, I call for backup. Chantelle is the first to arrive. When I point the girls out to her, Chantelle realizes that Jay is Jasmine.

I tell her to go up to talk to Jasmine and say she wants to join them. This'll create an opportunity for us to speak with them and find out why they're stealing. It doesn't seem like it's just for fun. Chantelle smirks and walks over to meet Jasmine. They talk for about ten minutes before Jasmine gives Chantelle an address for Chantelle to meet with the rest of her crew.

Now that we have our in, it's time to plan our next steps to make contact with the three of them. Jasmine leaves before everyone else arrives, but we come to a consensus that Chantelle is going to meet the girls while the rest of us wait outside. We're confident in her ability to handle herself, but back up never hurt anyone. When night falls we go to the address that leads us to a huge mansion.

"Why would they have you come here?" Omar asks.

"I don't know," responds Chantelle. "But it's a little weird that they are hitting licks when they obviously don't need the money."

"Maybe, they're still going through their rebellious years," Braheem mocks.

"Aren't we all?" I laugh.

"Not me, I'm too old and set in my ways," he jokes.

We get into position and Chantelle walks up to the house. Before she can knock, the door opens and Jasmine is in the doorway.

"Welcome sister," Jasmine says smiling.

"*Thank you?*" Chantelle says awkwardly.

Chantelle walks into the house and Jasmine closes the door behind them. We listen in on their convo, hearing everything that goes on. Jasmine asks Chantelle to turn off her phone, stating that she doesn't want anyone to listen to them while they speak. I said it before and I'll say it again, these girls are smart.

I hear their footsteps as they walk from the foyer to the large living room. We circle around so we can get a better look, finding a spot in the bushes that we can hide. As they walk into the large living room, we see the other two girls watching TV, eating snacks and smoking.

"What is all this?" Chantelle asks.

"This is freedom," Chantelle responds.

"Meaning?" Chantelle questions.

"The power we wield. We're stronger than everyone else. We're faster than everyone else. We can take whatever we want and no one can stop us," Jasmine smiles as her arms spread out to either side of her.

"No one?" Chantelle asks innocently.

"No, no one. We can take as we please, like this house," Jasmine says confidently.

Chantelle begins looking around, "This place doesn't belong to you?"

"Nah, but it's nice right?" Jasmine smiles proudly. "Oh, where are my manners? I forgot to introduce everyone. Over on the couch is Nichole and in the lazy boy is Kiara. We've been together since the beginning. Now we go from house to house just like this, so we always have a warm place to lay our heads."

"Yea, welcome to the unofficial lifestyle of luxury," Nichole says. "I've never felt better than I do now." Nichole jumps from the chair before lifting it up over her head with very little effort and putting it down.

"Don't be a show-off, let the girl breathe," Kiara asserts. "Let me guess, you've only been a werewolf for a few months, so this must be all new to you right?"

Chantelle nods her head. She's playing her role perfectly, trying to see what their agenda is. The three of them have no clue that we're outside and that's just what we need. If anything goes wrong, Chantelle will say the word takedown if she needs help. If our plan is successful, she's going to steer the conversation so that we can enter the house to try to talk to them. She'll put her hair in a ponytail when she thinks it's the right time. Lucky for us this place is full of windows.

"I have two questions," Chantelle states. "How did you know I was a werewolf and how do y'all make money?"

"You're cute," Kiara says. "Since you don't know, we give off very distinctive smells compared to humans."

"I never really thought about it," Chantelle responds.

"Once I confirmed your scent, I knew I had to get you to join us, so I told Jasmine about ya." Kiara smiles.

"We do whatever we want, running scams here and there, or staying in places like this while the family is gone," Nichole responds.

"We typically don't stay in any place for too long, it's best to keep on the move whenever we can," Kiara continues.

"But that seems a little lonely. Don't any of you have families?" Chantelle asks, solemnly.

"We used to have families, but that's all over now. Together, the four of us will be a family," Jasmine announces.

Chantelle stares at her feet trying not to draw too much attention to herself. I look at Braheem Darius and Omar. We know what it's like being alone after being turned and just like them, we found people to rely on. The difference is we don't go around robbing people.

"I'm sorry that you all had it so rough. My brother and I were the same way." Chantelle says in a soft voice.

"You have a brother?!" Kiara asks excitedly.

"Yea I do and we both were bitten by our alpha

who only wanted power and didn't care about anyone but himself," Chantelle says in an annoyed tone.

"Been there, done that," Jasmine says as she waves her hand.

"I do have a question though, aren't you worried about other werewolves or possibly hunters?"

"Hunters?" asks Nichole. "What do you mean hunters?"

"There's this group who call themselves Tailors and they hunt and kill werewolves indiscriminately." Chantelle answers.

"I'm not worried," Jasmine says, proudly. "There's nothing that can hurt us."

"Yes there are. I know we feel invincible, but we're far from it. We can still be hurt by silver, but there's also this plant called wolfsbane that they use to poison us."

"There's no way," Nichole says in disbelief. "I always thought that was a myth."

Nichole tries to pick up one of the silver picture frames on the end table. In less than a second her hand starts to sizzle and she drops it. When she screams in pain, Jasmine and Kiara run to assist her. Upon inspection Nichole's hand is slightly blistered and the three girls are almost mortified.

From then on Jasmine, Nichole and Kiara believe what Chantelle tells them. They spend the next hour or so talking and sharing stories. Chantelle goes into detail about how she and Omar were bitten and how they were held hostage to do their alpha's bidding.

They were sent to either kill or recruit other werewolves to build his army. While Chantelle is talking, I hear the regret in her voice.

She's almost trembling by this point. I look at Omar to clarify if what she's sharing is an act or not. His expression says everything. We didn't go over what they did before we met them, but his demeanor speaks volumes. Each of us put our hand on his shoulder, to tell him he didn't have to suffer alone anymore.

Jasmine, Nichole, and Kiara all stop for a moment. The air around us changes. Kiara gets up and hugs Chantelle before guiding her over to the couch to sit with them. They then comfort each other as they talk about how Nichole, Kiara and Jasmine met each other.

It takes a few minutes, but Jasmine is the first to share their story, "The three of us were bitten by an alpha named Jake who wanted his own werewolf harem. Apparently, he's part of a prestigious family and was next in line to take over. Jake turned young women like us into werewolves. He finds us at clubs and bars and waits for us to be alone before biting them. Then waits a few days before showing up revealing that he is also a werewolf. Then apologizes, saying it was another wolf that bit us before offering help."

Jasmine, Kiara and Nichole hold each other close as Kiara continues telling the story, "Using our fear and confusion against us to get close. Overtime, he taught us how to control the change. So of course we felt indebted to him and thought he loved us. It wasn't until later that many of us realized who he truly was," Kiara's voice begins to break. "Jake was not the good natured man he portrayed to be, he was something worse. The three of us were the first among many other women who were used by him and his friends for whatever they wanted. Whether it was sex or a random beating just because they felt like it. Even to go as far as to make us serve them hand and foot."

Wiping her tears, Nichole carries on from there, "That was four years ago. Any time any of us tried to fight back or stand up for ourselves, we were beaten worse or locked in what Jake called the dungeon. Because we're werewolves, the wounds healed, but the psychological scars will always remain."

Braheem, Omar, Darius, and I stare at the ground. Even though we aren't the ones that went through it, the emotions they were giving off are felt by all of us. Their pain is traumatic to say the least. I now see why they attacked me in the alley. No one should have to go through that. I know there's some darkness inside of people, and even with werewolves it can get really bad, but this is tragic.

Jasmine, Nichole and Kiara, all bonded and so did a lot of the girls that were imprisoned there. The unfortunate part is not many girls stayed there long. Some overdosed, while others took their own lives due to the abuse. Jasmine, Kiara and Nichole agreed that if it wasn't for the bond they shared, they wouldn't have survived as long as they did.

One day Jasmine had enough and decided that it was time for her to leave. In the dead of night, she decides to escape. Jasmine asked Nichole and Kiara to get out with her. They of course jumped at the idea. Neither of them wanted to die there, they knew that a better life awaited them.

On the night of a new moon, they broke free of their restraints and under the cover of night, left their captures without ever looking back. They cover their tracks and scent by covering themselves in mud and crossing a few state lines making sure to look over their shoulder every step of the way.

The scams they ran were good for money, but they had a hard time finding a place to sleep. Eventually they decided to stay in homes that were vacant with no alarms. None of them want to keep living that way, but what choice do they have? They want more out of life, but have yet to find anything.

They went through years of hell. I can't imagine it even if I try to. We all have our demons, but theirs are in this world. A piece of me wants to leave and tell Chantelle to abort the mission. However, no matter how hard I try, I can't just leave them like this. I have to get them to trust us first.

"I think I've heard enough," I whisper, quietly. "I think it's time to let the wolf out of the bag."

Chantelle nods her head through the window and puts her hair in a ponytail, while stretching to make it seem like she's getting more comfortable. She clears her throat before saying, "Look girls, I'm sorry you went through all of that, I truly am, but I think that you could benefit from being in a pack."

"Why would we want to do that?" Nichole asks.

"Well, if you were a part of a pack the three of you would be protected if someone were to attack. *And* you could stop looking over your shoulder."

"Who said we were looking over our shoulder?" Kiara asks. "Who are you?"

"I'm just someone who wants to help, that's all," Chantelle responds calmly with her hands in the air.

"Are you here to take us back?" Jasmine asks sternly.

"No, no I'm not, I just don't want you three to have to worry anymore," Chantelle says, putting her hands down.

"Why would we?"Kiara asks.

"Because if Jake is as connected as you say he is you're going to need back up and robbing banks is a dead give away."

"How'd you know about that?" Jasmine asks impatiently.

"Because my alpha told me," Chantelle responds. "He's also the reason my brother and I are still alive. He's the one who told me about the Tailors and the fact that they hunt and kill werewolves."

"Why should they matter to us?" Kiara questions.

"If you're alone, who would you turn to?" Chantelle asks. "We all had someone we could turn to and depend on. Wolves are pack animals by nature, the fact that the three of you stayed together through all of this proves that."

"We don't need an alpha!" Kiara screams. "We had one and look at the good that did us!"

"Okay, okay, just listen for a moment, hear what he has to say please," Chantelle pleads.

Jasmine pauses for a moment looking at Kiara and Nichole. She and Chantelle go back and forth for thirty minutes before Jasmine agrees to speak with me. Jasmine is pretending to be strong, but she's really hiding her fear. I sense that she has a little hope and that it's hidden under her feelings. I'm not sure if I'm the right person for the job, but I will try my best to help these girls.

Jasmine clears her throat before she speaks, "Even if we were to entertain this idea of meeting your alpha, what does he want?"

"Just to talk, that's all," Chantelle says, softly. "He helped my brother and I. I know he can help you."

Kiara, Nichole and Jasmine exchange looks, before reluctantly allowing me to meet with them.

Chantelle opens the door revealing Braheem, Omar, Darius and myself. As we walk in Jasmine looks at me and immediately recognizes me, "That's the guy from the alley," Jasmine exclaims.

I nod, "Yes that's me. We're just here to talk, that's it. My name is Damien Nichols, it's nice to officially meet you. You know Chantelle, over there is her brother Omar. This is Darius and Braheem. I am here because there's been a misunderstanding. None of us are here to take you back to Jake or anywhere else," I say calmly.

Nichole stares at me with disbelief, "I don't care either way, but I don't trust you."

"Aight fair enough. Just like you, I was bitten by a werewolf and left on my own," I begin to say. "It didn't manifest until a few years ago. Along the way I met Braheem, then Darius and finally I met Omar and Chantelle. Darius escaped his alpha just like you did. Chantelle and Omar's alpha actually sent them to kill me because he thought I was trying to build my own pack to take over his territory and he wanted to stop it."

I see Chantelle and Omar looking at their feet, in regret. I explain that I didn't blame them for following what they were told, especially since they were manipulated. The looks on the girls' faces softens as I tell our history.

"Listen no disrespect, but I love being a werewolf and free one at that," Jasmine says proudly. "Being a werewolf makes me unique and ever since we escaped that hell, my eyes have been open to how the world really works. I'm able to get what I want when I want and no one can stop me."

"I can stop you, the Tailors can stop you, and the Werewolf's Council can stop you," I exclaim, my eyes illuminating with the passion of my words.

She gasps as her eyes react to mine. Nichole and Kiara stand behind Jasmine as their eyes react the same way hers are.

"Woah, woah, woah everyone settle down," Chantelle says, as she gets between us.

Kiara sighs, "She's right. We shouldn't let things get out of hand. We should hear them out."

Jasmine glares at me, then turns her attention to Chantelle and finally looks at her friends. She calms down and her eyes go back to normal and so do mine. Usually when I get passionate like that, it doesn't trigger my eyes, nor have I triggered anyone else's. I'm not sure what's happening here. There's so much tension between us. When emotions settle, we sit down and begin again.

"Could we possibly talk this out?" I ask.

On the other side of the room sits Kiara, Nichole and Jasmine, who crosses her arms, rolls her eyes and says, "Five minutes."

I take a deep breath and begin explaining what happened when I was kid. I explain the fear I went through and how I was alone when I had my first turn. Then Braheem talks about how he was bitten at 14 and had to leave his family and was on his own ever since. He talks about how he was betrayed by those like Jake and hunted by the Tailors. Braheem goes over how he didn't let anyone in. Then he met me and he's been able to learn how to accept who and what he is.

Darius speaks up and says the same thing. We went to the same high school, but we weren't friends initially. After the incident with a few old school bullies, I helped him. He told them how I initially tried to talk to him, but he brushed me off. Even when I insisted that we not be alone. He's happy to have met both Braheem and I because he was always alone, even before being bitten and now he's not.

Omar and Chantelle talk about Darnell. Darnell fed Chantelle and Omar the lie that he could and would cure them if he did his bidding. They hunted and watched others be killed for him for a few years before meeting me, which was the first time either of them hesitated to kill anyone. After finally getting the chance to talk to them, I told them that there isn't a cure and he was using them.

When they found out the truth, I fought for them alongside Braheem and Darius. I didn't just do it for them, using people is wrong. I wanted them to be free and not used. They explain that Darnell and I fought and I killed him, becoming an alpha myself. I didn't kill him for power, I did it because I had no other choice. Nichole and Kiara listen to us and notice that we're telling the truth. Jasmine is still very critical due to everything they've gone through.

"Listen, I know why you would be standoffish about this, but it's good to have a pack," I begin to say. "Humans and wolves are social creatures by nature. It only makes sense that we join together."

"I still don't know if I can trust you, either of you," Jasmine says. "But if this is in the best interest for my friends then I guess we can work something out."

Jasmine walks over and extends her hand out to me. I stand up from my chair and shake her hand in return. For the remainder of the night we talk about what things would look like moving forward, knowing that there is more to come. I know the girls are still paranoid about joining us, but I have high hopes for the future.

Chapter 6

Our little pack continues to grow, now having eight total members. It's been five years since my first change now and I'm the alpha of my own werewolf pack. Attempting to balance my normal life with Catalina, and being a werewolf is getting difficult. She keeps asking me to turn her into a werewolf, but I don't want her going through the same pain I did. I've shown her the videos of me changing, but that hasn't stopped her from asking.

Having Kiara, Jasmine and Nichole in the pack seem to make us better. The three of them are very tactile. If an infiltration mission is ever needed, their skill would be the ones we'd turn to get things thoroughly planned out.

I've been talking to Tevin a lot since that night with Darnell. We've become very close. I figure that he's met a lot of werewolves, including alphas and wondered if he would mentor me. I didn't think he'd do it, but to my surprise, he happily accepted. In one of our first talks, he explains to me that the wolf is as much a part of us as we are a part of it.

Every now and again we have to let the wolf be free, it's an outside animal, so we have to let it be free. When I thought about it for a while, I remember spending so much time suppressing the wolf that I didn't think about it other than when I turn. I saw it as a beast, and nothing more. Tevin mentions that all wolves love to hunt like every other predator and usually hunting on the night of a full moon is enough for it.

I've been going over to his house for bi-weekly session and today is no different. I spend a few hours here learning all I can. Toward the end of our lesson, I see him bringing a book over to me.

"Damien, here's something new," he begins to say. "There are different wolf forms that we can tap into that you haven't used yet," he says, placing it in front of me.

"What do you mean haven't used yet?" I look at him puzzled.

"While human, it's called Homid, when you're fully transformed it's called Crinos," he says pointing at the page. "However, there's an in between form called Glabro. It's…a pseudo transformation."

"Really?" I ask. "I hadn't thought about it," my eyes widen as I stare at the page.

"From what you shared, you've already been doing a low scale version of this already," Tevin continues. "You've used the glowing eyes and claws, but that's not all. The glabro form will also elongate your ears and make certain changes to your face."

I remember how Darnell transformed in our fight. How his facial features changed, resembling the beginning of a full transformation, but stopping mid-way through.

"Using this form, you can better hide your identity from Tailors and other werewolves," Tevin adds.

As he tells me more about this form I grow in excitement. I can use this form like a mask. I want to try it out for myself and fail immediately after. Instead of stopping mid-way through, I almost transform into my crinos. I stop myself before I do, but my clothes are torn.

"I have a lot of work ahead of me," I joke as Tevin lends me a spare pair of clothes. I start to head for the door, since our time is up.

Before I leave, Tevin stops me and asks, "Have you come up with a name for your pack yet?"

I stare at him puzzled, "A name for my pack?"

"Yea, every alpha that's recognized by the Council, is able to name their own pack," Tevin smiles. "For now your pack name is the D.Nichols Pack, since your last name isn't an uncommon one."

"I never thought about it, but I guess I'll have to now won't I?" I say putting my hand on my chin.

"Yea, you should. Come to me when you've figured out a name and I'll put the registration through to the Council."

"Thank you, I appreciate it."

Later that night, I tell everyone what Tevin shared with me earlier. I suggest the first thing we should try to do is come up with a name for ourselves.

"We're all black werewolves, so why not just call ourselves The Black Pack?" Jasmine asks.

"That's a little too on the nose don't you think?" comments, Chantelle.

"Yea, but what else would we call ourselves? The D.Nichols Pack is so bland," I admit.

"Ever see that trend online for the Night Skins?" Darius asks everyone.

"Oh yea, I saw that!" Exclaims, Kiara.

Everyone's eyes lit up at the thought of calling ourselves the Night Skin Pack. We take a vote and it's unanimous. I text Tevin and tell him our pick. Within minutes, he responds that he'll put the request through, and he'll let me know if it's approved.

Now that naming our pack is settled, we talk about today's lesson. Everyone agrees that we feel stronger whenever we transform and run together. Despite that fact we all think that one day isn't enough. We need more than once a month. Normally, we strive to meet on a full moon, but now we'll add one other night in the month.

As a sign of trust and respect, we'll also let the wolves have control, to further deepen the bond with ourselves, our pack and each other. For the next two months, we work on shifting into our glabro form. It was tough at first, but by working together, we learn how to use it.

In the days that follow our mastering glabro, I finally hear back from Tevin. He calls me to tell me that our name change has been approved. A few other packs were trying to make their name the Night Skins, but we were given the name since this our first name change. I thank him and hang up.

Despite the pack's relationship with Jasmine, Kiara and Nichole getting better from when we first met, I still get the sense that they haven't recognized me as their alpha. I didn't get the same feeling I got from Braheem, Darius, Chantelle and Omar when we became a pack. With the four of them, we felt like a unit. Sometimes I swear we can read each other's minds. However, I think Jasmine, Kiara and Nichole were still resisting me as their alpha. It's not like we don't get along, but it's like I'm ringing their line, and no one's picking up.

Chantelle did what she could in helping them get on their feet. She helped them get a job and eventually get their own place. Since Kiara, Jasmine and Nichole have always been together, they live in an apartment together, giving up robbing and stealing for money.

Otherwise, we're melding quite nicely with one another, but I still sense that they aren't ready to trust me as their alpha yet. Jake and his friends left a huge scar on their hearts. I'll never stop trying to gain their trust, not just as their alpha, but also their friend. I just have to give it time.

One day Catalina comes to me saying she's noticed that something has been bothering me for a while now. When Catalina asks me about it, I tell her everything that's going on. Catalina tries her best to help and give me suggestions, but isn't too sure what she can offer, since she's not a werewolf. I kiss her on her forehead and thank her.

In an effort to take my mind off of everything, Catalina buys tickets to a circus to help me relax. They're for this weekend and she thinks it'll be a good idea for us to go out together. She says I need some fresh air. I'm excited to go and spend time with Catalina. Between our jobs and my werewolf life, we've barely seen each other. A normal night together is needed.

The week came and went, and it's finally the weekend. Time for us to sit and enjoy our time together at the circus. We see so many incredible acts, from daredevils, animal trainers and acrobats. When the final act comes, we see a family of performers, called The Powerhouse Jones'.

We see a mother, a father, and their children. We watch them do amazing things. From acrobatic to contortionist and powerlifting. They're lifting almost three times their own body size, jumping on trampolines and bending their bodies in ways that look like a Mortal Kombat fatality. They don't have the same edge I do, but that makes the show better.

I lean in to tell Catalina saying I want to join the circus. She tells me to keep dreaming. At the end of the act, the youngest son performs. Unlike the rest of his family, he's lifting five times his body weight. He's leaner than the rest of his family, so he shouldn't be able to, especially since everyone in his family is considerably more muscular than he is.

The crowd is loving the show. His family tries to lift the weight and even invites some audience members to try as well. When no one else can, he steps in and lifts the weight with no issues. I wasn't sure until now, but I'm sure he's a werewolf. The audience cheers as he continues to lift incredible weight over his head and move them around the arena. It's remarkable to see that he was doing all these things in plain sight while the crowd cheers.

Honestly it's impressive. Do his parents know or anyone in the circus? To end the show they bring out two one ton barbells that he proceeds to lift. I see why spider-man became a performer. I must be the only one who knows that he's really lifting all that weight. I can smell the metal from the weights and sweat that came from his father when he repeatedly tried to lift the dumbbell. This guy couldn't be more than 145 lbs.

"What's wrong?" Catalina asks.

"N...nothing," I reply.

"Are you sure? You have this serious look on your face," Catalina asks in a worried tone.

I try to keep it from her, but I can't do it for long, "That kid over there, he's like me,"

"Are you sure?" she asks.

"Yea, the bar he's lifting is real, it's not fake," I explain.

"How do you know?" she ponders.

"I can smell the metal from here and hear it when he's putting it back down, the barbell is actually real. I could lift that back when I was a beta."

"You mean when your eyes were yellow?" she asks.

"Yea, you can get stronger naturally, like with everyone else, but there's baseline strength when you're first bitten."

"Do you think he's dangerous?"

"Honestly, I don't know, but I have to watch him to find out."

After the show, we walk toward the car. When we get outside the tent, I see some performers signing autographs. The son is one of them. From the posters I see that his name is Kahlil. Kahlil is showing his strength a little more for his fans, mainly the girls, to get their attention.

Before he signs anything, they ask Kahlil to do something powerful. He rips some bark from a few trees and then some girls would sit on his shoulders and he holds them up while posing for pictures. I watch as his eyes flicker back and forth between his human and werewolf eyes, I don't think he notices.

"Wow, that's so cool," says one of the girls.

"What are you talking about?" Kahlil asks her.

"Your eyes, they changed color for a second," she smiles.

"Oh," he laughs nervously. "Yea that sometimes happens at night," he plays it off nervously.

He then announces to everyone that he needs to get back to his family and clean up for the next show. Kahlil thanks everyone for their time and leaves. I can't take it anymore, I have to say something, because what he's doing is dangerous. I don't know if he lost control for a second or he's still learning, but it won't take long for the Council or Tailors to find out about him, with him performing. The Tailors will be here in minutes if someone posts that online. I tell Catalina about what I saw and with a sorrowful expression she kisses me and says she understands. I sigh because I feel so bad that I have to leave her again.

"Baby...I don't want to leave you," I apologize. "I promise. I just want to go back home with you."

"I know Mi Amor, but this is something you have to do," Catalina smiles back at me, putting her hand on my face. "You're the type of person that can't turn anyone in need down, you're always there to help and that's why I love you."

"I love you too. we'll talk more when I get back, I promise," I say as I hug her.

Catalina nods with a brave smile before driving off. I let out a big sigh as I watch her drive away. Normally I don't do this, but I listen to her in the car. She's softly whimpering in the car. Now I feel even worse. I have to make sure she knows that she's a priority not secondary. I have to make it up to her.

I close my eyes to focus before going toward the tent where Kahlil entered. After a few minutes of searching, I can't find him. The smell of animal poop is everywhere, so I can't pinpoint his location. I let out a growl strong enough to let him know that another werewolf is around. I'm not sure if he can tell if I'm an alpha or not.

"Who are you?" he asks.

My ear twitches as I hear his voice, "Don't worry. I'm not here to hurt you. I'm just here to talk. That's it."

"How do I know?" Kahlil questions.

"Because instead of attacking you, I let you know I was here," I respond.

"I don't trust you, all werewolves are the same," Kahlil says. "They want me to join their packs and I'm not a pack wolf."

"That's only going to get you so far," I explain. "I don't need you to join my pack. I came here to tell you that you have to be careful. I found out you're a werewolf from just watching you perform. It doesn't take a rocket scientist, just someone like me or hunters."

"What do you mean hunters?" he asks.

Rather than answer Kahlil, I slowly start to walk out of the tent, hoping his curiosity will make him follow me. After a few minutes, I hear his footsteps following a few paces behind mine, I must have piqued his interest. Thanks to the training from Jasmine and the others, I'm able to sneak around a little quieter, stay just ahead of him so he can see me. Also, just far enough so he couldn't catch up. When he tries to catch up I circle around to get him off guard. Just as he rounds the tree, I step from behind another and surprise him.

Kahlil stops abruptly, "Who are you?"

"My name is Damien," I respond.

"The guy that I was talking to was you?" he asks, condescendingly.

"Yea, why? Is that a problem?" I challenge.

"No, but I imagined someone a little scarier based off the aura you gave," he admits.

"Tch, I don't know what that means, but I am the one that growled," I growl once more, showing him it was indeed me. "The reason I wanted to talk to you is because I saw your show and I was going to let everything slide, because everyone believes it was all a show. But then I saw your eyes flicker as I was leaving. You have to control yourself better than that. Someone could see you."

"Why should I?" he asks furiously.

I tell him about Tailors and the Council. He of course is skeptical of everything I tell him. He doesn't believe Tailors or the Council exist. I try telling him that I've met both parties, but unlike the Council's people who, while stern, accepts all werewolves. They want to keep our race a secret. The Tailors on the other hand want to exterminate us. I try my best to explain the danger he'll be in if the Council ever perceives him as a threat to our secret. Worse if the Tailors find out about him, they'll hunt him down and kill him without hesitation.

"Why do you care?" he asks. "I'm not in your pack."

"I just don't want anything to happen to you or any other werewolf. Pack or not we should be sticking together."

"Nigga, I've been a werewolf for almost a year and half and ain't never run into your Council or pfft Tailors," Kahlil turns around and starts walking back to the circus.

"Ard look, I'm not trying to get you to join me. I just want you to be safe."

"Leave me alone!" he exclaims. "You have no idea what it's like to be the only one in your family with no talent," he turns around and stares me in the eyes. "My family *is* this entire circus. My Dad and brothers are strongmen. My other brother and sisters are the acrobats and though my mom is on the stage with strong women, she's also double-jointed and is a great performer."

Kahlil's facial expression changes, "Sometimes, I hear them late at night talking about the shows. Each time they leave me out of the conversation because I couldn't contribute anything to the show. When the morning comes, they smile and act like everything is perfectly fine."

Tears swell in his eyes as he speaks, "Ever since I was bitten, it's been the best thing that could have happened to me. They don't look or talk about me like I'm a failure. I can contribute now," Kahlil says softly.

"And no one is going to take that away from me!" he expresses in a serious tone.

I pause for a moment, processing what he told me, "Kahlil, I'm sorry you went through that. I know what it's like to feel like a failure, believe me I get it. However, I can't take the wolf from you even if I tried. As far as I know there's no cure. All I'm saying is be careful. From what I've seen the Council doesn't take lightly those who could expose us. On the other hand, you're putting a target on your pack with the Tailors and on the other it's the council," I caution him.

"The Council and the Tailors know nothing about me!" Kahlil shouts. "I'm free to do whatever I want," Kahlil says happily. The tone of his voice changes, "The only reason they'd find out about me is because you were seen talking to me. Now go before your imaginary council finds you."

Kahlil turns around laughing. I try to reach out and grab Kahlil's arm, hoping I can get him to listen. I hear something snap in the distance. I look around trying to find out what it was. I search everywhere, but I'm unable to see anyone. I open my ears, and I hear footsteps nearby. Suddenly, I hear Kahlil screaming.

Chapter 7

I sprint in search of Kahlil, hoping I can get to him in time. I run through the woods desperately trying to find him. Did I bring this on him? Did someone follow us after we left the grounds? I can't worry about that now, I have to get to him first. When I find Kahlil he's pinned to a tree with an arrow in his shoulder. I try to pull it out, but the second I touch it, it burns my hand. I shake it trying to cool it off.

"Ahh, it must be coated in silver," I groan.

"Damien, what's going on?!" Kahlil asks frantically.

"I think it's the Tailors, the Council doesn't use arrows," I respond.

"Are you sure?" Kahlil asks.

"He's right young man, it's not the Council," we hear a voice in the distance say. I turn around and saw a man emerging from the shadows, "You can say we're something much... much worse."

I can't let them see my face. My eyes glow and I bring out my claws, the bridge of my face changes, and my ears peak at a point. Glabro is very useful.

"Haha, look what we have here, an alpha trying to save his beta," The man says smugly. "We wondered how long it was going to be before you showed up."

"Who are you?" Kahlil asks scarcely.

"It's obvious isn't it?" The older man says. "We're Tailors and you... you are our prey. We're better hunters than you mongrels."

We pause for a moment, Kahlil stares at me before saying, "Tailors? You're telling me they're real?"

"Indeed we are real dear boy. And just in time to put you dogs down,"a female Tailor responds.

"My life may be in danger, but to call yourselves Tailors is kinda funny," Kahlil laughs. "Who came up with it? An angry seamstress?"

"Tch, you dog!" The leader screams at him. "Becoming a Tailor is the highest honor a human can have. We keep you whelps in check and yet you multiply every year. Let me put this in a way you flea carrying dogs can understand. We're just like your tail, dogs like you like to chase us and you can bite at us all you want, but we'll be forever out of your grasp. Just like a shadow we're always behind you, always at your tail."

In all of my run-ins with the Tailors, it's never been this dire of a situation. Moments later, all the charisma Kahlil had fades. The seriousness of the man's words and the seriousness of their faces make it very clear that we are in danger. We have to get away from here.

All of their weapons are aimed at me, keeping me from moving. Their lasers show me that I'm dead in their sights. Maybe I can find a way to pick them off one by one and we can escape.

I focus on their leader, "Y'all must be pretty afraid of us to send seven of you for just the two of us."

He smirks at me, "Afraid?" he responds. "Kid, it's not like either of you are even human anymore. One of you is stronger than the seven of us put together. Two of you can wipe out a small town in a matter of hours if you wanted to. Second, two of them could take your beta over there. And finally, lucked out that your beta drew you out, it's like Christmas came early."

He obviously has a disdain for werewolves, so there's no way to talk him out of this. Perhaps I can use his anger against him. The angrier he gets, the more likely I can manipulate him. He begins stepping closer to us. As I watch him, I wait patiently for an opportunity to take him down. I know there's a flaw in him somewhere.

"Kahlil, I have a plan, Just stay close to me when I make my move," I whisper.

He nods while keeping his eyes directed at the Tailors as they approach us. I stand tall with my hand on Kahlil's shoulder prepared to rip the arrow from him and set him free. It'll hurt like hell, but he'll heal. As the leader draws near, I notice even though I'm standing tall he towers over me. My heart begins to pound in my chest with anticipation.

The leader stands directly in front of me smiling smugly, "Would you look at that, he still has some fight in him," he looks me up and down. "I'd expect nothing less from an alpha. I'll tell you what, I could use the exercise, you can get the first hit."

"Sir, do you think that is wise?" One of the soldiers asks.

He stands there with a welcoming challenge in his eyes at me, "Yea I wanna see what the kid's got, there's something in him. Looks like hope and I want to be the one who tears it from him right in front of this beta, so he knows who the real apex predator is."

I smile back at him, "Oh you'll get your wish."

I fake like I'm going to throw a punch, thinking he's going to block or counter. Instead, I use my strength against him by sweeping his leg and pushing him as far back as I can. As he falls to the ground and in the confusion, I rip off my shirt and use it to grab the arrow and pull it out of Kahlil's shoulder.

Once it's out, I grab his other arm and scream, "C'mon, let's go!"

With the Tailors still staggered, we run through the woods. But they won't stay that way for long. The leader screams at them to shoot and chase after us. They must've anticipated a chase because I trip over a tripwire that sends arrows flying at us. I can dodge them, but I doubt it's the only one out here.

Kahlil stops and breathes heavily, "H... h... hold on f...for a second. I need to catch my breath."

"We don't have time, we have to go," I insist.

"Okay... just give me a second," he says.

He inspects his arm, "Why aren't I healing?"

"You were shot with a silver arrowhead that's probly laced with wolfsbane. It's not like any normal injury, it takes us longer to heal."

"That's real?!" Kahlil exclaims.

"Yes nigga, just like we're real. *Now get your ass up and move*!!" I scream.

I peek from behind a tree, looking to see if we were being followed. From what I can tell, the coast is clear and we have nothing to worry about. I get a better look at his shoulder. It's trying to heal, but it's going to take some time.

"It doesn't look that bad. It's already starting to heal," I assure him.

"Thanks, but it still hurts like a bitch," he groans.

"Yea it's going to for a little while, because of how long it was in you, it might take a few hours," I advise.

"A few hours?!" he shouts.

Before he can say anything, I cover his mouth when I hear Tailors catching up to us. I tell him we need to go and we start running again. I tie the rest of my shirt around his arm and we keep running. With Kahlil hurt, we aren't going to get very far. He keeps nearly passing out. I howl to call for the others, because we need back up. I hear them howl back and they aren't far.

"Damien, we...we... I need to stop," Kahlil says, heavily winded. "I can't run anymore."

"Just a bit longer, we're not far from my pack," I urge.

Kahlil closes his eyes before dropping onto his face into the grass. I check his pulse, he's still alive, but barely. I take off the shirt again and the wound is getting worse. Whatever strain of wolfsbane they used is making him pass out. I'm out of time and options. I put him on my shoulders and begin running 65 MPH.

"Where the hell are y'all?!" I scream.

Not long after, I'm confronted by Tailors who shine lights in my eyes, stopping me in my tracks. They turn on other lights that illuminate the entire area.

"Did you really think that you could get away from us?" One of them asks.

I bare my teeth and growl at them. I'm ready for a fight, but I have to also protect Kahlil. As they step closer, I take one back. All I can do is watch as they surround us with the intent to kill. Suddenly, the lights go out and screams of the Tailor's are heard one after another. Finally, I have some help.

"I can't believe you, of all people are being punked by Tailors," I hear Braheem mocking me.

"Nigga, It's not like I was playing tug of war with them," I retort.

Jasmine starts leading the charge in attacking the Tailors. Seeing Kahlil was on my back, they come over to help me with him as the squad of Tailors rush toward us with weapons drawn.

"Jay, hold back," I command.

"D, you might be afraid of them, but I'm not," she responds, pridefully.

She charges forward without a second thought. I hoped I could stop her, but she's too headstrong. In less than a few seconds, Jasmine knocks out three Tailors under the cover of darkness. However, her triumph doesn't last long. They turn on another set of lights that blind her before they tase her. I give Kahlil to Kiara and Nichole and tell Omar and Chantelle to join me in rescuing Jasmine.

Braheem stays behind to protect them. With them having weapons, we have to be smart about how we move. My priority is getting us all home safely, no matter how slim the chance is. That includes getting to Tevin if he needs to patch us up.

The Tailors tie up Jasmine and starts taking her away. I'm not having it anymore, I tell Omar and Chantelle that it's time to play offense. We use our speed to our advantage, howling in one spot before maneuvering to another, taking out the rest of the lights, in an attempt to keep them guessing.

Each time one of us move we get closer. The goal is to get to them without killing them. We don't kill, unless provoked. We're in sync, not needing to say anything, almost able to hear each other's thoughts. A few months ago, we saw our wolves using this as a hunting technique and since then we've been waiting to use it. We fight hard pushing to get Jasmine back. It takes a little longer than expected, but we succeed at the last second.

When Chantelle removes the gag, Jasmine couldn't wait to talk, "Ugh, took ya long enough."

"You try fighting to knock out lights, then against bullets trying to save your ass," Chantelle responds.

They laugh as Nichole helps Jasmine up. That's when we hear a few shots go off. It's then that we realize that we fell into their trap. They were trying to separate us. By the time we knocked out the Tailors that took Jasmine, we were too far away from everyone else. We race back fearing the worst, to only see Nichole, Kiara and Braheem limping toward us. Braheem has a few bleeding wounds, while Kiara and Nichole are holding each other up and blood coming from their heads while also having a few knife wounds of their own. I know they fought hard, but were out matched.

"Where's Kahlil?" I ask.

"Damien, I'm sorry they got him," Braheem says defeated.

"It's ok, we'll get him back," I say. "Where's Darius?"

"We don't know, we called him when we heard you howling, but he didn't answer, so we left him behind," Kiara says.

I don't know what to do. I lost a werewolf to a bunch of hunters who outsmarted us at almost every turn and now we're down a pack member. I start pacing back and forth in the grass. I thought to ask the other Tailors we fought where they took Kahlil, but they're nowhere to be found.

"What do we need him for anyway?" Jasmine scoffs. "I could have taken all those hunters down myself."

"ENOUGH!" I yell as I swing my arm backward, hitting a tree and knocking it to the ground. "I am so sick of your attitude. It almost got us killed just now and you're still sitting here being arrogant? We're a pack, we're supposed to work as a unit, but noooo you always have to go off half-assed and look where we are!"

Jasmine takes a step back, but keeps the same demeanor. I didn't care, I had to say something to her. Not every plan can just be won by brute force. I'm the alpha not her, she needs to respect that. Jasmine crosses her arms and pouts before turning away from me.

"Damien calm down, we'll get him back," Omar says.

"Jasmine, Damien is right, Kiara chimes in. "We have to focus and work together, not fight amongst ourselves."

"I don't feel that way," Jasmine says. "I still don't like the idea of someone telling me what to do. Do we really need an alpha?"

I get where she's coming from but I'm the alpha, she needs to respect me. As annoyed as I am, we needed to get our wounds looked at. We head to Tevin so he can stitch us up before our healing kicks in. We go home for the night and then schedule to meet at the Den tomorrow night, hoping to figure out our next move.

The following day, we finally manage to get a hold of Darius. He says that he heard my howl and wanted to run, but couldn't. He was at a dinner with his grandparents and wasn't able to join us until now. Braheem lays into him pretty hard about not letting us know. Eventually we get down to business.

Since we know nothing about where Kahlil was taken, the best we come up with as a plan is for one of us to get captured by the Tailors. Hopefully we can find him and that person will signal the others for the cavalry to break in and save them both. While we all were in agreement with the plan, one question remains, who would be the one to get captured? Though everyone steps up, the first to volunteer is Jasmine. The aura she's giving off is arrogance and pride, she doesn't care about Kahlil at all.

"We have to beat them at their own game," I say proudly.

"Let's lay a trap for the hunters to become the hunted," Jasmine begins to say. "Since no one wants to back down, how bout this, we all get captured Trojan Horse style and then free Kahlil that way."

Everyone pauses for a second before looking at me.

"Jasmine, you are out of your mind!" Kiara exclaims. "Are you trying to get us all killed?!"

"I still don't know why we're even talking about this, the guy's not one of us," Jasmine snarks.

"Risking our lives like this is going to get us all killed. And I don't want to die."

"No it won't, he may not be a part of our pack, but he's a werewolf," Nichole Interjects. "This is the only plan we have to get Kahlil out safely without killing the Tailors or any one of us getting killed."

"We're werewolves, we should just bust our way inside and take Kahlil back by force," Jasmine declares. "We got the power, we're faster, stronger and can get more ferocious. We get in, grab him and get out before they know what happened."

"Jasmine!" I snap. "You don't get it. You've been held against your will and what Jake did to the three of you is nothing compared to what they'll do to Kahlil. He's not being used for sex, he's going to be used against other werewolves. They'll possibly kill him or worse, they'll use him for experiments. Yes we're werewolves and we may be stronger and faster, but they'll have a fortress with better numbers, guns and armor that they *will* use against us!"

Everyone is frozen, not sure what to say next. I inspect everyone's gaze before continuing, "You talk a big game about going full wolf, but I can tell you've never been there. I've fully let go and given into my primal instincts in order to save Chantelle and Omar. The power is amazing and yes you feel unstoppable, but there's more to it."

My tone changes to a softer one. "You have to be able to come back from it. You know I killed Chantelle and Omar's alpha, but you don't know how I did it. He lied to them and made fun of it like it was some sick joke. He kept hurting them while laughing and talking about power like it was the end all be all. He was beating them and laughing. When I couldn't take it anymore, that's when I killed him. I overpowered him and punched into his chest, ripped out his heart and took his power for myself. I watched the blood roll down my fingers."

I stare at the ground as I continue to speak softer, "I wanted to let him live, I tried to let him live, but when he came at me for the final time, it was either him or me. No it was all of us or him, because he would have killed Braheem, Darius Chantelle, Omar and myself, if I hadn't let go and given into that anger. And you know what he said to me before he died? *'See, I told you that you were a killer.'*

"That was the last thing I wanted to hear that man say. I don't want any of you to take a life and kill with the type of anger I had. You know why? Because all you'll do from that point forward is suffer... like I have. Taking someone else's life, stays with you. I know it's stayed with me. Even though I know he would have killed us, I still feel there could have been another way."

Jasmine, Kiara and Nichole all stare at me then at everyone else. Intensely focusing on Chantelle and Omar. Everyone's silence corroborates my story. Then everyone's attention turns to me. The intensity of our emotions left all of us enclosed, attempting to find out where we all stand with one another.

Omar clears his throat, "Dame... I'm so sorry you had to go through all of that just for us."

"Yea...neither of us knew that you've been carrying around so much guilt all this time," Chantelle says tearfully.

I sigh heavily, "I guess...it is what it is," I turn my gaze to Jasmine, "I'm sorry, I didn't mean to snap. I just want to protect y'all and I want to get Kahlil back before they do something to him. I need a second."

I walk away leaving everyone behind, so I can cool off. I hope we can figure this out calmly. I go over everything in my mind, from meeting Darius to Braheem, to Omar and Chantelle, Jasmine, Nichole and Kiara and now Kahlil. I thought about getting attacked by that werewolf when I was a kid and how it's affected my life. I then picture Catalina and how much I love her. I don't want her involved in any of this.

I'm happy she knows about all of this, but there have been times when I come home and she's needed to patch me up. It doesn't matter that I healed, it's the fact that she needs to wrap my wounds at all. She still asks me to turn, but if she ever got seriously hurt, I don't know what I'd do.

I begin to slowly breathe deeply as I peer into the darkness of the woods. Then I gaze at the stars, trying to focus on the task at hand. We have to get Kahlil back, but we can't if we can't agree on anything. I sit on a rock trying to find a way to get everyone together. I put my head in my hands trying to figure out if the plan we came up with will even work. In theory it could, but going into unknown territory there's still so much about the Tailors we don't know. Suddenly, I hear someone walking behind me. Without turning, I know it's Jasmine. The sound of her footsteps, the smell of her perfume, it wasn't hard for me to determine it was her.

When she gets close enough, she says, "Damien, I'm sorry. I get what you were saying and I didn't know you had that much to live with."

I sigh, "It's ok, it's not your fault. I know you and the girls didn't know."

"I want to work together with you all, and get Kahlil back," Jasmine says softly. "It's just that I've been the one that Nichole and Kiara look to when things got rough. When we were going through that hell, all the girls turned to me when shit hit the fan."

I stand up and turn around, "Jasmine you're headstrong and you're fearless. Qualities that are unique to the pack, but you can't let your past and your emotions get the better of you. You have to stop fighting me. I asked you to join the pack not only for your protection, but also for ours."

"I just have a hard time letting that go," Jasmine admits. "I don't want to feel powerless again." Jasmine's face, softened with her words, almost quivering.

"I'm not telling you to let go of your anger, but to use it," I say softly. "You have keen senses and can see when things are about to go wrong," I respond.

120

"Everyone here has a role to play. A pack is only as strong as the members in it. Everyone has a voice in my pack, and no one gets left behind. I don't know what it'll take to trust that but I'll never stop showing that to the three of you. For right now, let's get back to finishing coming up with a plan."

I walk past her and start heading back. She then stops me before turning me around. Jasmine steps closer to me and stares directly into my eyes. The glimmer in her eyes was something I hadn't seen before. She suddenly hugs and thanks me, no longer side stepping around her feelings about me and the pack. Jasmine is entrusting herself and the other two to me.

That's when I feel it, I know everyone else does too. It's like a missing piece was finally being put in a puzzle, almost completing it. We go back to join everyone else, to see the smiles on their faces as an indication that we're finally all in sync. Our pack is stronger, our family is stronger and now I know we can save Kahlil together.

"Ok everyone, let's make sure our plan doesn't get our alpha killed while he's inside," Jasmine announces.

It's the first time she's called me alpha and it makes me feel good about it, "You heard the lady," I say smiling.

Chapter 8

It takes a few days, but we finally manage to reach an agreement on how we can save Kahlil. The simplest plan is to send someone in and while they're inside they'll signal to the rest of the pack when they find Kahlil. It's going to be a battle on two fronts. Everyone else will fight the Tailors on the outside while the inside person fights the Tailors on the inside and somewhere in the middle we'll meet up and leave together.

Now that Jasmine is on board with the rest of us, she votes that I be the one who goes in to save Kahlil. She requests that she be the one to lead the charge from the outside. She and everyone else will watch from the outside after I'm taken into the Tailor base. Braheem, Darius, Omar, Chantelle and Kiara will follow Jasmine's lead. They'll stay in the shadows, watching until I give the signal. I tell them to stay in glabro the entire time.

Coming up with this plan and seeing everyone's strengths made me happy to have Jasmine, Braheem, Darius, Chantelle, Kiara, Omar and Nichole be a part of my pack. I know I can trust them with my life. The only thing we couldn't figure out is how to get the Tailors to chase us. Neither of us know how to draw them to us, we've always been the one hunted by them, never the other way around.

At first, we try to track their scent to their hideout, since it still lingers in the woods, but it's very faint. We follow the smell, but lose it after twenty minutes. No matter how many times we go back and start again, we lose their scent at the same spot each time. These Tailors know how to hide from us. Whatever they're using to hide their scent, it's very good.

In the hopes that we can draw them out, Kiara comes up with the idea to create a bunch of dummy accounts online that reports a strange animal running around the woods scaring people. It takes a few days, but we finally get them to take the bait. Every report that we created, the Tailors follow up on. We use disguises to watch as people show up asking specific questions about the *animal* rather than focusing on the people who reported it.

We run them around town for three days straight to verify they're Tailors before letting them catch up to me. Kiara and Nichole make the final reports online and the Tailors react quicker than they ever have before. When we hear them approaching, I'm already in the woods waiting for them. The report states I'm attacking campers, who are really Chantelle and Omar are in disguises. When the Tailors show up to save the two campers, they tell Chantelle and Omar that they are animal control and for them to go somewhere safe.

"You're on D, good luck," Omar says as they leave the grounds.

I hear the Tailors approaching and prepare to give them the best show ever, "Alright you mutt, we know you're there," one of them calls out.

I hide behind a tree, "Who are you and what do you want with me?" I ask.

"We're here to make sure beasts like you don't terrorize any more nice people," the other threatens me.

I run away so they chase after me. I figure they'll do the same thing they did earlier, so I'm on the lookout for any traps they may have set for me. The first one I find are claw traps hidden under a pile of leaves. I'm prepared to give them an easy win, but I didn't want to be mangled, so I run around it to find another trap.

Then I find an electrical trap. Before I run into it, I turn around when I hear them drawing close. I glare at them, while baring my teeth. I can't believe how easy this became. Things are going exactly as planned. We're the ones with the upper hand this time. I hit the trap and am shocked with a convulsing amount of electricity. I'd prefer not to do it this way, but I'm wrapped in the wires and fall to the ground.

"Well look what we have here boys, an alpha, without a pack," says a third Tailor.

"You took a werewolf a few days ago and I want him back. Now!" I demand.

"We may have killed him, it would be nice for you to join him," the female Tailor says.

"Wait, let's take him alive," the male Tailor suggests. "You know alphas have a thing about them where they can force betas to do their bidding. It's a primal thing, and if we can take him alive we can see what he does with the other one."

That's it, they told me all I need to know. I'm pretty sure they're talking about Kahlil. I begin smiling to myself. This is easier than I thought.

"Yes, let's take him alive," the female Tailor says.

"I'm not going anywhere with you, you'll have to kill me first," I sneer.

"Aww, the little doggy doesn't want to play with us. I'll make him heal," the male Tailor threatens.

I lean toward the Tailors, pretending to attack. They shoot me with their tasers, I could have easily dodged them, but I let it hit me. It stings worse than I thought and the tasers force me to lose consciousness.

When I awake, I'm bound to a gurney and my mind is hazy. I don't know where I am or how long I've been out. They have me in some type of containment box with a fluorescent light at the top. I try to, but I can't break free. I smell something funny, that stings my nostrils. Whatever it is, it making it hard for me to focus. I try looking around, but my eyes won't concentrate on anything. I can only guess that they're using some type of airborne wolfsbane to keep me from regaining my senses. A few minutes later I fall back to sleep.

I wake up again, unable to tell where they're taking me. I hope it's the same place they took Kahlil. I hope the others are close behind, because I keep drifting in and out of consciousness. The world around me swirls every time I open my eyes until I inevitably phased back out. The final time I wake up, it's a few minutes before we stop. I don't know how long we drove, but it must've been a while. This last time I wake up, the smell starts to fade and my hazy mind begins to clear.

I feel the truck jerk forward, we must have stopped. I listen to everything around me, hearing the soldiers get out of the truck and brag to the others about how they caught an alpha. Whatever they were pumping into the back of the truck must be wearing off. I have to pretend to still be asleep, since I'm in no shape to fight, but I'll listen to everything. As the doors open, I lie still. I figure I'm where I need to be, but I can't be sure.

As they take me out of the truck, the Tailors tighten my restraints. I hear so many people, as they wheeled me into the facility. Though it's still hard to focus, I hear people speaking different languages. I hear some people speaking Spanish, French, and what I think is German.

"Be Careful!" one Tailor screams.

"Why?" asks another. "He's just another dog about to be put down."

"NO, he's not," the Tailors warns. "He's an alpha. If we can get him on our side we can use him to control others. And because he's an alpha, that kb wolfsbane will only work on him for so long. Keep him tied down before he wakes up."

"A kid like him, an alpha? Please," scoffs another.

"He might have killed his alpha and started a new pack, who knows. *Just get him in a cell.*" I hear a familiar voice say.

Whoever he is, he's someone important. They aren't taking any chances. They secure my restraints before wheeling me further into their compound. Just before the door closes, I hear Jasmine howl, letting me know they're close by. I feel relief knowing they followed. I'm wheeled into what I think is an elevator and we proceed to go down. I'm not sure how far we go, but it's deep underground. Probably to stop any of us from breaking out.

It takes a little time, but the elevator finally stops. As we pass through the elevator doors, I'm welcomed to the stench of blood. It's so overwhelming, I smell burnt hair, silver, wolfsbane, blood, and other bodily fluids. They don't care what they do to us, but whatever torment they subject werewolves to makes my skin crawl. I sense the fear and hopelessness lingering all over. My heart begins racing the further they roll me in this place.

I try not to react to the putrid smells, but it becomes difficult. When they set me in my cage, I feel them draw blood. I barely flinch, hoping they think it's my body's natural reaction. Then they take my fingerprints, I guess they want to find out who I am. These people are thorough, but what can I expect from a group of people who hunt werewolves for a living? Good thing I've never been arrested.

When I hear them get back onto the elevator, my eyes shoot open. It's time to put the plan into action. After a few minutes, I stand up from the bed and look around the cell. I'm not all the way there yet, but I have enough strength to stand up. The cell isn't big, but small enough so I can't turn while inside. I try to find a weak point in the bars, but there isn't one. As soon as I grab one, I'm immediately hit with an electric charge. One strong enough to make me jump back.

"Ah ah ah, we wouldn't want you escaping and causing havoc now would we?" I hear the familiar voice on the intercom say.

"Who are you, where am I?!" I ask, in a panic.

"Well my dear boy, you're here in one of our finest experimental buildings," the voice responds. "You're the first alpha we've ever had here. Sorry if we didn't roll out the red carpet for you." he patronizes me.

I inspect the cell once more, now seeing the camera in the corner of the ceiling next to an audio box.

"We're going to have a little fun with you now that you're our honored guest," the voice says menacingly. "I was hoping we'd meet again after that night in the woods."

There's no longer any doubt in my mind. He's the same guy I met that night with Kahlil. He must be the one in charge here.

"What do you want from me?" I ask confused.

"We only want to contain and then exterminate your kind, however, we still don't know everything about you yet. So you and many like you will be subject to tests for us to kill you all off in the very near future," I can't see his face, but I feel the smugness in his tone.

"I haven't done anything to you!" I shout.

"Maybe not yet, but you always give into the beast at some point. It's been like this for millennia. Our king's mission is our mission."

"What king? What are you talking about?" I question.

He doesn't respond. I'm alone in silence. Suddenly, the lights in my cell turn on and in comes three Tailors with cattle-prods. I try to fight them off, but the wolfsbane isn't out of my system yet. They easily overpower me using the cattle-prods and I drop to my knees as they strap me to another gurney and wheel me out of the cell.

This time, they bring me into a medical room with a few nurses. I notice that one of them is wearing a bracelet and another is wearing a necklace with an insignia that my mom wears a lot. I asked my mom about it once before, but she told me she got it from her time in the military. I've also seen the same symbol on Jakobe and Davion's sweaters when they came home a few weeks ago.

This has to be a coincidence, because there is no way that my mom and two of my childhood friends are werewolf hunters. Jakobe and Davion went to the military after high school. My heart starts racing as I start to looking around to try to find the same symbol anywhere else or on anyone else's uniform. Luckily, while looking around, I can't find the same symbol anywhere else.

"Damien focus," I tell myself.

Eventually, I find myself alone. I sit in the room for a while, even though it's only a few minutes, it feels like hours. I attempt to sit up, but the straps won't budge. It shouldn't be this hard for me to rip them, what's going on? Are they trying to see if I'll try to break free? What are they waiting for? Where are they? I start singing some songs, counting random things in the room, anything I usually do when I'm bored. In counting the tiles on the ceiling, I see another camera fixated on me. I'm not going to give them any satisfaction.

I thought about the possibility of guards outside waiting for me. I feel safe knowing I'm not alone, because if I was, I'd be terrified. I start to think about how I got here and if I could get back to the cells, hoping I get the opportunity to find Kahlil. Eventually, I got tired of waiting for them and decide to break free. I've regained a good amount of my strength back, so I sit up, breaking the straps with ease. Soon after, I walk out of the room and peek into the hallway. There's no one in the halls, but there's a rotating camera. I pause until I'm sure it wasn't going to see me when I leave the room.

After leaving the room, I tiptoe through the hallway all the way to the elevator. Listening to my surroundings with every step I take. To my surprise, no one is in earshot. Am I a few floors from the cells or fight on top? Once I get on the elevator, I figured to start two floors down and go from there. When the doors open, I realize this is the wrong floor. It takes a few tries, but as I descend lower, the grotesque smells grow stronger. I know I'm getting close.

Finally, I make it to the cell floor, and it's dimly lit, I can see in the dark, but I still have to be wary of my surroundings. Using my wolf eyes, I carefully search each cell, hoping that Kahlil is in one of them. I hear someone faintly breathing, but I can't pinpoint it. This floor is huge, I hope to find him soon and get out of here. By this point, I've searched three quarters of the entire floor and found nothing, but I won't give up. As I walk toward the last section of cells, the sound of breathing grows louder. I grin as I rush over. When I approach the cell, I see someone in the cell, hiding in the shadows. Upon further inspection, I see the person groaning was in fact Kahlil.

"I FOUND HIM," I say to myself excitedly.

The light in the cell makes him barely visible, but I can tell he's been badly beaten. It saddens me in the realization that some of the blood I've been smelling is his. I feel sorry for him, Kahlil doesn't deserve any of this, he's just someone trying to fit in with his family and the Tailors did this to him. His wounds are still fresh, but not healing. What did they do to him?

"Hold on Kahlil, I'll get you out of there," I whisper to him as I look for a way to open the cell.

"What do you think you're doing?" I hear the voice on the speaker says.

Lights all over the cell floor turn on all at once, illuminating everything around me. I turn around ready for a fight. I knew they were watching me, but I hoped I had more time.

"Sir, we have to make sure he doesn't get close to the other one," a Tailor says as he's walking toward us. "You want me to stop him?"

"You idiot, he's not like the other one, he's an alpha," the voice responds. "You're young, your ability to tell the difference between them will come in due time."

I observe the man standing in front of me with his weapon drawn. He's a tall, skinny, average looking man with light brown skin. There's nothing remarkable about him, and he didn't seem as much of a threat.

"Who are you?" I ask him.

"Listen kid, we don't have time to chit-chat," he responds. "We have other werewolves we'd like to hunt, like that little pack of yours."

"I won't give up my friends!" I scream. "We haven't done anything wrong, don't put us into a category we're not!"

"All of you are abominations of nature. All your kind does is murder," the man states.

"I haven't killed anyone," I declare.

"Your kind has been killing people for centuries. All of you are cursed dogs who needs to be put down," the man asserts.

I sense the conviction of his words in my soul. I've never killed any humans, or terrorized anyone and neither has anyone in my pack, but he may be right about that. I don't know much of our history nor do I know what many other wolves are like, but I do know one thing. It wasn't me who did those things.

"That's not me!" I scream. "Not all of us are the same, so don't lump us all together like that. I don't have it in me to kill without reason," The passion in my words emanate from me. My eyes glow crimson red. "Kahlil over there didn't deserve any of this, look at him, he's barely breathing."

"Who cares about him, he's gonna die like all of you," the young Tailor says.

"You're going to sit there and tell us that you've never killed anyone?" The voice on the speaker asks. "How'd you become an alpha?"

I looked down at the ground remembering how I gained the power of an alpha. Even though it was to protect Omar and Chantelle, I still killed Darnell and became an alpha. I thought it was ok, since I took a life to protect theirs. The fight in me leaves almost instantly once the realization sets in. If he wasn't a werewolf, he wouldn't have turned them and I wouldn't have had to kill him.

"I wondered how you became an alpha at such a young age without being from one of the families," the young Tailor concludes.

"I didn't kill him to take his power, I did it to protect two of my betas," I cry out. "I killed him to protect them."

"Kid, the reason behind it doesn't matter, you killed another werewolf," the speaker disproves. "The crimson color in your eyes is a physical and constant reminder of the blood you spilled."

I drop to my knees as I lose myself within the self reflection of their accusations. The pit I fell in my stomach is enormous. Am I just a monster like they say?

"Timothy, put down your weapon, he's ours now, take him to room 5 and bring the other one to the infirmary so he doesn't die. We're not done with either of them," the speaker box says.

Timothy steps closer to me and puts very thick chains on my wrists and ankles. A few Tailors come behind him to pick up Kahlil and take him along with me to the elevator. I watch as they wheel Kahlil out onto another floor. As the doors close, I flinch.

An animal, a killer? I thought so at first but I know that's not the entire truth. They take me to a large empty room and just like the cells, there's a strong smell of so many other things. They walk me into the room and hook my chains to another chain that hangs from the ceiling in the center. I can't help but think about what I did to Darnell. As they leave the room, they close the door behind them.

"I... I didn't want to kill him," I say softly.

I did what I thought was right. There may have been another way. I had the power to stop him, but I killed him. I don't know what I could have done differently. I watch as the door closes behind them and the room becomes dark. I'm alone with one small light above my head slightly swaying back and forth.

Chapter 9

They leave me in the shadows of my forebearers. I don't know about the werewolf who bit me or how many people they've killed. Am I any different from anyone of my kind? The Council is supposed to keep us all in check, but if they were, would the Tailors exist? So many questions that don't have answers.

Suddenly, Timothy and his mentor come bursting through the door. The lights in the room blind me for a moment. As my vision adjusts, the leader grabs my shirt and screams in my face.

"What's with you kid?" he asks, aggravated. "Our database can't find you. Nothing in the DNA results for your family history or fingerprints. You're a ghost, who are you?!"

"W...what are you talking about?" I ask confused.

"Our database is connected to the police, the FBI, CIA and even Interpol, but none of them could find a record on you," Timothy explains.

"Who are you working with to hide you from us?" the captain asks.

"I… I'm not working with anyone," I respond. "I've only ever run from hunters. Why would I work with people who want to kill me?" I ask frantically.

"Bullshit!" the leader screams in my face. "There's no way you don't have an accomplice running interference for you."

"I don't know what you're talking about!" I scream leaning in to match his energy.

"Captain Bruce, sir, he's obviously protecting someone," Timothy suggests.

"I'm not protecting anyone!" I exclaim.

Timothy backhands me, but when I turn my face back toward him, I'm glaring. I want to be free of these chains, so I can beat his ass. Bruce walks out of the room angry that I didn't give him the answer he wanted.

Timothy smiles as he gets closer to me, "We'll find out who you are, then find your pack, your family and anyone who gets in our way and kill them all."

The grin on his face is devilish, Timothy thinks they've won. I hear Bruce say that he wishes Shadowcat was still with them because she could make me talk. I don't know who Shadowcat is, but I'm glad she's not here.

Anyone in any organization with a certain nickname like that can't be good for me. Suddenly I see a vision of everyone lying dead at my feet because they were found by the hunters and I couldn't do anything to stop them. Even though they don't know who I am, it doesn't mean they won't eventually find out. I'm not going to lose any of them.

They look to me as their alpha and that's what I'm going to be. My job is to protect them. I'm going to get Kahlil and we're getting out of here. Bruce threatened my family, I can't take that lightly. There's no time to wallow in self-pity. My strength starts rapidly returning. Soon after, Bruce and Timothy come back into my cell. I have to make the fact that they don't know who I am work for me. They unhook my chains and carry me down a narrow hallway.

"Wh...wh..." I begin to say, pretending to still be weakened.

"What's that runt?" Says Bruce, leaning towards me.

"What's your last name, so I can make sure to write it on your gravestone?" I ask in a menacing whisper.

Timothy laughs uncontrollably, "Did you hear that sir? He's making idle threats against you."

"Never take a wolf's threat lightly," Bruce says in a serious tone.

I smile viciously, "He's right."

Bruce and Timothy look at each other. Now's my chance. The chains they have me in are no longer a problem. I break free and begin to struggle, so I can get the keys from one of their belts. I scream at them asking where Kahlil is as a way to distract them. I give them the appearance that all my strength isn't back yet. I let them wrestle me to the ground as I grab a set of keys.

"Where's Kahlil?!" I scream again.

"Don't worry we're taking you to him, so you both can be together," Timothy mocks. "We'll train you dogs to bring us to others of your kind, like your pack. Then we'll go after the Council. You're going to be our secret weapon."

"I'm going to light this bitch up before that happens," I exclaim.

"We'll see about that," Timothy laughs

He gloats at the fact that I'm going to be turned against my own kind. When they stand me up, I subtly resist, careful in not letting them know I'm close to full strength. Timothy then punches me in the stomach as hard as he can. It didn't hurt, but I pretend it does by hunching forward and coughing. We go down the elevator and back to the cells. This time they put me in a cell right next to Kahlil.

I can hear him breathing, but it's very shallow. Whatever they did to keep him alive worked, but also could be preventing him from fully healing. I'm not sure if he's awake or asleep.

After Bruce and Timothy get onto the elevator, I listen to see if I can hear anyone else on the cell block other than Kahlil and myself. I smile knowing it's just us.

I whisper to him, "Yo Kahlil. Kahlil, can you hear me?"

He wheezes before answering back in a hoarse voice. "Yea, just a lil ruffed up."

"How are you feeling?" I ask concerned.

"Not all the way there, but I'm getting there," Kahlil coughs.

"Think you can walk?" I inquire.

"Probably, but not on my own," he admits.

"That's fine, but we have to get out of here," I say, determined.

"How are we going to do that?" he ponders.

"We're going to turn and break our way out. Doing that should trigger your healing and help you escape," I respond.

"I don't know if I can," he says softly.

"Why not?" I ask.

"Besides the pain, they put a collar on me and told me it'll trigger if I change. The collar will grow spikes and they'll go into my neck."

"I'm sorry," I say softly, thinking for a moment. "The collar is to only prevent you from changing, not stopping you from using our claws, strength or speed, right?"

"I guess not," he answers.

I inspect the set of keys I took, "Maybe one of these keys works on the collar,"

"What about the cameras?" Kahlil inquires.

"We'll have to take them out before we unlock the cell," I say.

Kahlil agrees with me and we talk about our plan with more detail. We're going to wait until he feels strong enough to walk. Then rip down the cameras in our cells and escape. The Tailors will be forced to come to this floor and we'll fight them. My hope is that'll also lead to them sounding an alarm, telling the others to ambush the front door.

After a few hours, Kahlil says he's ready to go. On the count of three, we remove the cameras in our cells and unlock the cells right after. Now we're free and I can remove his collar.

Immediately, the alarm blares within the building, "Dammit, I thought we'd have more time!" I say looking around.

"Damien, do you think we can really escape?" Kahlil expresses.

"Yea, I do," I smile. "My pack is waiting outside for my signal and this alarm is as good as any, don't you think?"

"You have a point." Kahlil laughs.

We head toward the elevator, since it's the only way out. No more than 10 feet from the doors when four guards come rushing out with stun rods.

"Well, we'll have to think on our toes won't we?" Kahlil asks confidently.

The hopeful look in his eyes tells me he believes we really had a chance of getting out. He's still a little shaky, but ready to fight. I take point against the guards coming after us. They're easy enough to defeat since their combat training is nothing like what I learned from Chantelle, Omar or my Mom.

After I knock them out, we grab a few of their ID cards and get on the elevator, heading for the top floor. Neither of us know which floor leads to the way out, so we're shooting in the dark hoping it's correct. As the elevator scales the shaft, our anxiety grows the higher we climb.

Before we reach the top, the elevator suddenly stops at a random floor. When I try the ID card again, nothing happens. They must be able to control the elevator remotely. The doors open and we rush out. Thankfully, there are no guards around us. Unfortunately, there aren't any windows and all the doors we try are locked. My heart pounds with every moment that passes. We hear footsteps all around us. Kahlil finds a door that isn't locked and we hide inside, closing behind us.

"The mutts were last seen running down this hallway, we have to head them off," we hear a Tailor command.

"What should we do?" asks another voice.

"What do you think? Find them, subdue them and *get them back in their cells!*" the first voice commands.

I listen to their footsteps fade down the corridor. We wait for a few more minutes before leaving the room. There has to be a way off this floor, unfortunately for us the elevator is locked. Try to open other doors and go down the hall. Somehow we end up at the same place we started.

"This place is a maze. Dammit!" I exclaim as we encounter the guards from earlier.

After knocking them out, I was ready to run, but Kahlil stops me, "Damien wait, this place isn't a maze, it has a certain layout like any other building. It's meant to confuse us so we can get caught. I think this used to be a hospital before it was converted into whatever the hell it is now."

"Great, but how does that help us now?" I ask.

"Using architecture," Kahlil responds.

"Meaning?" I ask confused.

"I've been in and out of hospitals my whole life, living with a family of performers. I would walk around and sometimes get lost while waiting to hear about my Mom, Dad, or my siblings after they were injured. In doing so, I got pretty familiar with them and architecture as a whole."

"I'm impressed," I say excitedly.

"Don't be, my brother told me this hobby won't amount to anything," Kahlil sighs.

"Not true, look at how this hobby of yours is helping us right now," I retort.

"Well let's wait to see if this *hobby* of mine can really get us out of here," Kahlil mumbles. He walks over to a map on the wall and shows me, "Usually the main floor is the one with an entrance, but they'd want us to think that, so let's try to two levels above that. More than likely, it'll be the most heavily guarded."

"Oh let my pack worry about that," I insist. "I'm sure they're here already anyway. You ready?"

"Yea, lead the way captain," Kahlil laughs.

We move forward as we talk about how he got into architecture as a way of trying to find his own identity. Before he was bitten, he wasn't as good as the rest of his family when it came to the circus. Since becoming a werewolf all his natural abilities like his mind has increased. I tell him that's what his gift is.

I figure by now Jasmine is leading the charge to get us out. Kahlil tells me that he's confident that he'll find the door. He leads us to floor after floor, climbing the uncertain enemy base. Every guard we encounter we fight and move on. I follow behind him because I see the confidence in his choices.

Suddenly, with every fiber of my being, I feel the same sensation I did when everyone else joined the pack. It feels like leveling up in a video game. Us trusting one another and our ability to work together is stronger than I thought. We have another pack member.

Kahlil wasn't kidding about being able to figure out how to get us to the entrance, he points us in every direction, never second guessing himself. He's so focused on finding the door, that his other senses are slightly dulled. A few Tailors have nearly taken him out. Kahlil can brawl, but that doesn't really do him that much good in a surprise attack. He wins his fights, but that was due to him being stronger than the Tailors.

"Two floors left before we reach the one we need," he says.

Before I can say anything, we round a corner and encounter everyone else. Instinctively, Kiara judo throws him over her shoulder. Before she knocks him out, I grab Kiara's hand to stop her.

"Wait. It's okay!" I shout. "That's Kahlil, remember we're here to save him."

Kiara's face becomes remorseful, "Oh I'm so sorry! I didn't get a good look at you before I attacked."

N...no worries. It's all good," Kahlil groans.

"Damien, thank God we finally found you," Jasmine says, relieved.

"Are y'all ok? You look terrible," Omar asks.

"Yea, we're good," I respond. "We took a few licks, but nothing major," I put my hand on Kahlil's shoulder. "For those who don't know this is Kahlil, he's our newest pack member," I announce.

"Damien, we know," Chantelle reveals.

"Yea, we felt the same thing you did," Kiara says happily, as she helps Kahlil back to his feet.

"Let's save all the kissing and hugging for when we get out of here," Braheem urges.

"Damien, are you sure?" Kahlil asks as we run through to the next floor.

"Yes, we're sure," I reply. "Thanks to you, I remember why I love being a werewolf. We may be able to turn into monsters, but that doesn't mean *we are* monsters."

Everyone looks at me then at him and I can feel that the pack is together at last. We have all the family together, but I sense that there's still someone missing.

"Ight everyone, let's get out of here," I direct.

"We've been trying, but we're lost," Nichole responds.

"That's why we have Kahlil, it's his thing, he'll guide us out," I say proudly.

Kahlil shyly laughs as he takes the lead in getting us out of this labyrinth of a hospital. Just like earlier, Kahlil dictates which route we take. After ten minutes, we are finally able to get to the main floor.

"We're almost out, stick together," I command. "We move as a team."

"Yes Sir," Everyone cheers.

I expect the lobby to be full of Tailors that stand between us and our freedom. That we'll need to make one last stand and fight our way out. As we rush to the lobby, I spot the door. It's so close that I can feel the open air. Surprisingly, the coast is clear. I order everyone to stop since this is too easy. I spot a few chairs sitting close by and ask Darius and Braheem to throw them at the door. Just as they cross the threshold, the chairs are shot by rubber bullets flying from all angles.

"Motion sensors…greeaat," I say sarcastically, "How'd y'all get past that?"

"We didn't, they weren't there when we came in," Darius replies.

"Damn, freedom is right there," I say, almost defeated.

"I got a question," Darius says. "Nigga, how'd you know that was going to happen?"

"Ehh, saw it in a movie, didn't think I was right though," I respond.

"Well...it's a good thing you watch so many movies," Nichole adds.

Just as we take our first step, the lobby fills with twenty or so Tailors with stun rods and guns. I look at everyone and smirk, "Think we can handle this?"

"You know me," Jasmine says, as she begins to put her hair in a bun. "Always ready for a fight."

Chantelle, Nichole and Kiara follow behind her. Omar stretches for a second while Darius and Braheem roll their shoulders and throw a few jabs. I crack my knuckles, looking at the Tailors in front of us. I turn glabro and loosen up my shoulders.

"On my count, we're going to take them down!" I announce.

"Don't worry bro, no one will get through us," Braheem asserts."

"Yea, we're *all* getting out of here," Omar acknowledges.

Kahlil can't use glabro yet, so he bares his fangs, and grows his claws.

"On my count everyone, let's go!" I scream.

"Right!" Everyone replies.

"One...two...three!" I say running forward.

We roar at them, these Tailors have no idea what they are dealing with. We successfully dodge all of their rubber bullets and stun rods. For every punch that's thrown and every bullet that's fired. We slowly make our way closer to the front door and to our freedom.

Most of them are wearing body armor, so we have to punch a little harder. No matter what, we're determined to take them down one by one. Before long, all the Tailors are lying on the ground. Just as we thought everything is over, one of the Tailors springs up and shoots Omar, Darius, Nichole and Kiara. They scream and almost fall to the ground.

"You son of a bitch!" Kahlil screams as he lunges and kicks the gun away before punching them repeatedly.

"Kahlil, enough!" I say, breathing heavily.

I look around at everyone else, who are just as hurt and tired as I am. Upon inspecting their wounds, we realize that they were shot with rubber bullets. Thankfully they're all going to be ok. Kahlil apologizes saying he reacted to seeing them being shot, he thought the worst after seeing them hit.

"After we get out of here I'm going to sleep for a week," Braheem says, coughing.

"Yea, I feel you man," Omar replies, holding his shoulder.

"Everyone sound off!" I exclaim.

One by one, everyone responds letting me know that they're still alive, hurt, but still with us. Some of them aren't able to stand up properly, so we help each other up and slowly exit through the front doors. I prepare for us to still have to fight, but to my surprise, there's no one outside. I sigh in relief, thankful that I can finally get home, see Catalina and sleep.

Chantelle and Omar start talking about how we're going to party once we get home. One by one we add in our own ideas of what to have. As we walk out of the building, the smell of the fresh air is so breathtaking that I almost collapse. Hearing everyone talk about celebrating and how things are going to be now that Kahlil has joined us makes me smile. I feel lighter now that we rescued Kahlil and what's more we didn't kill anyone. I gaze to the sky happy that I'll see Catalina soon.

That's when we hear the gunshot. It echoes throughout the openness of the night. An intense pain burns in my chest. I look down to see my shirt filling with blood. I've been shot. My hands tremble as I touch the wound and see my own blood on my fingers. We turn around to see Bruce standing in the open doors with a gun smoking. I drop to my knees as everyone cries out for me.

"Did you kids really believe I'd let you escape?" Bruce asks with a devilish look in his eyes.

"Damien!" Jasmine screams.

"NOOOO!" Shouts Omar.

"How could you do something so cruel?" Nichole shrieks.

"It's nothing personal, kids, I've got a job to do and one of them is to kill and or contain dogs," Bruce asserts. "You may not be bad, but I will not let an alpha go that easily. If you won't sit and stay like good little doggies, then I'll just have to put you down."

I'm bleeding out, my body starts to feel cold. I fall on my face coughing up blood. Darius and Nichole do what they can to stop the bleeding, but I know I'm going to lose my life. My vision blurs as I watch Jasmine charging towards Bruce with tears in her eyes. Braheem, Omar, Chantelle, and Kahlil follow behind her.

They attack him with a fury of rage for shooting me. Furiously throwing punches, kicks and swiping their claws in an effort to take him down. I can only watch as they're seamlessly outdone by Bruce. He's a better fighter. They may have had speed and power on their side, but that doesn't amount to much against his skill. It's like he can predict their movements. I try to move, but my body won't let me.

"D...don't -cough– kill him...just..." I try to tell them to run away, but my words can't reach them.

I fade while watching my friends fight for me. My heart beat starts slowing down before stopping completely. My eyes close and I can only see the cold empty darkness.

Chapter 10

I'm surrounded by darkness, unable to see, hear or feel anything outside of the endless void of cold. I didn't know it was possible to feel this cold. I try to reach out to find where I am, but I can't. I can't feel my hands, arms, legs or toes. The pain in my chest is gone, but I don't know what this means. Am I dead? What happened to my body? What's happening to everyone else? I start freaking out, I can't see or hear anything. The bitter cold that surrounds me is suffocating.

"Damien…" I hear someone calling my name.

It's very low, like a whisper from a far distance. I search all around me, trying to find out who or what said my name. Unfortunately, there's nothing, but darkness. Suddenly, something attaches itself to me, attempting to direct me. How can this be possible without a body? Where am I? What is all of this?

"Damien…." I hear the voice once more.

This time it's a little louder. Where is the voice coming from? Who or whatever is calling me, I sense that it wants me closer. Strangely, I'm not afraid. The presence this thing is giving off, doesn't seem like it wants to hurt me.

"Damien…can you hear me?" the voice calls out again. This time it's like someone's calling me from across a large crowded room. I can barely hear the voice.

The connection between it and I grow, and for the first time since I've been here I can speak. The only thing I can think to say is, "Who are you?"

There's no response. I have no sense of time, not knowing how long I've been here. I wait for a while longer, and there's nothing, but the cold silence. Whatever attached itself to me starts pulling me toward a small light that's very far in the distance. What the hell is happening to me?

Is this where the voice is coming from? I can't tell. The speed at which I'm pulled slowly starts increasing. As I get closer, I finally get a sensation of something other than the cold. The light starts to get brighter and I feel a warmth like never before. Soon after, I faintly feel my fingers. The coldness dissipates the closer I get to the light. I hold up one hand, finally capable of seeing it. However, it's transparent, like I'm a ghost.

The light grows brighter as I approach the light's source. I'm not sure how, but I'm able to control my movements, like I'm floating. Still unsure if I should, I make my way to the direction of the light. Pretty soon, I get so close that I'm finally solid, free to touch everything around me. Just before I reach the center of the light, a platform materializes, like it was created for me. I firmly plant my feet before taking a few steps to the center.

A giant screen appears in front of me, it rises over my head and starts showing everything that happened tonight. Me being caught and put into the cell, then finding Kahlil. Then me being interrogated, before showing us escaping our cells. And finally Kahlil and I meeting with the others, and before fighting the Tailors in the lobby. The video ends by showing me getting shot and falling.

"What is goin on here?" I ask.

"Damien," this time when I hear the voice it's clear as day. The same voice that has been calling out to me, came directly from this light source. A man steps onto the platform and begins speaking to me. "I was wondering when you'd be able to hear me," he says in a strong, calm tone. Yet his accent, I can't place where he's from.

The man before me is a tall brown skin man with long curly hair that reaches his shoulders. He has no facial hair, but I see his eyes are green. I've never seen him before, but I feel I can trust him.

"What is all this, where am I?" I ask him.

"You're safe," he responds.

"I thought I was dead," I admit.

"You are dead," he says with a seriousness in his eyes. "I pulled you here just before your soul crossed over."

"Why would you do that? Who are you?" I question.

"You will learn who I am in time, but for now your friends need you," he answers. "The reason I pulled you here is because you have enormous potential and I want to give you a chance to save your friends. The same one that was given to me."

"Wait... why?" I ask puzzled.

He smiles before saying, "Since becoming a werewolf, you've lived only for your friends, trying whatever you could to keep everyone safe. Trying to make sure you didn't hurt those you loved when you turned and creating a safe space for everyone in your pack."

"All the good that did me. I was still killed," I say in a low voice. "You've been watching me?" I ask confused.

A smile appears on his face, "That's not important, what is important, I can't explain right now, because we are low on time. You have a decision to make."

"Decision?" I look at him puzzled.

"Yes, I can give you the power to not only revive, but, in return, I ask you to lead our people into a new age. Do you accept?"

"Hold up, hold up, lead our people? What are you talking about?" I blurted out.

"In order for you to revive, you'll need the power I can give you. If you do not accept, you will stay dead and your friends will soon join you." he then gestures to the screen, showing my friends getting beaten by Bruce and the reinforcements of other Tailors with weapons drawn. My anxiety races, unsure of what to do.

"I'm still not sure about this, I don't know who or what you are," I say. "As far as I know you could be a demon trying to get me to make a deal."

"All I can tell you for now is this is the power of your ancestors. My power, the power of the Tremauré, the first werewolf."

I freeze upon hearing his words, I never thought of the first werewolf before. It never occurred to me to ask about our origin. I try to ask more about him, but he stops me, saying all my questions will be answered in time, but this isn't it.

"Do you accept the responsibility to take on the role of the Tremauré?" he asks again.

I pause for a moment, seriously considering the offer I'm being given. Become the Tremauré and save my friends or watch them die? "To protect them, I will accept," I say without hesitation.

"You must be sure," he advises.

"I am," I say standing tall.

The man holds out his hand, I'm not sure why, but I'm confident in everything he's telling me. I reach out and grab his hands with an assured look on my face. The man nods as he begins to glow. A blue light starts emanating from his eyes and warmth washing over me.

The light instantaneously fades and I'm back in my own body again. My eyes shoot open, as I take my first breath of life, like I had been holding my breath underwater for an extended period of time. I inhale and cough up the blood that filled in my lungs, before attempting to stand up. Kiara and Kahlil are amazed to see me awake, trying to prevent me from getting to my feet.

"Don't push yourself," Kiara warns. "You've already lost so much blood."

"Don't worry, I'm fine. I just need a sec to catch my breath. I got this."

I look up at the full moon to take in its light, feeling this new power start from the bullet wound and spread through the rest of my body. It slowly flows throughout every vein and skin follicle. This is like nothing like I've ever felt before. After the bullet drops from my chest, the wound heals almost instantly. This is incredible.

I then hear Jasmine scream in pain. My attention darts over to see Bruce repeatedly kicking her in the ribs. Everyone else is already lying on the ground, either in pain or unconscious. The pain from the gunshot is still present and strong, but I have to do something to save them. I try taking a step and almost fall over, my body's not as ready as I thought.

"Don't embrace the power and ignore the pain," the Tremauré says. "This is the only time you can revive, make it count."

I take a deep breath and exhale slowly, "I, Damien Nichols, accept the power of the Tremuaré to save my friends and protect my people, the werewolves of this world, until my dying day."

156

Suddenly, my body pulses with an even greater surge of energy, similar to when I became an alpha, but much more potent. My body feels jittery as it tries to adjust to this new power. It takes a few seconds, but now I'm ready to go, full of energy I could only dream of having.

Only a few minutes passed here, but in the void it seemed so much longer. Now I have the power to save them. I roar at Bruce and his men, shifting into my glabro. Bruce stops hitting Jasmine and stares directly at me in amazement, accepting this new challenge. His soldiers however, were in a panic after seeing the werewolf he shot in the heart now standing.

"Don't just stand there gawking at him, kill him before he kills us!" Bruce screams at them.

All of them aim their weapons at Kiara, Kahlil and I. I pick them up before they fire and move us out of harm's way. I'm faster than before. I want Bruce and his Tailors to pay for what they had done to my pack. They deserve to feel the same hopelessness we did. I retreat into the shadows before telling Kiara and Kahlil to hide and that I'll take care of everything.

I hear one of them call out to him, "S…s…sir, his eyes are blue. I thought you said he's an alpha. Alphas are supposed to have red eyes. What type of werewolf has blue eyes?" The Tailor panics.

"Get yourself together, soldiers! You shoot and kill that wolf now!" Bruce commands.

I jump out of view, using the shadows of the night to my advantage. I take the soldiers out one by one as they come after me with ease. I'm able to punch right through their armor. I throw their unconscious bodies out of the shadows every time I defeat one. Many of which landed at Bruce's feet. Eventually he orders the remaining hunters to fall back and stay close to the base.

"Alright, you made your point," Bruce calls out. "C'mon out and we'll settle this."

"I see you finally see the turn of the tide," I say confidently as I emerge from the shadows. "Let me pick up my pack and we'll settle this. Just you and me."

"Deal," Bruce says as he takes a few steps back. He shifts his attention to his soldiers and says, "Tailors, no matter what happens on this field, do not engage or help me! Turn on all exterior lights."

"But sir...." Timothy interjects as he pushes through the crowd.

"That's an order soldier!" he shouts. "Stand down and turn on the damn lights!" Bruce exclaims.

"Yes sir," there's worry in Timothy's words.

I know Bruce is a man of his word and isn't one to use underhanded tactics, so for the moment I trust he'll keep his word, but I know better than to drop my guard. One by one, I pick up everyone and move them to where Kahlil and Kiara are hiding. Braheem, Chantelle and Nichole are able to stand, but not walk, so I carry them.

Once I get everybody to a safe enough distance away, I tell them to take care of each other. Now that we're all together, I sense all of their injuries. All the hits they've taken tonight trying to rescue and then avenge me. Even through my death they stand beside me. In the very next moment, my eyes glow and so do theirs. Their cuts and bruises vanish before my eyes. Is this the power of the Tremauré?

"Damien...y...you were dead, how'd you?" Omar asks as he opens his eyes.

"W...what's going on?" Jasmine asks. "You shouldn't be alive, you were shot in the heart, we all thought you were dead."

"I don't know how I healed you, but now I have the power to end this," I reply.

"Bro, y... your eyes..." Darius stammers.

"What about them?" I ask.

"T... they're blue, what happened?" Braheem questions.

In a soft voice, I say, "We'll talk about it later, for now, rest, heal and wait for me here. I'll deal with Bruce."

"That's suicide, we couldn't beat him and we jumped him," Chantelle exclaims.

"Don't worry, I got this," I say, confidently.

Even though each of them are still in awe that I am still alive, and walking. They nod and agree to sit there and watch me as I approach Bruce. I rip off what's left of my shirt and drop it on the ground.

"Damien, don't go," Kahlil pleads. "It's cuz of me you're here in the first place."

"Nah, I would've been here either way. This has to be done, not just for us, but for all werewolves."

I start staring daggers at Bruce, as I walk toward him. Unsurprisingly, he starts making his way toward me. I snarl at him as a warning. I don't want to fight him, but I know there's no other choice. Before long we're standing 5 ft from each other.

"Hey kid, I killed you, not more than ten minutes ago," he says. "How is it that you're up walking around?"

"Let's call it a power up," I answer smugly.

"I see... those blue eyes of yours," he says curiously. "There's this legend that the first werewolf to ever exist had blue eyes, just like yours. He was known as the Tremauré. He's said to have possessed immense strength, speed, and power we never could dream of, especially for a werewolf. He's the reason your kind exist in the first place. The one who usurped the throne from our king."

"Meaning?" I ask.

"It's not important,

You'll be dead soon," he asserts. "So there's no point in explaining the history to you now. Though I never thought I'd see those blue eyes myself. I always passed it off as a legend, until now."

"I don't know much about the Tremauré other than the fact its power is going to help me kick your ass," I declare.

"Hmph, well I guess I get to finally let loose and go all out, since it's clear you're about to," he says confidently. "Let's see what this legendary power can do against me."

For a moment we just stand there staring at one another. Eager but also anxious at the same time. Bruce takes off his shirt and tells me that he'll only use a knife in this fight since I have my claws. I agree. Everything is different from before. I can smell a little better, I can feel the emotions coming from all around me. Calmness emanates from him. Bruce doesn't have one ounce of fear.

He knows he can't win this fight, but he's going to put his all into it. Admirable, but only one of us may be walking away tonight. I'm confident that the winner of this fight is going to be me, but will I end his life, or can I find another way?

"Don't get cocky, kid," Bruce warns. "A second ago you were bleeding out. Now's not the time to slip up or my knife could be entering your heart and this time I'll make sure you stay down."

"Oh I'm sure," I reply. "By the way, I'm confident, not cocky. Confident that there's no way you can win this fight. I have the power of my predecessor flowing through me, which means I have the upper hand now."

"We'll see about that," Bruce smiles.

Less than a second later, we're charging at one another. He swings his knife at me and I dodge without thinking. He tries once more and throws a punch followed by another thrust of his knife. I block and maneuver around his first attacks. With each strike he throws my way, he tries to catch me off guard, showing me his higher level of training. He seems to be moving in slow motion, it's easy to dodge and block his strikes.

Though Bruce's hits aren't landing, he doesn't lose his composure or doubts anyone of his strikes. He's still a better fighter than I am, always ready for my counterattack. When I throw a punch, he strikes almost immediately after he blocks. I won't give up, he's giving it his all, so I won't disrespect him by not honoring that.

"What happened to all that talk?" I ask in an attempt to bait him. "Seconds ago you were talking about how you were going to kill me," he throws another strike. "Oh my, that was slow. My granddad could do better than that."

I hoped that my teasing would be enough to throw him off, even if it was only for a second, but it doesn't work. Bruce's conviction hasn't changed since we started. It doesn't matter how hard I try. He won't comment on anything I say.

Whatever Bruce has gone through in his life left him with this unwavering principle. Honestly, it's unreal how good of a fighter Bruce is. His ability to combo his moves right after another would have made anyone else fall. I'm tired of being on the defensive. I foolishly hoped that he'd be an easy opponent to take down, by tiring him out, but I was wrong. Bruce's stamina is greater than I expected.

It's time I start hitting back, I catch his fist with my hand. The look on his face changes, but only for a moment, there's my chance and I'm going to take it. He follows up with a kick to my thigh, but I block it with my knee before throwing him back a few feet.

Bruce lands on his back and handsprings to his feet shortly after, "Damn kid... I wasn't expecting that," he grins.

"I know you weren't, it's time for round two, no more will I stay on the defensive," I reply.

Bruce takes a second to gather himself before charging back at me. This time when I counter it's with a punch. I'm still pulling my punches, so I don't kill him. I'll only knock him out if I can. My next punch lands and that makes him take a step back, however he is still trying to bring me down.

This guy is relentless. The knife he has still plays a role, he hasn't cut me with it nor will I want to give him the chance to. Bruce tries to swipe at me with the knife and I duck. Then he follows up with a kick. I catch his leg before forcefully pushing him hard enough to get him to the ground once more. Before Bruce has the chance to recover, I pin him. He pulls out another knife from his boot and uses my momentum against me to thrust the knife into my leg, before rolling out of my path. I scream in pain as I drop onto the grass.

"Relax kid," Bruce says. "The knife isn't made of silver. I want this to last, I can't have you dying on me just yet," Bruce smiles as he stares down at me.

I pull the knife from my leg and inspect the wound, which is already healing, "Haha. Well, would you look at that, you're right."

Bruce stands up once more with two knives in each hand. I wait for a few moments, giving my leg enough time to heal. He's ready to die tonight and I'm still playing nice. I can't do that anymore or he'll kill me. I look back at everyone watching him and me. This isn't about me, it never has been.

The second my leg heals, I growl at Bruce before coming at him with furious intent. I hit him with a slew of combos, one right after the other, not giving him a chance to defend himself. I land a few punches to his face and then a few punches to his chest and abdomen. Even though he's still a better fighter, he can't defend against my speed and power.

Bruce's mountain-like stance and indomitable will is starting to crumble. Bruce is finding it hard to stay on his feet, swaying back and forth. I stop, realizing I've won and I know he knows it. Seconds later, Bruce finally falls. I turn back to the others with my eyes glowing their new royal blue color. I raise one arm in the air showing my victory over Bruce and the Tailors. My presence as the Tremauré triggers their eyes to glow in response to mine.

I shift back into my homid form after taking a short breath and begins walking back toward them. The power is still surging through me. Just like when I became an alpha. Is it just the adrenaline? No, I'm becoming one with it. I'll have to train with this just like before.

Before I get too far away, I stop and walk back to Bruce, offering my hand to help him to his feet. His glares at me before brushing me away, deciding to get up on his own even though he's having trouble doing so.

"Why would think I need your help?" Bruce sneers. "You had the upper hand and I was on the ground. You should have killed me or just walked away. I told my men not to do anything even in the event that I lost."

"I told you," I respond. "I'm not what you think I am. All me and my pack want is to live in peace so we can run free like wolves should be able to. My pack is my family and we protect each other. I've been given the power of the Tremauré to change the world and it begins here."

Bruce stares at me, not saying a word. I may have wanted to make them suffer, but I don't want to kill him. Even though he shot and killed me, I can spare him and maybe his thoughts about us can change. True power is being able to defeat someone, but choosing not to. And in sparing Bruce, I am moving in the right direction to change the future.

"This new power will be used as I promised, to bring about a new way of life for werewolves," I declare.

I thought that everything was done, so I begin walking back toward everyone, ready to tell them that we can go home. My body, though now healed, is exhausted. After that first step, I almost collapse. I take a moment to catch myself before continuing.

In my weakened state, I let my guard down. Bruce turns me around and throws me over his shoulder. Upon hitting the ground the wind is kicked out of me. He stabs me in the leg with one of his knives. I scream in pain. Just because I was willing to walk away, he thinks he has me. He mistook my mercy for a weakness. Almost falling over doesn't mean I don't have any more fight left in me. Before he makes his next move, I use my strength to throw him off me and handspring back to my feet.

I pull the knife from my leg and throw it down, "I thought you and I had an understanding!" I roar.

"Yea, we do. I respect you as a man and as a warrior," Bruce states. "However, that's not stopping the fact that you're still a werewolf. Did you really think that little speech of yours was going to make things better? I can't let you roam free, especially now that you have that power."

I sigh heavily and close my eyes. A millisecond later, they shoot open glowing blue and I barrel toward him furiously. It's time to show him what werewolves can really do. That's the only way to end all of this.

I came at him as fast, I'll need to in order kill Bruce and scare the Tailors in a way that they'll think twice before hunting us anytime soon. Before Bruce can react, I punch straight into his chest and grab his heart. A familiar feeling of the warm blood covers my hands. It pumps twice before I tear it out. Bruce didn't expect me to kill him, he thought my naivety was going to be my downfall. I'm the Tremauré and I need to live.

A second later, he falls to the ground, dead. I hold up his heart as I transform into my crinos form and roar. It's loud enough that every single Tailor starts backing away. I stare at each of them dead on, challenging any of them to attack me. I put Bruce's heart in my mouth, as each of them watch. I chew a few times before swallowing it. It tastes horrible, but this is a show of power. All the hunters drop their weapons. All except Timothy, who keeps his glance trained on me.

I shift back to my human form. Now we can go home. They wouldn't dare attack us for the foreseeable future. They rush to their cars after gathering their defeated soldiers and drive away as fast as they can.

Timothy is the last one to go, his eyes like daggers trying to pierce my heart, "We've disgraced ourselves and our king!" he shouts. "Mark my words, I will avenge my mentor and the disgrace you've brought upon us!"

"I'll be waiting," I say back. Even though I know he couldn't hear me. I sense he knows I'll be waiting.

I wonder what he meant about what we did to their king. Bruce mentioned the same thing earlier and I still don't know who they're referring to. I walk back to the others and then past them. Braheem, Jasmine, Darius, Chantelle, Omar, Kiara, Nicole and Kahlil all follow. For the first few minutes I sense that they're terrified. Even though I'm ahead of everyone, I feel their eyes on me.

"D, what exactly did you do?" Braheem asks.

"What needed to be done." I say quietly, yet firmly.

"Is that what you meant?"Jasmine asks.

"Yea…that's *exactly* what I meant," I respond "This is why I stress so hard on us not losing control, but *if* you do make sure *you* are the one in control *not* the wolf."

"But we are the wolf aren't we?" Chantelle asks.

"Yea, and there's power in anger, but you have to know when and how to use it," I respond.

"Damn nigga," Braheem exclaims. "Where'd you learn that?"

"The Hulk, I figured the best way to learn to control rage from a monster is through the one character on this planet that has to."

"Never thought about it that way," Kahlil admits.

I stop walking and turn around. Each of them has fear and uncertainty in their eyes, "Don't think I don't feel bad for what I did. If I saw any other way, I wouldn't have killed him, but he chose his fate."

A few more seconds of silence passes before Kahlil steps toward me, "Bro... thank you," he daps me. "Noone's ever done anything like that for me."

"Don't worry Dame, it's just a lot to take in all at once," Darius adds.

"I know, I'm still trying to figure this all out myself," I say.

"Seriously, I didn't think it could ever be this bad. I was careless about when and how I used abilities," Kahlil acknowledges.

"Kahlil, this isn't your fault," Kiara states. "Trust me, you're not the only one that this happens to. Jasmine, Nichole and I were just like you. We escaped our captures and went around doing whatever we wanted to. If it wasn't for Damien, we would've been caught just like you. It took us 'til now to realize what he's been saying all along."

Kahlil looks at everyone's assured faces, hearing Kiara's words, unsure if he's really a part of our pack, "Thanks everyone, but do I have what it takes to be a part of your pack?" Kahlil asks. "I don't have what you all have. Damien, you're an amazing leader and you have all of them to fight with you. Each of you has something special about you. I don't."

"You're already in the pack," Nichole says proudly. "Now, let's go."

I get the sense that Kahlil is still unsure, and doubting himself. He seems like he doesn't think he's worth the effort of us saving him and asking him to be in the pack. Kahlil starts walking away from us.

Before I can stop him, Darius grabs his arm, "Hold up, I was like you too. In the beginning it was just Damien and Braheem. I was picked on in high school and everyone always made me feel worthless. One day after I had gotten bit, the usuals were picking on me and I thought, '*Why not just let go and kill them all?*' I definitely could lure them away and kill 'em, no one would find out. They'd probably chalk it up to an animal attack. As those thoughts entered my mind, Damien was there to help me. He saw what I was going through and wanted to end it. I was cold to him at first, but Damien still tried to talk to me. I'm glad I did because I don't know where I'd be if it wasn't for these two. We've learned and grew so much together."

Braheem shares his story of how we met and what happened to him when he was bitten. Then Chantelle and Omar and finally Jasmine, Kiara and Nichole share their stories as well. Afterward, I tell him about how I was bitten, and how each of them helped me.

"We all are outsiders, just looking for our place," Jasmine begins to say. "And we feel as though we found it in each other. There's nothing remarkable about any of us separately, but together we've achieved great things."

I realize I don't need to say anything further, they were doing everything for me, saying exactly what Kahlil needs to hear.

"Kahlil, we're not just the sum of our parts," Nichole says.

"We all contribute by working together," I add in. "I'm a better fighter because of Chantelle and Omar. I wouldn't have had the strength to protect others if I hadn't fought their alpha, Darnell. We've all met at random, but we learned to work together by figuring out what works and doesn't work. Especially since neither of us really knew how to control the change in the beginning. Jasmine, Kiara and Nichole came as a package deal, and I learned what patience as a leader is."

Kahlil's still doesn't seem very convinced that we want him to join us, "I don't know man. I haven't really done anything special. All I've ever done was make things worse, like getting you shot and almost killed."

I start laughing, everyone else is puzzled. Tyler has the strangest look on his face.

"What's so funny?" Kiara asks.

"I think he finally lost it," Darius says.

"Yea, maybe," Jasmine agrees.

"D, maybe you should sit down because you got stabbed a few times," Braheem says. "And you've also lost a lot of blood."

"Dude why are you laughing?" asks Omar.

I look at everyone, attempting to calm down, "Okay, okay. I'm laughing at Kahlil. He thinks he has nothing to offer. Dog, if it wasn't for you, we wouldn't have found a way out of there. You have so much knowledge on architecture that you realized that their base used to be a hospital. That's your special skill.

They don't have to always be physical to be exceptional."

Everyone agrees, their once confused looks are overcome with the same realization. The building was like a maze to us and no one could easily find their way out, except for him.

"D's right," Omar chimes in. "We're not going to twist your arm with this. It's your choice no matter what."

Kahlil watches everyone's cheery expression, then looks at the sky and finally at me. "I'd be more than happy to join your pack."

Braheem steps closer before putting his arm around Kahlil, "You've been a part of our pack since like 3 hours ago."

"Uhh... what do you mean?" Kahlil asks.

Jasmine explained that we all got a feeling, like a pulse of energy that ran through each of us. We could all feel when he became a part of the pack. She then told him that we didn't want to tell him at first in an effort to not influence his decision.

Kahlil says he felt the same thing, but wasn't sure what that was until now. We talk all the way back to the city. It is not very far, but it's more than enough time for us to enjoy the night. More than anything, it's a time for celebration, we're alive, we got Kahlil back and we're heading toward a new future. The night sky soon turns to the twilight of the day. The start of a new day, with a new pack member. I'm still torn with how things turned out, but I think I can live with it. We're safe and that's all that really matters.

Chapter 11

After we were safe and back home, I was so exhausted that I slept for almost a week. Catalina did all she could to help me while I slept, taking great care of me. I don't know where I'd be without her. She called my job and told them that I was sick, and had to take some time off. Catalina told me she was afraid I'd never wake up.

When my friends Jakobe, Davion and Terrance heard I was in a coma, they called to check up on me. I'm sad I didn't get the chance to speak to them, it's been a while since we really talked. I asked my mom where they're stationed, so I could send them a thank-you letter, but she said she doesn't know. She told they complained about having to do the grunt work, but more recently, they've been given orders for reinforcements after one of their strongholds had been ransacked. I know the three of them are capable of protecting each other.

The day I awoke, I see Mom and Catalina by my bedside. After a few hours of doctor's running their tests, they allow me to go home. A day or two later, Mom and Catalina urge me to see the doctor again. No regular doctor can help me with what I'm going through, so I go see Tevin with Catalina. Though I felt fine, I bring her along so she knows I went to see someone.

Tevin tells me he's been waiting for me to reach out after Braheem told him what happened. He checks all my vitals and gives me a clean bill of health, but isn't sure why I was asleep for a week when everyone else was fine after a few days. There's nothing physically wrong with me. However, he has seen cases where dying and coming back does take a toll on the body. He suggests that I take it easy for a few more days.

Hearing Tevin tell me I'm going to be alright, Catalina hugs and kisses me as we leave his office, "See I told you I'm fine, you can't get rid of me that easily."

"I know, I just hate how you put yourself in these situations. I'm worried because I never know where you are or what you're doing. I could help you, if you turn me. I could be with you while you're fighting."

"I know..." I sigh. "I've gone back and forth with this for so long. I want to keep you as far away from this violence as possible. Because if I lose you, I don't know what I'd do. I'd rather you stay out of harm's way," I say looking in her eyes.

"Okay, but think about it," Catalina insists and kisses me.

I can tell she wants me to turn her, but I have to question if my hesitance is protecting her or myself?

Two days later, I go see Tevin again to ask him what he knows about the Tremauré and what this means for me. He tells me that he's still in disbelief after hearing about what happened. Before telling me anything he asks me to show him my eyes. He didn't ask before because Catalina was there. I oblige him by showing my once crimson alpha eyes are now royal blue. Tevin is in awe, he explains that he's been working with werewolves for the last 15 years and even he thought the Tremauré was a myth.

"The Tremauré was the first werewolf," Tevin begins explaining. "I don't know the entire history, but what I do know is that the first werewolf was granted the power to save his kingdom and his people, after it was taken from him during a rebellion. To fight the usurper and his followers The Tremauré was granted the power of the wolf. When the Tremauré and his knights, who were then werewolves, took back the kingdom, the remnants of the traitor's army created the Tailors. The Tailors believe the Tremauré killed their king and took over. The descendants of the usurper and his warriors have been hunting werewolves ever since. The most notable thing about the Tremauré is the blue glow, no wolf in history has had them since. Not even his own children."

Tevin suddenly stops, stating he doesn't want to overstep by revealing too much, "You now have the power to change the world. That type of power doesn't come without a price. It attracts those who wish to control it."

"Could…anyone take this power from me?" I ask, somberly.

"I… I don't know," he says with concern in his eyes. "If someone were to kill you… it might be possible that it could work the same as if you kill an alpha. But since the Tremauré hasn't been seen in over 3 thousand years, I can't say for sure," his tone shifts "I will warn you that you now have a huge target on your back, and the only way to ensure you and your pack are safe is for you to be ready for a fight. And in that fight, it could lead to killing a few of your foes. Are you okay with that?"

I remain silent as his words reach my ears, "I'm going to have to be ok with killing. Even if I don't like it. I'll always try the civil way first, but I can't let that stop me, because if I do, I'll die," my tone becomes serious. "I don't want to die again. Thank you Tev, I appreciate all the info, your advice and mentorship you've given me. You're a huge portion of why I'm alive today. As much as I hate to disagree with you, I can't," I reach out to shake his hand.

"I can't take all the credit, ever since Darnell, I've seen great potential in you, but this is something else entirely," he says, as he reaches back to shake my hand.

"Last question, does the council know?" I ask with fear in my voice.

"Of course they do," Tevin responds quickly.

"I haven't heard anything," I say confused.

"You won't, not until they figure out what to do with you," he responds.

"I wonder when that'll be," I say as I start walking towards the door."

Tevin Sighs, "No one can really say, they're mysterious when they want to be. I guess you're going to be called the Pack of the Tremauré now?"

"I don't think I'm ready for that yet," I laugh as I walk out of his home.

After I leave, I can't help but think about what he said to me. My power could be taken away from me. We could be under attack, not just from the Tailors, but also from other werewolves. I can't figure out what to do. Should I tell the others? I don't want to frighten them. Since I'm meeting them tonight and it's supposed to be a celebration, I don't want to ruin it with any bad news. By the time I get to the Den, everyone is already there.

"Well look who it is, let him sleep for a few days and he thinks he can just show up on C.P.T," mocks Braheem.

"Ha...ha..." I reply. "Yea I get it. I'm late cuz I was checkin in with Tevin to see what he knew about this Tremauré stuff."

"What did you find out?" Kiara asks.

"Other than this being the power of the strongest and first werewolf in history, he doesn't know much about the history of the first werewolf other than he used to be a king, was overthrown, then turned into a werewolf, and took it back. Those he overthrew then

178

became the Tailors we know today. Besides that, nothing much."

"Ooh yeeaa, nothing much," Jasmine says sarcastically.

"We know one thing, bro we're jacked now," Omar says, excitedly.

I ask Darius what he means. He explains to me that after I became the Tremauré each of them were given a strength increase. Though neither of them know how to explain it. They're able to do things that they weren't before.

Jasmine points and tells me how they moved a huge boulder over from one spot to another in an attempt to redecorate, but it only took two of them to move it while in their glabro. They estimate that it weighs close to 12 tons, which was close to my previous limit in my crinos form. Just two of my pack members can lift 8 tons easily in glabro.

My eyes grew wide as I watch them pick it up, "Y'all been leveling up like crazy. I want to see what I can do."

I walk over to the boulder they moved, which was lighter than I anticipated. I'm able to push it on its side no problem. I'm making this 12 ton boulder move it like it's almost nothing. I continue to push it like I'm lifting and flipping a huge tire, not a 12 ton rock. I turn glabro and I lift it over my head. I feel it's weight, but it's not anywhere near my limit.

"Dog, that's crazy," Darius says in amazement.

"Yea I know," I say as I set the boulder down.

"Just being able to do that is more than I thought possible," Omar walks over and daps me. "Since this isn't anywhere near my max, I'll have to see what happens when I shift."

"I don't even want to know," Omar laughs, backing away slowly.

After talking for a little while longer and throwing boulders around, we get back to business. The purpose of today is to set up the party for Kahlil. We set up our tables, chairs, cups, and food. Everything we need to officially celebrate Kahlil joining the pack. I see Kiara and Chantelle setting up tiki torches to light the area. I still think it's funny having them since we can see in the dark. This is a great way for us to unwind after fighting the Tailors. Right now it almost seems like a distant memory.

For the next few weeks, we'll have to look over our shoulders. I don't know if the council knows about what happened to us before I became the Tremauré. My conversation with Tevin lingers in my head. He tells me that we'll be attacked from both sides. The last thing I want is for my mom or Catalina to get caught up in this.

Omar notices the intense look on my face and asks if everything is ok. I snap out of my trance and realize everyone is staring at me. I chuckle nervously and tell everyone that I'm okay. I don't want to worry them while we're having a party. We'll celebrate for a few more hours before I say anything.

A few hours later, Chantelle walks over to me, "Damien what's wrong?" she asks sincerely.

I sigh heavily before I get up to turn down the music and speak to everyone, "I was thinking that maybe we need another place for us all to meet. We're deep in the woods, but we're still in the open."

"Honestly, I've been thinking the same thing," Kahlil responds.

"Me too," Kiara adds. "We're too exposed out here. We can get here pretty easily, but so can other werewolves."

"Lil, is there anywhere we can go that we may still be able to still meet?" I inquire. "A place that we can be away from prying eyes and ears? Something we can call our own?"

"Hmmm..." Kahlil ponders. "They're a few places that I've looked into just in case this convo ever happened," he says, smiling.

"See, look at you, using your gift," Jasmine says, while patting Kahlil on the shoulder.

Kahlil pulls a stack of pages from his bag and shows us all the buildings he's been looking into. We look at quite a few of them, noticing most are old abandoned warehouses. After inspecting each of them we take a vote on which one we'll visit. We pick one that we won't have to put much work into.

"Okay where is this place?" NIchole asks, pointing at the picture.

"Just follow me," Kahlil laughs before running off.

Seeing Kahlil just take off running, surprises us, but doesn't stop us from following him. He takes us through the woods moving like I've never seen, running 65 mph through the trees, dodging and dipping in between them with ease. When it comes to Kahlil and architecture, we've learned it's best to just go along. It's tough to keep up, he must be really excited about this place.

After running for twenty minutes, Kahlil finally slows down, showing us the building in front of him. At first glance, it's nothing special, but it's solid. Upon inspecting the structure, we notice it has strong doors and is very secluded, even I'm not exactly sure where we are.

"This place'll need a lil elbow grease, but what do you guys think?" Kahlil asks with a grin.

"I think it'll work just fine," Nichole nods.

"Just don't expect me to kill any mice," Chantelle says as she shivers.

"I've seen you eat a moose and you're worried about a mouse?" Omar asks, turning to his sister.

"*Yes!*" Chantelle shrieks.

We all laugh at Chantelle's reaction, "We aren't very far from our spot in the woods, we're just a town over," Kahlil explains.

"What about anyone who might come by?" Jasmine asks.

"Since the city shut this factory and the others around it down 40 years ago, most of the time it's homeless people who can't get inside. The windows are strong and we can get a lock for the door. I've been scoping this place out for a while now. And with it being right next to a pier, so if we need to, we can escape by water."

The confidence in his voice is something to be inspired by. The man we met a few weeks ago compared to the man we see now are two different people. Nichole suggests that we give our place in the woods and this place code names, for secrecy.

"Since we already call that place the Den, we should keep that name and call this place the Basement," Kiara proposes.

We laugh when we hear the name basement, asking why she picked that, "No one would think of it as a warehouse, but an actual basement," she says, pouting.

Nichole goes to comfort her, "It's okay. It's not a bad idea. We were just caught off guard by the name. *Right everyone?*" Nichole glares at us.

Hearing Nichole's tone, we apologize and think about calling this place the Basement. After a few minutes of deliberating, we agree to call this place the Basement and the Den is keeping its name. The next thing Kahlil asks caught us off guard. He says he's been getting better at tracking and even though he's been with us for a while, he doesn't really have our scent yet. He asks each of us to give him a piece of our clothing so he can get familiar with our scent. A simple request that we happily oblige.

Before we leave, I ask Kahlil about how he's handling everything with his family and how they're handling everything. He reveals that even though it was rough, he told his parents that while he enjoys performing at the circus, he doesn't feel it's for him. He got a job as an assistant at an architecture firm that agreed to help him with school. When his parents heard this they were sad, but happy he's following his dream.

I congratulate him, because I know that wasn't an easy thing for him to do. He says that there were a lot of tears, but he will see his family again and promised his mom to call twice a week, which was non-negotiable. We head back to the basement to finish our celebration before going home.

Chapter 12

Over the course of the next few weeks we play out scenarios where things would happen and we break apart and regroup at either the Den or the Basement. We got pretty good at it after a few hurdles. We even worked on getting the entire building soundproofed, so no one outside can hear us.

Pretty soon after we've gotten pretty comfortable with the way things are going, but I couldn't help but have this uneasy feeling. My work, my werewolf life and my relationship with Catalina are starting to get more and more complicated. It feels like whenever I'm out in public, I'm being watched. It doesn't matter who I'm with, I sense malicious intent, but I can't find anyone. I start thinking I'm being paranoid, but everyone else told me that they've been sensing the same thing.

Out of the blue, we randomly start getting attacked by other werewolves at the same time. We're all attacked by a set of two werewolves. Our suspicions are confirmed, but we didn't know who they were because they always wear hoods. No talking is involved, just a random attack followed by an immediate escape, when they can't win. This reminds me of the first time I met Chantelle and Omar. It's like they're testing us, not trying to kill us. I order that no one goes out alone, everyone has to have a battle buddy.

Everyone has a partner except for me, Braheem and Darius are a team, Chantelle and Omar are a team, Jasmine and Nichole, and finally Kiara and Kahlil. I'm the only one who walks alone. It makes me rethink my stance on turning Catalina. Every time I think about it, I remember that I'll be putting her in danger because of what these blue eyes represent. The only way I can see myself biting Catalina is if there was no other way.

A few more attacks follows into the next week, then nothing for the last two weeks. We figure that it's okay to go back to our normal lives, but our guard will remain up at all times. Since there's been nothing out of the ordinary for a while, I figure it's safe enough for Catalina and I to go on a date. She's been asking to go out for a while and I told her it wasn't safe, due to the attacks, but now we should be able to go on one. There's a rescreening of the Twilight movies at a small theater across town and I thought it'd be a good idea for us to go.

The theater is doing a marathon of all the movies and each night we go to see one right after the other. After watching the last one, Breaking Dawn Part 2, we walk out of the parking lot and back to the car. I stare at the sky and see a full moon. Since it no longer affects me like it used to, I feel like it's sort of nostalgic that tonight was the full moon for our date.

"Look baby, the moon is full," I say, pointing.

"Yes it is," she giggles. "It's beautiful."

"Nothing compared to you," I say with a grin.

"That was corny," Catalina mocks.

"Yea, but you liked it," I chuckle.

"Yea I guess so," she kisses me as we continue walking toward the car.

"How was it rewatching the movies?" I ask.

"Just like before, it was good, and vampires are cool and everything, but werewolves are still better," Catalina says, grasping onto my arm.

"*Oh really*?" I ask intrigued.

"Ah huh," she smiles really big.

Suddenly, I notice we weren't the first ones to leave the theater, but the parking lot is strangely empty. I search around, but I don't see any cars or any other people. This is a fairly busy area, so I'm a little surprised that no one is around. The surrounding air changes, I feel someone or something lurking around us. This ominous feeling of malicious intent, I've felt it before.

"Baby, get in the car, now!" I say sternly.

"Why what's wrong?" she asks.

"Yea honey pie what's wrong?" we hear a female voice say in the distance.

My sears twitch, as my eyes dart around searching for the voice. I see a woman emerging from the shadows across the parking lot. When I see her face,

I notice that she looks vaguely familiar. I can't place where, but I know I've met this person before.

"What's wrong Damien? You look like you've seen a ghost," the woman says in a high-pitched tone.

"Who are you?" I ask.

"You know me, you've been my best friend for a while now" the woman says with a sinister smile.

"What are you talking about? Why are you here?" I interrogate.

"I just wanted to see an old friend," the woman says with a grizzly smile. "I see you're playing with your food. Why don't I take her off your hands?"

"Leave her alone!" I shout, baring my fangs and snarling. My eyes glowing with the passion of my words.

"That's right you live amongst the humans," she patronizes. "Pretending to be just like them. Purebreds like me don't understand the mingling of mutts and humans."

She must be one of the werewolves that allows her pack to hunt and eat people for sport. It makes my skin crawl thinking about it. When I ate Bruce's heart, I found it hard to keep anything down. I could never be that cruel on purpose.

"What's with the hostility?" she asks, innocently. "I didn't come here to fight. I just wanted to talk, that's all. You got something I want and I'm here to ask for it nicely," as she says that, her pack appears from the shadows. Her voice told one story, while her actions say another.

"And what would that be?" I question as I turn glabro.

"For one thing, it would be the title you stole from my brother and the other would be the power of the Tremauré," she reveals. "You don't deserve it, you're low life trash. How Darnell lost to a lil nigga like you, I'll never know. You've cost my family and I dearly and you're going to pay!" she screams.

"D... Darnell is your brother?!" I mutter. That's why she looks familiar.

"Ahh, you've noticed the family resemblance. Now give me what I ask," she demands, trying to intimidate me.

I'm pretty sure I can fight them all, since it's almost midnight, but I know they don't have enough strength without the full moon to back them up. However, Catalina is here and she's my priority.

"What is she talking about?" Catalina asks, in a scared voice.

"Remember how I told you I became an alpha?" she nods. "That's the sister of the alpha I killed."

She has the most frightened look on her face that I've ever seen. I look at Catalina then back Darnell's sister and her pack. They're giving off an immense, imposing presence. I have to wait for them to attack me, hoping that I can defend myself and Catalina from all of them. This is the first time she's seen me fight another wolf.

"Where are my manners?" Darnell's sister asks. "I never told you, my name is Monique and I should be the Tremauré, not you. I'm going to take what's mine, her eyes emanate the alpha's crimson glow.

Right after she says that, Monique and her pack start inching closer toward Catalina and me. I stand there anxiously awaiting them. I tell Catalina to get in and to cover her eyes and ears, so she can't see what was about to happen. The nearby church bell rings 11 times. Each time the bell rings, I feel the sound in my chest.

I'm ready for them, but I don't think they're ready for me. Monique has 8 other people with her, who come at me in pairs. The first set is easy enough to defeat and so was the second. The third pair are better fighters, but when they throw a punch, I dodge and kick them out of the way. The final two, I use their own momentum against them, knocking them on their backs with my fist, sending the air from their lungs, while simultaneously cracking the concrete.

Since they're not a threat to me, I'll let them live. So, I only knock them out. One by one, I pick them up with one hand and return them to sender. I won't chance that they'll wake up and attack Catalina. Tevin once told me about her, and I always thought she'd come after me, but not like this.

The listings of the most dangerous werewolf is controlled by the council and there are at total of 50 around the world with the title. After Killing Darnell, I became number 23 and Monique is 30. I never wanted any part of this, it only put a target on my back and now since becoming the Tremauré it could be lower now.

To protect everyone I care for, I'll fight whoever to keep them safe. Once Monique acknowledges that her pack is no match for me, she snarls. Rather than waiting, I go after her, taking the offensive. The farther this fight is from Catalina the better. I throw the first punch that sends her flying. Monique may also be an alpha, but I'm stronger than she is.

Monique rushes toward me, each one of her strikes are easily blockable. I dodge all the ones she sends my way and go for the counterattack. Before I can throw a punch, Monique kicks me in my balls. Out of the sheer pain, I drop to my knees and scream. Monique starts laughing as she tells me to get up. After a few seconds, the pain subsides enough so I can get back to my feet. I slowly stand up, looking Monique in the eyes.

This time when we engage each other she comes at me stronger than before. I expect her power to be that of an alpha, but she's stronger. Has she trained all this time? Monique's movements become faster. She sees the look on my face and smiles devilishly. She thinks the dynamic of the fight has shifted compared to how it started. She starts taking full advantage.

"Haha, look at you. I know you're wondering how I've gotten so strong aren't you?" she asks condescendingly.

I take a deep breath and smile, "Yea, you could say something like that," I egg her on.

"Well if you must know, all those attacks that you and your pack have been experiencing weren't just my pack," she explains. "They were coordinated by me and three other alphas. When we realized y'all caught onto us, started walking in pairs and continued to fight us off, we needed a new tactic. When we couldn't agree on a new plan of action, I came up with the best idea to take you out and killed them all. Taking their power for my own. Their strongest joined me in my pursuit, while the others ran away. The only way we are going to get this done is to do it together," I see the madness in her gaze as she speaks.

"Why would you do that?" I ask frantically.

"I was the only solution, I took all that wasted energy and I put it into one container...*ME*," she points to herself. "I want to be the best and once I take you out, I can be." a devilish smile appears on her face.

"Why do you need to be the best?" I question.

"Because it's my destiny!" Monique screams. "My grandfather was the best before he was and I'm going to take the title back!"

Who is she referring to? She then lunges at me. I catch her before throwing Monique 30 feet in another direction. Sadly, that is the same direction as Catalina. She lands against the other car next to mine. When I hear Catalina's scream along with the sound of shattered glass, I run over to them both. I throw

Monique in another direction before checking on Catalina. I shift back to my homid terrified.

"Catalina, are you ok?!' I ask, desperately.

"Yes I'm fine," she responds. "I was just startled when I heard the loud bang and glass breaking."

"I'm so sorry, I wasn't looking when I threw her."

"It's ok, I'm glad it wasn't your car," she says happily. "Thanks for protecting me," Catalina says, putting on a brave face.

"Of course," I say with warmth in my eyes. "I love you."

"I love you too," she smiles. "Damien look out!" Catalina screams.

Before I can react, Monique digs her claws into my back before throwing me away from her.

I catch myself and land, before seeing Monique charging after me, "Give me my power, it belongs to me!"

Seeing the fury in Monique's eyes, I'm reminded of Tevin's words, "The only way to ensure you and your pack are safe, is for you to be ready for a fight. And in that fight, it could lead to killing a few of your foes. Are you okay with that?"

"I have had enough of this!" I shout. "You want the power of the Tremauré? I'll give it to you," I roar as I turn back into glabro. "Catalina, look away now!!" I scream.

I see her shut her eyes and cover her ears. As Monique approaches me, I grab onto her shirt before swinging my arm backward as hard as I can, sending her head flying off of her neck and into the nearby forest. I watch as the blood pours from her neck and onto my hands. Seconds later, I let go of Monique's lifeless body. I feel a surge rushing through my body just as she hits the ground with a thud.

Immediately, I go to Catalina, "Hey are you ok?" I ask from outside the car.

"Yes, I'm good," she says, getting out of the car. "Don't worry about me."

"I'm sorry I let the fight get that close," I apologize. "I was trying to protect you."

"But you did," she acknowledges. "But you wouldn't have to worry about protecting me if you bit me. I look after you and you look after me. That's the deal."

"I want to, it's not like I don't, but I don't want to include you in this," I respond.

"Too late for that," she responds. "You're strong, but you can't always protect me, so please turn me. Catalina pleads."

I sigh, "The first turn is the hardest, it's so painful and will breaking."

"It'll be fine Damien, I promise. "Please, please turn me," she pleads again.

"No I can't," I say, as I wipe blood from my hands.

I use all the napkins and hand sanitizer from the glove compartment. After I'm cleaned up, I get in the car so we can go home. On the way, I call Tevin and tell him about Monique's body, and the other wolves lying in the parking lot. He tells me that he'll take care of all of it and asks if I needed help. I tell him that I'd be fine.

After I get off of the phone with Tevin, Catalina looks at me and asks, "Why Can't you bite me Damien? You know how strong I am, so why don't you do it?"

"Because of times like now, it's not easy," I answer. "There's something about being a werewolf I didn't tell you," I begin to say. "After your first change when you don't have full control, sometimes you're left with the memories of what you did. You get to see the terror you inflict on those poor animals. The wolf might go after people and you might kill them too. I'm lucky that I haven't hurt anyone, but that doesn't mean I couldn't have. You'll get blood on you and you'll start to like the smell. Those I've killed are still with me. I don't want this life for you. If I could choose another life for myself I would, but I can't," tears start forming in my eyes as I relive all the memories of killing Darnell, Bruce and now Monique.

Catalina puts her hand on my arm, "I'm sorry. I didn't realize how difficult of a position you were in. I can't know what you're going through, but I want to know, so you don't have to keep me at arm's length." she says in a loving and considerate tone.

The car is silent for a moment, I don't know what to say. I know she wants this and she seems to be accepting of everything I've told her.

"Abucheo, I know you were alone at first, but I won't be," she begins to say. "I'll have you and your pack there to show me how to control it right?"

"Yea I guess so, but still," I doubt. "I've never turned anyone before and I don't want to be the one to make a deadly mistake in turning you."

We come to a stoplight, "Look at me..." Catalina says, turning my face towards her. "I can do this, you can do this. I can be of better help to you in all parts of our lives if I'm a werewolf."

"Alright, alright, I hear you... Let me think about it and run it by the pack," I respond.

"The pack? Why?" she questions.

"Because if I turn you then you'll become the queen of the pack," I explain.

Catalina sheepishly smiles. We sit quietly until I drop her off at home. As I open her door and walk Catalina to the door, I jokingly ask how she feels about her clothes potentially being ripped and or being soaked in blood. She laughs and rolls her eyes as she goes inside after kissing me good night.

I go home to take a shower to wash the remainder of the blood off of me. The entire time, I'm thinking about what happened. What I could have done better and even if biting Catalina is the right thing to do. Honestly, I know she's right about being able to take care of herself. I just have to have faith in her the same way she always has faith in me.

It takes a few weeks, but I finally get the courage to finally bite her. Just like before, I went back and forth with the idea. I talk to everyone and they tell me it's my decision, they won't give me an answer. I go to Tevin about it, who says, the bite won't kill her, but the first change could. He also tells me I could have turned her as a beta, anyone can turn a person into a werewolf.

Upon hearing this, I'm more fearful of turning her, Catalina is ultimately right about her helping me. She's with me and because of that, she is going to be in danger. It's the best thing for the both of us, if while I'm fighting, my queen protects my neck. I finally come to terms with turning Catalina.

She suggests that I bite her 3 days before the full moon, so she could get a jump on her training. I plan an all day date for us. It starts in the morning and ends tonight with me finally biting her. I start the day off by making her breakfast and from there we go to the mall, have lunch and then a few other places. I don't think I've ever felt more normal than I have today. I love seeing Catalina smile and enjoying the time we're spending together. I wish every day could be like this.

The day comes and goes, and the night is fast upon us. We go to her bedroom, in an attempt to have some privacy. Close by I have bandages ready. The resolve on her face tells me she accepts what's about to happen. The closer the time comes for me to bite her, the louder our heart beat becomes. I hesitate when I go to bite her the first few times.

I don't want to hurt her, but I know there is no backing out now. In order for me to turn Catalina, I have to bite her and it *will* hurt.

"Baby, last time, you sure about this?" I ask, a little timid. "There's no turning back. I'll also need to break the skin when I bite you."

Catalina's gaze meets my own, "This is what I want. I trust you," she responds. "One question though, can't you just scratch me?"

"Even if I did, I'd still need to break the skin," I reply. "You still need to bleed even if it's just a little."

"Do you want me to bite you or scratch you?" I question.

"Bite me, we have to make sure this works," she answers. "You were bitten right? Just give me a second," Catalina gets up from the bed, and grabs a belt for her to bite down on. "Just do it," she demands as she bites down.

She raises her arm and I elongate my teeth before biting down into her forearm. I made sure to bite hard enough that my fangs dig into her arm so I can break the skin, causing her arm to bleed. Catalina screams in muffled pain the entire time my teeth are in her arm. 10 seconds later, I release her arm from my jaw before grabbing the gauze and bandages. After wiping her bleeding arm, I wrap it in an ace wrap. I feel so bad seeing my teeth marks in her arm.

The tears she's shedding tonight will be the only time I make her cry. A few minutes following the bite, she grows very weak. Catalina is unable to stand up on her own and starts to get a fever and chills at the same time. Her vision becomes extremely blurry in one eye. I help her get ready for bed, washing her face before tucking her in.

"Do you want me to stay?" I ask in a soft voice as she lays in her bed.

"It's probably better if you went home." Catalina responds in a weak voice.

I knelt down next to her, "that's not what you really want is it?"

"No," She holds back tears as she speaks.

"Then I won't go," I say as I get under the blanket with her before wrapping my arms around her.

Catalina lays in my chest crying for 45 minutes before she settles enough to goes to sleep. I hold her the entire time, falling asleep shortly after.

The next morning, she feels better than ever. Since the full moon is in two days, I keep a close eye on her the entire day. Catalina has been happy and full of energy, all her senses are heightened, including her libido. I go right along with it. The next day she levels out and I barely notice anything different. On the third day, she's been moody, almost getting annoyed at every little thing.

Tonight's the night of the full moon, she mellows out and starts to realize why I love being a werewolf. The power it gives you is amazing. When nightfall comes and the moon rises, Catalina notices how everything isn't as easy as she thought. Her emotions are all over the place, she asks for her first change for it to be just she and I.

I understand why she asked and told the others that we'd use the Den for her first change. They tell me I didn't need to ask. I take her to the Den, which is close to where she found out I'm a werewolf. It's kind of poetic.

It's half an hour to midnight and she's already feeling the effects of her first change. I tell Catalina to breathe and concentrate as it's almost time. We take off our clothes so we don't rip them. I've shown her all the videos and gone over the pain she'll experience during this, but no matter what I can't prepare for what is to come. Ten minutes til midnight, the excruciating pain of the first change hits her hard.

Catalina drops to her knees screaming, admitting that this is worse than anything she's ever felt. I stay close to her for the first few minutes before she turns, but now I have to step back. It saddens me that I can't help her get past this. I watch in horror as my girlfriend's body changes.

As she transforms I hear the sound of her bones breaking. The blood-curdling screams of her body transforming for the first time. What feels like an eternity of pain, is really only five minutes and experiencing it for the first time is terrible. I've seen this so many other times watching my own transformation, but it never gets any easier no matter how many times you see it.

After Catalina finally turns, I can tell she isn't the one driving, nor do I expect her to be. She lunges at me and roared at her in asserting that I am her alpha. Catalina immediately backs down. Afterward, she lowers her head, bowing to me, acknowledging me as her alpha. Using a few growls and my own body language, I let her know everything is fine and she's safe. Her wolf is still young and untamed, it's not going to know anyone around her and if they are friendly or not. It's my job to watch her through this first turn and the next few after.

Without wasting any more time, I turn so we can run together. That night we run all through the woods. Normally I'd be the one controlling while in crinos, but I figure it's better if I let my wolf run free. We've had an understanding with one another for a long time and I trust him. I take the back seat and let my wolf run free with Catalina's.

The next morning when we wake up, we're cuddling like normal when we sleep together. There's a fresh deer carcass a few feet from us, the wolves have eaten their fill. When she wakes up, Catalina is freaked out at first, but I calm her down slowly. The first change always leaves a person a little weak at first, so I have to help her up to her feet and back home. Afterward I get her showered and then into bed. After I tuck Catalina in, I kiss her. I smile as I walk out of her room. She has a long road ahead of her, but I know she can do it.

Chapter 13

Unfortunately for us, the attacks didn't stop while trying to teach Catalina how to control the change. It's crucial for us to teach Catalina everything about being a werewolf. I'd rather be working with her one on one, but she has to learn on the fly. Even with all that's been going on, Catalina is a natural, absorbing everything we're teaching her.

After a few more weeks, the attacks finally stop once they realize that they can't win. When the coast is finally clear, we decide to celebrate Catalina joining the pack. We meet at the Den to have a party, finally able to relax and blow off some steam. Tonight's a full moon and we're going for a run. It's been so long since we could just let loose.

I stand on our large rock to announce Catalina's initiation into the pack. Everyone seems happy, but I can tell that something isn't right. I see it on all of their faces. Everyone is side-stepping around her. Though we've been fighting and teaching as a team, something is off. I've talked about Catalina with them or I'd tell her about what's happening within the pack. Everyone knows about each other, but this is supposed to be a party. I thought it would be different.

The two lives I kept separate for so long are now one. I thought they'd treat her like a long-lost family member, but that isn't how they're acting.

As the moon reaches its peak, I bask in its light before stripping and transforming. Catalina transforms right after I do and everyone else follows. We stare into the starry night sky before howling at the moon. Soon after we move through the woods for a few hours before returning to the Den and changing into homid.

Once we clean the blood off of ourselves from a deer we ate and cloth ourselves, my thoughts from earlier creep into the forefront of my mind. It's been almost six weeks since Catalina joined us and the relationships between Braheem, Omar, Darius, Kahlil, Chantelle, Kiara, Nichole and Jasmine are rough. I hope that they can get along, but I'm not sure what to do to help the situation. Is it that we've been a pack for so long and they're trying to protect me? Honestly, I'm not sure, but I do know we can't be effective if I let these feelings fester.

I first noticed that something was off a couple of weeks ago when that pulse didn't come. The feeling that came when everyone else joined. I never found a name for it, but I thought it would have happened by now. I thought we were whole, like the final the piece had been put in, but I guess we still have some work to do.

I'm sitting alone when Catalina comes up and expresses her concerns, "Abucheo, I don't think that everyone likes me," she says in a low voice.

"What do you mean baby?" I ask.

"Well… I mean, I still feel like an outsider," she responds. "They've been a part of the pack for so long and I've only been with the pack for a little over a month."

I kiss her on her forehead, "It's okay baby, I think they're just trying to look out for me. I've noticed how they've been towards you and I wouldn't take it personally. I think they're trying to feel you out," I say, trying to make her feel better.

"So you think they'll warm up to me?" Catalina asks quietly.

"Without a shadow of a doubt," I smile. "Soon you'll find that you can get along with everyone," I say confidently.

"Good, I was beginning to think that I was being added to your harem," she jokes.

"Well a harem would be nice, but that would mean everyone is a woman," I laugh. "Braheem, Darius Omar and Kahlil would also need to be women."

Catalina smiles then kisses me. However, I sense she's still worried. She's been there to bandage me, but she hasn't seen the other side of my life until the fight with Monique. I know she has what it takes to be one of us, I just need to get everyone else to see it too.

For the next few days, I think about how I can get everyone's opinion without them feeling like I was forcing the conversation. Since day one everything with us is open to discussion and Catalina's being in the pack is no exception. I text Darius, Braheem Omar and Kahlil to meet me at the Den the following afternoon, in an effort to get their honest opinion. I don't think the stand-offishness is strictly from the girls. That's creating a cliché drama. We all arrive at the same time.

"Yo Dame, wassup man, why'd you call us here?" Braheem asks after we sit down.

"Yea bro wassup? You never ask just us here without everyone," Omar adds.

A serious look appears in my face, "Ight, I asked you here because I wanted to ask what y'all think about Catalina?"

One by one, they tell me how pretty she is and how smart they think she is. Then going on to tell me that they feel like she's a good fit for the pack. I could hear the sincerity in their voices, but I could also hear that they are holding back.

"Ard I heard y'all. Now honestly, tell me what you think of Catalina," I respond. "No matter what y'all say, it won't hurt my feelings."

Each of them took their eyes off of me and look at each other before looking at the ground. I know there's something they want to say, but they also want to spare my feelings.

"Y'all it's me," I say earnestly. "Tell me the truth."

Darius sighs, "Aight... It's not that we don't think highly of her, y'all have been together for years."

"*But...*" I urge him to continue.

"But, she's still new to the werewolf thing," continued Braheem. "Do you really think that she can handle this after being on the outside for so long?"

"Yes I do," I say, confidently. "I've been around this girl since we were kids and some of the things I've seen her do are incredible. If anyone can handle this she can."

"It's not just that though," Kahlil inputs. "She's still learning to control herself under the full moon. It's a lil scary knowing she's that much of a wild card."

"You think that's bad?" I ask. "We've all had our hiccups. You didn't have that much control when we first met. Neither did I nor Braheem or Omar in the beginning. These things take time."

"My bad D, you're right," Braheem admits. "We didn't think about all of that. We never gave her the chance we've given each other. I don't know what it is, but it's not fair to her, you or the pack."

"He's right," Darius says. "You wouldn't have bitten her if she couldn't handle being a wolf. You're our alpha and our friend. We trust you on this."

We dap each other and I thank them for telling me the truth. After they leave, I sit for ten minutes before texting the girls. I want to talk to them about the same thing, to get their perspective. When I see them coming toward me, I see them dolled up, with makeup and somewhat revealing clothing. I laugh at first, thinking it's a joke.

"Well, well, well, don't the four of you look beautiful today," I say. "Are y'all going somewhere later?"

"No, no, we just like looking cute as all," Chantelle answers. "You caught us on our weekly outing. We like to dress up nice every other week and today was just so perfect that we couldn't resist."

"Yea, we were just feeling cute. It is what it is," smiles Jasmine.

Looking at each of them, I catch a lump in my throat. Before I speak, I clear it, "The reason I asked you all here is because I want your honest opinion about Catalina joining the pack. I noticed that there hasn't been a lot of fair treatment towards her like there has been for everyone else. And before you say anything, I've already talked to the guys about this."

Jasmine lets out a little sigh, "It's not that we don't like her, we just don't know her."

"I figured as much, but have either of you *tried* to get to know her?" I ask.

"... Not really," Nichole acknowledges.

"I'm sure if either of you try, you'll find out that all of you can get along," I advise.

"How could you know that?" asks Chantelle.

"I don't, but I do know that you'll never know if you don't try," I respond.

"Fine, I guess she *is* your girlfriend and we have been a little cold towards her and that's not fair," Jasmine says.

"It's fine," I chuckle. "Lead by example and show the rest of them how it's done."

Chantelle steps closer to me, "Are you sure she's ready to deal with all of this after being on the outside for so long?"

"Braheem asked me the same thing, and I'll tell you what I told the four of them earlier," I stand tall. "I've been around this girl since we were kids and some of the things I've seen her do are incredible. If anyone can handle this she can."

Each of them smile at me. Even though it was hard to bring up the subject with both groups, it needed to happen. We may not always be on the same page, but a pack that works together, stays together. I know Catalina is still new, but she needs all of us to train her. I can only show her so much by myself.

They left to go back to town. I sit down on my rock. I never knew that being a werewolf would be so much work. I thought it was only fighting and blood, but seeing as there's a Council, purebreds, mutts and the need to keep everything secret was a lot more like a secret society than what they show in the movies.

Feeling satisfied with today, I leave the Den and go to my car. Since it's getting late, I decide to get to a fast food restaurant to grab something to eat. As I park and get out of my car I caught a whiff of something. My head perks up and I start surveying the surrounding area. Are they an enemy? What is this ominous aura surrounding me? My gut is telling me that whoever this is, they're going to be a problem.

"I'm surprised you picked up on my scent so quickly," I hear a voice say. "It is because of the power of the Tremauré or is it you're just that good?"

"I'd say it's because I'm just that good," I respond.

"Well in any case, I'm here because you have something I want," he says.

"The power of the Tremauré?" I question.

"Oh, nothing so trivial." he answers.

"I want my beta back," he demands.

"*Your beta*? Whom are you referring to?" I ask.

The person speaking emerges from the trees, "I'm referring to Darius. You see the little pup has gone astray and I've been so worried," he says sarcastically. "He hasn't answered any of my calls the last few years. All this time I was wondering why and what do I find? He's been following a subpar alpha. You."

"Subpar?" I chuckle. "Well if you were that concerned about him, he wouldn't have left."

"Not only will I have to take him back, but I'll also avenge my friends," he says.

"Friends? What friends, Andre?" I question.

"I see he told you about me," Andre says smugly. "The friends I'm referring to are Darnell and Monique. I may not be a purebred, like them, but on some level I had their respect and you took them from me, and my business has suffered severely."

My eyes begin to illuminate, "You obviously know who I am, but you have no idea what I'm capable of."

"I'm well aware and that's why I didn't come alone," he laughs.

Seven other werewolves come from behind the trees. Which is a surprise to me, because I didn't smell them. They must have hid their scent from me to keep the element of surprise.

"If you don't give me what's rightfully mine, then I will take it! Beta and power in all!" he exclaims.

Before I can say anything, his pack rushes toward me. I'm going to have to defend myself against the 8 of them. It sucks because I really like this shirt and nothing good ever comes from a fight against werewolves like them.

Before any of them throw their first punch, I hold my hands up to stop them, "Wait!" I scream. "Before we start, let me take off my shirt because it's hard to find."

Andre sneers, "Ard, I guess we can grant you one final request, but don't try anything stupid."

At the same time I remove my shirt, I howl, signaling the others that I need help. Panicked, they immediately start attacking me. I defend myself while taking off my shirt. I'm forever thankful for all the training I went through with Omar and Chantelle. They never once pulled any punches, letting me know that martial arts is as much about offense as it is defense. I realize that I don't need my glabro for this fight, my homid is enough.

210

I knock out the first few, but the rest of them keep coming. After knocking out the other three, there's only one more left. He looks different from the rest of them. I can't explain it, but I can tell he's a much better fighter than the rest.

"Well, well, don't you look strong," I mock.

"Stronger than you and that would be alpha over there," he responds. "I'm just looking to get my money and killing someone you, I get a huge payday."

"You do know I'm not just an alpha right?" I question.

"I've taken down my fair share, so that won't be much of a problem," he says confidently.

"We'll have to see," I smile as my eyes glow.

That's when I see it, the werewolf in front of me, isn't just some other beta like the rest of them. He's also an alpha. From what he said, my guess is he's a mercenary and uses being a werewolf as means to be an efficient killer. Rather than using his glabro form, this guy transforms into crinos. He doesn't care about secrecy, but I can't let the humans see us.

The presence and aura he exudes is almost enough to intimidate me. I sense his will attempting to dominate my own, but being an alpha and the Tremauré makes my will stronger than his.

Without a second thought he charges and swings at me. I dodge by flipping away from him before running into the woods, hoping he'll follow. I'm correct as I see him charging after me with other wolves in tow. Being in homid he's gaining on me. I have to out think him before gets the chance to catch me off guard, I transform into my crinos and roar at them as my eyes glow brightly. For a moment, he stops after seeing me in crinos. Those following behind also slow down as well when they hear me. Andre tries to come up from behind and dig his claws into my back.

I stop his arm, just as it comes in reach. He then tries with the other arm, and stop that one as well. Andre's strong, definitely stronger than me was when I first became an alpha, but I'm stronger than he is. He's trying to overpower me by pushing even harder, but no matter how hard he tries he can't. He pulls his claws away from me and goes for another attack. I growl at him and jump out of the way as he goes for a tackle. I get behind him and throw him into a tree.

Andre howls in pain and tries once more to attack me. I look all around trying to make sure I know where all of my enemies are. Andre and his mercs circle me. I keep my guard up, but what's their next attack? As the merc goes in for the attack, I evade him, soon after Andre comes behind me. I throw him off and they circle again.

Andre's good but not as nearly as good as the merc, but them working together like this could end bad for me. Their plan to have one of them keep my attention while the other attacks will only work for so long. I growl at them both. Since Andre is considerably weaker, I go after him first. He isn't able to put up much of a fight, so I throw him to the ground and roar in his face forcing my will onto him. All his fight immediately fades.

With no time to react the merc thrusts his claws into my back and pushes me away. The pain is immense, but I'll heal. With the merc catching me off guard, I almost shift back into my homid form. I take a breath and focus, already feeling the wound healing. I'm ready for another round with him. Surprisingly, the merc goes from crinos to glabro and I did the same.

"What's wrong?" I ask.

"Nothing, I just want to ask a question," he begins to say. "I was curious about your eyes since the beginning. They're blue, I've only ever seen red or gold. What are you?" he questions.

"To be honest, I don't understand everything, but what I do know is I've become the Tremauré. The spirit of the first werewolf is inside of me," I answer.

"Interesting, I heard about that, but I didn't know it was you."

Seconds later, he howls and I'm met with an onslaught of arrows from all directions. I hadn't noticed that the other mercs he brought with him had stepped away. They're using arrows with the tips made out of silver. I dodge all the ones that I can, but there are so many that three of them end up in my leg. I drop to the dirt and scream in pain.

The mercenary laughs at me, "You think I'm going to finish this alone? I never hunt without my team. You're a good fighter, but this team isn't a one-trick pony. Most of them are trained marksmen."

A few of them come out of the shadows with their crossbows aimed at me. I try to pull the arrows out, but I'm not able to. The second I try, it feels like the rest of my leg is coming with it. My leg is trying to heal, but the arrow is preventing me. I'll have to leave them for now.

"Haha, very perceptive kid," he says. "The more you yank at them the worse it gets for you. I'm a hired gun, and a hunter, I always get my prey. I didn't want to have to fight this way since it's not really my style, but since you're stronger than I am, I see this as the only way. Before this was just another job, but now, I want that power. Killing you should be like any other alpha. However, the only way for me to be sure is to find out for myself."

"I don't think it works that way," I reply in pain.

"We'll just have to see now won't we?" he smiles devilishly.

The look in his eye is pure determination, something I've seen before. He sees a chance to get a power he's never had before. To him, I must look like a wounded animal that needs to be put out of my misery. I'm not sure what to do. I try standing up, but the arrows make it difficult. I can't put any pressure on my leg. I'm not going to go down without a fight, no matter what. I balance on one leg, putting my guard up to continue the fight.

The merc starts walking toward me. He brings out his claws and I know what he's going to do to me. I'll have to fight to stop him, and since I'm off balance, my chances are slim, but that won't stop me. As he approaches me, I look at his archers who have their aim still on me. No matter what, I'm not dying here tonight.

Just before he struck me, Catalina comes flying in and grabs him before throwing him as far as she can, "Get away from him!" she screams. Her stare could pierce the heavens. Her stance is very low, guarding me from him.

The merc stands up and watches Catalina closely. "Haha, look what he have here, the king has a queen. But the two of you won't be enough to take us all on."

"We're not alone. He has me and our pack," immediately after she says that, everyone else comes running from all directions, surrounding him and his archers. "Darius, Braheem, don't just stand there, help Damien."

They came to tend to me while she took over, "Damn, how'd you fumble this one?" Braheem asks.

"Long story," I reply.

()Catalina starts calling all the shots, telling everyone how they should move and how to take them down. She's like a general in active warfare. I couldn't be more impressed seeing them follow her commands. Everyone's working together just like we always do. Darius manages to find the switch on the arrow that allows it to be removed from my leg.

After they pull the arrows from my leg, I'm finally able to heal. A few minutes later, I get back on my feet. Once the anchors were taken down, I notice that Andre and the Merc are nowhere to be found.

"Catalina, keep everyone busy, I'll find them," I command.

"Right, be careful," she responds.

I go off further into the woods to find the merc and Andre. I have their scent now and I'm going to let them get away. First they come and try to take one of my pack members, then they try to kill me and take my power after shooting me with arrows. And finally, when my back-up comes and the real fighting starts they run, I'm taking them down. Chasing after their scent I find myself running for a few miles.

When I eventually catch up, I realize I've been in this area before. As I emerge on the other side of the woods, I see that they led me to a warehouse. Why would they take me here? I walk closer towards the building, unsure of what's to come next. A tree falls over, about to land on me. I catch it and throw it to the side.

"Really?" I ask "Is that the best you can do?" I bait them.

Moments later, Andre drops from a branch a few ft from me, "Remember this place? This is where you killed Darnell and all of my business died with him. Killed by a mutt, what is this world coming to?"

"Yea I'm a mutt, but so are you," I redirect. "Don't think that just because you hung with them, you meant something?"

216

"Don't patronize me nigga, I was working my way through the ranks. Trying everything to excel in this world and you ruined my plans. After I kill you, I'll take Darius back and I'll take the Tremauré's power for myself!" he declares.

"Well come and get it then," I challenge.

Andre lunges towards me, Catalina tackles him, catching him off guard. She then starts punching Andre in the face, knocking him out. The mercenary comes from his hiding spot.

"I knew you couldn't do what needed to be done," the merc says. "All of us have a job and you paid me to be the one to handle this for you."

"Oh yea?" I ask. "Then let's go."

He has this glaring look on his face. It reminds of my fight with Bruce and how his conviction and determination drove him. They are both soldiers, fighting their war the only way they knew how. Moments later he charges at me. Before he can reach me, Braheem, and Omar come up from behind me. He stops when he sees them. Everyone surrounds him, similar to what he and Andre did to me.

"How the tables have turned," I say confidently.

The Merc stands tall, pretending to be tough. However, I hear his heart racing. He knows he can't take on all of us at once. His tough act only lasts for a few seconds, but he raises his hands in the air to give up. Kiara finds a chain in the warehouse and ties them both up. Under Catalina's leadership, she successfully gets all the mercs subdued and accounted for.

We call Tevin and ask him what we should do. He calls some members of the Council who sent the DSF to get each of them. I ask what would happen to them, but I don't get an answer. I call Tevin back and ask him as well, he tells me that it would be best if I don't think about it. It's probably best I don't know.

When things finally die down and we have a chance to breathe we go back to the Den. I sit in the grass when Braheem comes up whistling. He starts talking about Catalina, "I wasn't sure before bro, but damn that girl is something else."

"Don't I know it," I respond.

Catalina turns around and blows a kiss in my direction. Locking eyes with her always makes me feel like we were the only ones in the world, "Thanks for the save," I whisper to her.

"Anytime," she whispers back.

From where I was sitting I see Catalina speaking with Jasmine, Chantelle, Kiara and Nichole. They're talking like they've been friends for years. It's nice to see them getting along. I knew they could be friends, even if it's under strange circumstances. It's kind of funny, but stranger things have happened.

Kahlil, Omar and Darius joined Braheem and I. end up sitting together around a fire, having the time of our lives. This is the true way to become a wolf family. Suddenly, a pulse washes over each of us. I hold my chest as my heart grows warm. We all feel the final piece of the puzzle has been added. Our pack is finally complete. Everyone looks at each other and then the rest of the group, it's like seeing the world in a different color. Jasmine then mentions that she's hungry, so we leave the Den and go to John's Burgers to get a bite to eat. The same place I left my car.

Jasmine raises her glass, "Here's to Catalina, not only for her ability to think under pressure, but for how she took charge when Damien was lying there like a wounded puppy."

"It wasn't that bad," I mumble. "You try fighting that merc and all his men."

"We did," Catalina teases.

"I know we didn't give you the warmest of welcomes, but I want to be the first to tell you I'm sorry," Jasmine smile.

"Don't worry about it," Catalina responds. "Anything to see the look on his face when I have to save his ass every time."

I stick my tongue out at her and everyone else laughs at us. We talk for a few more hours going over everything that happened that night and how we all feel about it. Everyone agrees that we should be on guard from here on out. Our pack has a target on its back and we will have to watch out for each other. Pretty soon, we eat all of our food and go back home. Catalina and I showered and end the night with some fun of our own.

Chapter 14

After the incident with the merc and Andre, there's been peace for the last few months. I guess everyone got the message that we shouldn't be messed with. I didn't kill them, but I seriously wanted to. I realize that with the power I was given, killing isn't always the only option. Sometimes letting them go changes the dynamic. I still don't know what it truly means to be the Tremaurè, but I think I have a better understanding than I did before.

We've also been getting a lot of werewolves seeking to join our pack. People are coming to my job, walking up to us on the street and even sending letters and gifts as a way to try to get their way in. It's a little overwhelming at first, but got annoying very quickly. Betas and omegas start coming from all over attempting to join us. Some are second generation purebreds trying to establish themselves by joining our pack.

Prestigious purebred representatives have asked me to join their pack. They tell me I'll have to give up my title as alpha, but I won't have to worry about money ever again. Immediately, I tell them no. This power is for everyone and being a part of someone else's pack means I won't have the free rein I have now. Some of them understand my reasoning, while others say I'll regret my decision.

Most wolves only want to join our pack to gain status or power. We aren't now nor will we ever be for that. We're a pack that protects ourselves, our loved ones and our race. With the amount of people attempting to join, Chantelle suggests that we could at least entertain the idea of letting someone else join the pack. She insists it's a great way for us to reach our goal.

When she first mentions the idea, I'm against it. I don't want us to get any bigger. I feel that we are big enough to spread our message. Things can be misconstrued very easily if we get bigger. We debate for a while and pretty soon Chantelle's idea grows amongst everyone else. First with Kiara and Omar, then Nichole and Darius and finally Jasmine and Braheem. Even though everyone else is in agreement, I'm still hesitant. Catalina is on the fence at first, finding it hard to make a decision.

I stay firm on my idea of not letting anyone else into the pack, but no one else is changing their minds. They wear me down and I agree that we can let more people into the pack. We start sorting through the people who came to us to vet each one of them as thoroughly as possible. There are 50 different werewolves who want to join us. Most of them want more power or tell us that they'll kill in order to join the pack.

When we explain to them that's not what we were about, they express their disgust. They spew the same bull about how we're werewolves and strength is the only thing that matters. Some of them even challenge us, I let them fight anyone they choose. Jasmine is ready to defend our message. It's amusing to watch many of them fall on their ass to someone they called weak. After the fight they leave with their tails between their legs.

Quite a few of the werewolves only want to join, because they see me as a deity. Once they get a look at my blue eyes, they drop to their knees and pray. I wasn't about to let any of them do that. I'm no deity, I don't have any special powers and I don't want them to see me as one. Like the others they too are turned away.

About five or six of them just want me to verify that I have the power of the Tremauré. When I show them my eyes they still disbelieve. The only way I know to show them was to do what any werewolf alpha would. I assert my dominance over them. As the Tremauré, I supersede even alphas. An ability that I hate using on anyone, but they want me to show my hand. I know I don't have to prove myself, but I can't have rumors spreading.

After meeting each one of them, my thoughts on the subject haven't changed. I think after speaking with all the werewolves that came to see us, Catalina Braheem Darius, Omar, Chantelle, Jasmine, Kiara Nichole and Kahlil still are for the idea to let others join, but glad we didn't let any of them join. It's not that we can't have more people, but I don't think we need it.

After a few days of meeting and talking to all those wolves I'm ready to relax my mind. Fighting Darnell, Bruce or the merc, was less exhausting than this.

I decide to go for a run to clear my mind. While running, I'm approached by a young woman, "A…are you the alpha Damien?" she asks sheepishly.

I slowed my pace and answer, "Yes that's me."

"Great, I finally found you!" she exclaims. "I've been working up the nerve to come out and ask you to join your pack."

She's a young dark skin woman with long braids. She's short but with an average build. Is she a werewolf?. What does she want with me?

"Oh, we uhh, we aren't really accepting new pack members," I say, nervously.

"I understand, I just wanted to ask since I was exiled from my family's pack, because my ideals didn't align with theirs."

"How do you mean?" I puzzled.

"Well…the things I want don't resonate with what they want," she responds. "I want the family to head into the future, but when I pleaded my case, it was quickly dismissed. Then I tried my best to fight for this new change, but I wasn't strong enough. I was beaten and then thrown out by my mother. I'm no longer next in line to take her place as leader of the pack."

"You're a purebred?" I ask.

"Yes I am." she answers. "You and your pack are my first and last resort. Hopefully we can work together to make a better future," she says smiling.

"Show me," I demand.

"Excuse me?" she asks.

"Show me you're a werewolf," I respond.

She laughs as her eyes glow before she holds out her hand and introduces himself, "DeShawna Cambridge. It's a pleasure to meet you."

I shake her hand and introduce myself, "Damien Nichols, it's nice to meet you. Why did you wait so long to talk to me? We held interviews days ago."

"I... I don't know. I didn't think you'd be willing to speak with me. I figured you'd met someone or multiple people and had them join already."

"No, sadly not," I respond. "We actually haven't added any of the people we spoke with, but I think we can definitely make an exception with you."

"Really?!" she asks excitedly.

"Yes I do," I acknowledge. "Out of everyone we talked to for the last few days, I only get a good feeling from you. Give me your number."

I take Deshawna's number and tell her that I'll be in contact with her after I speak with my pack. The entire time she spoke, I listened to her heartbeat. Never once did it skip a beat. She believes in what she's saying and even when she stuttered, it didn't show any signs of lying. I can't explain it, but Deshawna's words resonate with me. I think she'll be a good addition to the pack, but it's not just my decision.

Later that night, I call everyone together to the Den. I want to tell them that I changed my mind about the entire idea of adding another pack member. I'm the first to arrive at the Den and I sit down on my rock, looking at the stars. I think about what Deshawna said. I could hear the sincerity and her passion. She believes in change, just like the rest of us. It's hard to imagine what she went through after being cast out of her family's pack.

I've never heard of the Cambridges and I wonder what they're like. I pull out my phone to call Tevin wondering if he has any information. I'm interrupted by Darius and Omar walking towards me. I dap each of them and say we'll wait for everyone to arrive before I go over my ideas. Sure enough everyone arrives one after another. First Braheem then Kahlil and all the girls come together. It's good to see them getting along.

"Hey D, what's up man?" asks Omar, "You've been quiet this entire time."

"Alright since everyone is here," I begin to say. "I've been thinking about it and Chantelle may have had a point. I met someone earlier today."

"Ohh when were you going to tell me?" Catalina jokes.

"Not like that, she's another werewolf and she told me she was cast out of her pack and cut off because they had a falling out."

"What do you mean cast out of her family?" Jasmine questions.

"Well...she's a purebred," I answer.

"A purebred?!" Braheem asks. "Are you sure?"

"Yes I am, she has this smell on her, I can't explain it. Maybe I can sense it." I say.

"I know what you mean," Chantelle confirms. "Darnell had this smell on him too. Strangely so do you Damien."

"I'm not a purebred though. I was bitten like all of you," I say confused.

"All right, but I'm just telling you, your scent isn't like the rest of ours."

"Anyway... Deshawna tells me they have a difference of ideals and they kicked her out, so I want to speak to y'all first. I know what I said before, but I think she could be a good fit for us."

"Are you sure you're not saying this because she's a woman?" Jasmine asks.

"No, I'm not. We all know what it's like to be out there alone with no one to turn to and I want to prevent it where I can. Especially as the Tremauré. Besides out of everyone we've met, she's the only one who seems... I don't know...genuine."

"Are you sure you're not trying to increase your harem?" Nichole jokes.

I look at Catalina, "Y'all not allowed to hang out no more."

Everyone starts laughing. I just shake my head with my tongue poking my bottom lip. I know they have to mess with me a little, but they get on my nerves sometimes. For the rest of the night, we talk about what it would take if we were to have Deshawna join. I wasn't sure before, but now I'm hinting more toward the idea.

Catalina, Braheem, Darius, Omar, Chantelle, Jasmine, Nichole, Kiara, Kahlil and I talk for hours. Everyone shares their opinion on why they think we should or shouldn't let Deshawna into the pack. Jasmine and Braheem ask the same questions I did before.

We have an even number of pack members and our chemistry works so well. Adding in another only might change the dynamic, but that's sort of the idea. After that night, we decide that this isn't a choice we're going to make in one night. We spend a few more days deliberating.

What is interesting to me was I don't feel the same way about Deshawna joining as I did with everyone else. I could feel that we were all drawn together, but not with her. What's wrong? In order to change the world, I know we need to grow, but I can't feel it with her. Despite how I feel, I can't let her go just because I don't think she isn't drawn to us. The Tremauré is supposed to be a beacon of hope and I will strive to be that hope for all werewolves.

Since we couldn't come to a consensus while talking, everyone tells me that it's my decision and whatever I decide they will go with. It takes me a few more days for me to come to a decision. In total two weeks have passed since I met Deshawna, but I come to the conclusion that we should let her in. I can't let her stay out there fending for herself when in fact she can make a difference with the rest of us. I text Deshawna to meet us at the Den with its location. so she can meet everyone. I didn't tell her it's a welcoming party. Since we love our food and fire, we have everything prepared for when she arrives. As she walked to the Den there we were ready to welcome her.

"Welcome Deshawna!" we all say in unison.

"What's all this?" she ponders.

"What better way to meet everyone than to have a party with the entire pack?" I respond happily.

"I get it, but I wasn't expecting all of this," Deshawna says, sheepishly.

"Don't let it get to you," Catalina says. "Damien likes throwing parties and any reason we can cook some meat he'll take it. I'm Catalina by the way."

"Oh nice to meet you. How did you guys meet?" Deshwana asks.

"You know the old story, girl moves to a new town, girl meets boy, they go to school, date in college and then boy bites the girl, turning her into a werewolf."

"So you two are a couple?" Deshawna asks, confused.

"I know, hard to believe," Jasmine interrupts.

"She's so far out of his league they might as well be from different planets," Omar laughs.

"Ard y'all I think she gets it," I say out loud.

228

"Is this the entire pack?" Deshawna asks.

"Yes it is," Jasmine answers.

"Well let's get this party started!" Deshawna cheers.

We turn on some music and get the grill ready to officially welcome Deshawna into the pack. The music is going and we're dancing, playing games and showing off for Deshawna. We're trying to give her the best time, allowing her to feel a little more comfortable. It's nice seeing her smiling and enjoying herself with all of us.

Jasmine and Braheem start off reserved, even though this is supposed to be a celebration for welcoming a new pack member. It's like they're waiting for the other shoe to drop. I try to get them to relax, but they tell me that they are trying to protect everyone.

A few more hours pass and I finally see Braheem and Jasmine enjoying themselves. I have a few drinks, and I start to feel a little drunk. Before I have another drink, I drank some water to sober up. Catalina walks over to me shortly after. She asks me if everything is ok. I tell her that I'm fine, I just need a second. I'm just letting the drinks run their course.

I realize, everyone is actually tipsy. We usually drink and pretend to get drunk, but because we're werewolves we can't get drunk. The question is why am I tipsy? I drank some more water in an attempt to sober up so I can think straight.

That's when I hear someone whisper, "Be careful... Don't be fooled."

I look around, but I can't see anyone else around us. I take a few deep breaths as I try to regain my senses. Whatever is affecting me starts wearing off.

"Stay alert...," I hear the voice whisper again.

"Abucheo what's wrong?" Catalina asks.

Before I can answer, my ear perks up. I hear movement all around us. Something's wrong, we weren't alone. I can't smell them, but I can hear them. An arrow is suddenly fired from a crossbow directly at Deshawna. I grab a few napkins and snatch it before it hits her.

Upon further inspection, I smell the arrow is coated in wolfsbane. This has to be the Tailors, they're the only ones who use arrows like this. I stop the music and scream to everyone to be on alert. Soon after we are ambushed from all sides by Tailors. I growl at them and shift into my glabro. Though we are incapacitated, that won't stop any of us from fighting. Whoever these people were, they are more efficient than any group of Tailors we've met.

This attack is obviously designed to strike while our defense is down. While the fighting is going on, I hear everyone's screams of pain. This is the first time I can actually feel every time they're injured. We can't win this fight. If it wasn't for that voice, things would have been worse.

"Everyone stay in twos!" I command. "The no killing rule is in effect unless there is no other way!"

"RIGHT!" everyone screams in unison.

The more we fight, the more I can tell that we can't turn this around. I try to get everyone in formation, but we're being kept a part. I jump into a nearby tree and howl to everyone to stop and to fall back to the Basement. I hear everyone howling back to me one by one, acknowledging.

As everyone starts leaving the woods, I stay behind to make sure everyone gets out safely. I see everyone leaving. Everyone except for Deshawna. She stays behind fighting the Tailors.

"What are you doing, we have to go. NOW!" I shout.

"I'm going to try to protect everyone with you," she replies.

I admire the fighting spirit in her, but this isn't one of those times for us to go down fighting. I command her to join the rest of us.

We retreat to the basement, running as fast as we can in a formation of 95 MPH from the Den to the Basement. We don't usually run this fast, but to get away from the Tailors we have to. When we finally manage to get to the basement, we take a headcount to make sure that the 11 of us are all present. Deshawna is the last one to arrive and she's out of breath.

"How are you guys running so fast?" she asks, winded.

"What do you mean?" Omar asks.

"I mean I know I was going at least 75, but y'all were going faster than that."

"Catalina laughs, "Sorry about that, we're in glabro, our lives were in danger, so we took off."

"Yea, that makes sense," Deshawna responds. "Imma just sit down for a second. Where are we?"

"We're at our backup location," I respond. "We wouldn't have shown you this yet, but this is an emergency."

"Ahh ok got it," she nods.

Catalina comes up to me to ask if I'm ok. She looks at my hand. I told her that I used napkins, the arrow never touched my skin. Under the streetlight, she inspects my hand to make sure that I'm ok. She kisses my hand and gives me a hug. I tell her that everything is ok and we'll have to lie low for a little while.

The Tailors can't track us because they can't maneuver through the woods like we can. That is our domain which is why we're always there before going to the Basement. I thank Deshawna for staying with me while I fought off the Tailors. She tells me that she appreciates everything we've done for her. We stand outside the building talking for a few minutes, before going in.

"I'm still stuck on how they found us in the woods," Kahlil says. "From what you've told me, y'all have been going there for years and never once have they found you. I don't get it."

"Damien, some of us are clearly hurt, don't you have a vet to go to?" Deshawna asks.

"Yea we do, but we have to figure this out as well," I respond. "Let me call him and we'll get him to patch everyone up."

By the smell of it, it's a slow acting wolfsbane, but we don't know how poisonous it is. We have a few bandages and gauze stashed here just in case we need it and luckily for us this is one of those times. We set ourselves up pretty well under the guidance of Tevin. He even showed us a few ways to stop bleeding if we couldn't get to him right away.

We wrap up everyone's wounds and decide to barricade ourselves in the basement while I call Tevin. After half an hour Tevin hasn't called me back nor let me know he's on his way. He always responds to me even if he can't come.

"It's weird, he's not answering," I say confused.

"We'll have to figure it out ourselves," Catalina says.

"Watch out," the same voice whispers to me once more.

Just like earlier that night the voice whispered to me, warning me about the danger. Once more my ears perk up and I hear men in the distance speaking. I try to pinpoint exactly what the problem is. I focus and listen as best I can. I hear people talking just barely outside of my hearing range.

"Sir, we have them in our sights," The first voice says.

"Are you sure?" the second voice questions.

"Yes sir, we have the target locked and we are ready to fire," the first voice confirms.

"Then fire," the second voice commands.

I hear the sound of something being shot and it's barreling towards us. I scream to everyone, "We have to get out of here now!"

Everyone jumps up and tries to get out of the building as fast as they can. Since most of us are still hurt, it's hard for everyone to get up and move.

"Can we catch a break!" Omar screams.

"Deshawna, can you help Kahlil?" I ask.

She agrees to help him off the couch as we hurry out of the building. I watch as everyone leaves. I turn around and see Kahlil and Deshawna leaving the building. As they reach the doors, the Basement explodes sending silver spikes in every direction. I can't believe my eyes. I try to duck for cover, but I'm blown back by the force of the blast.

My ears are ringing, my body is aching. Dust and debris is everywhere. I have to get up, I have to see if everyone is ok. I try my absolute hardest to stand up and look for everyone. At first I can't, due to the silver steaks in my leg. I pull them out using what strength I have left and cough intensely as I try to stand. I examine everything around me and notice everything is either rubble, on fire or both.

"Hey, who's out there?!" I scream. "Is anyone still alive!? Please someone talk to me!!" I plead.

There's no response, I can't feel anyone's presence. The smell of smoke and the sound of everything burning is blocking me from finding anyone. My head is dizzy, and pulsing, I have to find them. Make sure that they are all ok.

While still in pain, I trudge as I search for everyone, unsure if they're alive or dead. The first person I find is Jasmine, she's conscious, but pinned under some rubble. I try to lift it, but I have no power due to loss of blood. Braheem comes up and helps me lift it off of her. We struggle as we cough to free her. Then we find Omar and Chantelle, they were blown into the water and just climbed out. Each of them had a spike in them as well. Other than that they are ok.

The smell of blood is everywhere, but hard to pinpoint. Soon we find Catalina, she's lying on top of some rubble, luckily she wasn't hit with any spikes. I manage to wake her up and get her moving. I'm careful not to move her too fast. Whatever was in that missile, it's stopping us from healing. One by one we uncover everyone else. First Kiara, then Darius and Nichole. Everyone is accounted for except for Kahlil and Deshawna.

"Kahlil, can you hear us?!" Kiara calls out.

"Kahlil, if you can, call out to us!" I shout.

"C'mon bro, let us know where you are so we can get out of here," Darius calls out in a hoarse voice.

We're all coughing, desperately trying to find them. Suddenly a gentle but strong breeze blows into our direction. It's just enough to allow me to discover Kahlil's scent. He was thrown furthest. When we reach him, we see that he's gasping for breath with several silver spikes and burns all over his body. He's obviously suffering. What can I do for him? I stand there trying to figure it out.

I drop to my knees with tears in my eyes, "NO! What did those bastards do to Kahlil?"

I dig deep and howl as loud as I can. Everyone else howls with me in pain.

"Damien," Catalina calls out to me, "Damien, we have to go, there's nothing we can do for him," Catalina pulls onto my arm, attempting to get me to my feet.

"What's the point?' I ask. "We'll just be hunted down. Even our best laid plans thus far have blown up in our faces." I say

"Damien, look at me, you're our leader, you can't fall apart on us now," Catalina cries out. "We need you more than ever. Baby. please pull yourself together!" she pleads.

I wipe my tears and place my torn shirt over Kahlil's face. I hear him nearing his last breath. I want him to go peacefully. The sound of the sirens are getting closer, so we have to leave the area. I tell everyone to go home and heal. To be careful of who may be watching them and it's radio silent until further notice. We all agree we go straight home.

Catalina and I limp back to our car that's parked a few blocks from the Den. We're healing, but it's a long walk. After we're sure the coast is clear, Catalina and I change clothes and I drive her home. There's no plan, nothing to do. We're lost in a wave of confusion. It's time to rest, heal and regroup. For the first five minutes, there isn't a word spoken between us.

I finally get the urge to speak, "Baby thank you for what you said. If you weren't there, I don't know what I would have done. Seriously."

"Abucheo, you don't have to thank me, it's what I'm here for," Catalina responds. "You support me and I support you. Werewolf and all."

I start to think about how the Tailors could possibly have found out about the Den. The only people who know about those places are us and Tevin. I know for sure he won't rat us out, so there must be a mole. Then it hits me that we didn't find Deshawna. She was nowhere to be found nor did she call out for help. Did she get killed in the blast?

"Could she be the one that ratted us out to the Tailors?" I ask myself.

I went to ask Catalina what she thought about Deshawna possibly being the mole, but when I turn to her, she's fast asleep. The more I think about it, the more possibility grows. I feel ashamed, I'm the one who recommended her to join and we were attacked. Until I find and talk to her, we'll never truly know, but I honestly hope I'm wrong. Maybe they'll find her body in the rubble.

I pull up to Catalina's house and check my face. We've already healed, but I'm exhausted. Instead of waking her up, I open the door and carry her to her door. I knock on the door and her mom opens the door.

"Hello Mrs. Suarez, I'm sorry it's so late, but while we were out Catalina fell asleep," I begin to say. "So can I carry her up to her room?"

"Oh hija, of course Damien, come on in," he responds. "What would Catalina and I do without your help?"

"Believe it or not I don't know what I would do without your daughter," I respond.

Mrs. Suarez chuckles before going into the kitchen after she lets us in. I proceed up to Catalina's room and lay her in her bed before taking off her shoes.

I kiss Catalina on her forehead and whisper, "Good night Baby, I love you."

I don't know if she heard me or it was just her subconscious responding back to me, but she responds, "Mi corazón."

I smile as I leave her room, closing the door behind me. I go downstairs where her mom is fixing herself a late night snack, "Mrs. Suarez, can you let Catalina sleep in tomorrow? She's exhausted. We had an... *interesting* night."

She laughs lightly and says, "Sure hijo, I'll let her know you asked me to let her sleep in. Can I get you anything?"

"No, I'm fine. Thank you. I'm just going to go home and sleep for the night," I answer.

With that I get back into my car and drive off. As I'm driving, I remember that I haven't heard from Tevin the entire night. I look at my now damaged phone and see that he hasn't read any of my messages, nor has he called me back. I continue thinking about everything that's happened so far. Nothing is been adding up. How'd the Tailors know about the Den and the Basement? They definitely have to be someone feeding them information.

Instead of going home, I decide to go to his house to see if he's there. Tevin has become one of my closest friends and my mentor. I need him to be ok, not only because he's been there giving me advice, but also because he may be able to help me figure this out. If I lose him like I did Kahlil I'm not sure what's going to happen to us.

As I pull up to his house, I see the lights in his living room are still on. I feel relief wash over me. I jump out of the car and head straight to his door. I knock intensely hoping that he'll answer.

"Tevin, Tevin answer the door, it's me," I call out.

Almost instantly he opens the door, "Damien what's wrong? Calm down before you dent my door. You break it, you buy it," he says.

"I'm so glad you're ok," I say frantically.

"Why wouldn't I be?" he asks, confused.

"We were attacked at both the Den and the Basement," I explain. "The Basement was blown up. And you haven't been answering any of my calls."

"What!? Blown up?" he exclaims.

"Yeah, the Tailors must have shot an RPG or blown up some C4, but it blew up sending silver spikes everywhere. We barely escaped with our lives," I reveal.

"You guys have had the place for a while now and have always been careful with who you let into their areas. What changed?" Tevin asks.

"Exactly, what I've been thinking. There has to be a mole," I confirm. "The only thing that's been different is we let Deshawna Cambridge into the pack."

"Cambridge… Cambridge. Cambridge, Why?" he puzzles.

"She told me that she was thrown out from the family due to differences of ideals," I say pacing.

"When did this happen?" Tevin asks.

"Within the last few weeks," I respond.

"Well don't know anything about her being kicked out, but do you think she's the one who told the Tailors what's going on?" He guesses.

"It's possible. She's the only one not accounted for," say.

"What do you mean?" Tevin asks.

"Everyone but her were found," I pause for a moment. "Kahlil was…was hit the worst. When the building exploded, he had spikes impaling him all over his body," I say, solemnly.

"Oh, I'm sorry," Tevin says, softly.

"It's fine, I just can't believe we had to leave him like that. A piece of me wants to believe Deshawna wouldn't betray us, because she was kicked out and alone like we all were," I declare.

"Even so you have to be cautious," Tevin warns.

"Could that be the reason she was kicked out of her pack?"

"I don't know, but we have to find out as soon as possible. I'll call the Cambridges tomorrow and see what I can find out."

I sit down on the couch to think about everything. I want to believe she told me the truth, but it could have all been just a sob story. I was just about to say something to Tevin when a smoke bomb is thrown through the window followed by a flash bang. The smoke is so thick that it instantly fills the room. My senses are thrown for a loop, I lost all ability to see or hear in any direction. I call out, but there's nothing I can do.

"There he is, get him," I hear a voice command.

I'm bound and gagged as I'm coughing and a sheet is thrown over my head. I'm so disoriented that I can't fight back. Whatever this smoke is, it's specifically used against werewolves. Out of the multiple voices, I hear a very similar one, but I can't place it. They hit I'm the face with what felt like the stock of a rifle and it knocks me out.

Chapter 15

I don't know how much time has passed, but when I awake, I find myself strapped to a chair in a dimly lit room with just a single lightbulb hanging directly above me. As I search around the room, I notice that I have the same spiked collar that Kahlil wore when we were captured. It prevents me from turning crinos. I don't know about my glabro and I'm not going to try it out. This has to be Tailors. How'd they find me?

"I hope these accommodations are…comfortable," I hear a familiar voice say.

It's the same as before, I know I've heard it before. Seconds later, I witness Timothy walking into the room with a smug look on his face, like he has me in his trap, "I'm going to ask you the same question my dear departed leader asked you. How is it you've eluded us for so long?"

I look at him with a fury in my eyes, realizing he's the reason that Kahlil and Tevin lost their lives.

"Oh, you're not going to answer me?" Timothy smiles as he sidesteps and pulls onto a rope, forcing me to stand up from my chair. He ties the rope to a hook to keep me from sitting, "Oh you're a tough one aren't you?"

Timothy punches me several times in my stomach. Even incapacitated, his punches are nothing. I'm going to make the Tailors pay for killing them. Neither of them deserved to die.

"Since you're giving us the silent treatment, I think it's time I step it up a notch," he says as he grabs a knife and stabs me in the abdomen with the blade. I scream in pain as he asks me who the rest of my pack was. Slowly gasping for breath I revert to my stone like demeanor. Giving him nothing.

"Don't worry, it's not silver, the fun has just begun," he explains. "You think that righteous act is going to save you? Show me you're the same alpha who killed Bruce two years ago."

I know what he wants, he may have forgotten my face, but I will never forget his, I won't give it to him. I stand there solid with my lips sealed, but my eyes remain glaring at him.

He grows impatient, "Deshawna get in here!"

Confidently, Deshawna walks into the cell with the two of us, "What do you want?"

I wish I could say that I was surprised, but seeing the way she walks into the room confirms that she's been working with them the entire time. She not only betrayed me, but her own kind.

"You told me this was the alpha that killed Bruce," he points at me.

"That is the same alpha, Damien Nichols," Deshawna assures him.

"Are you sure?" he asks.

"Here use this," Deshawna hands Timothy a small capsule that he breaks under my nose.

It smells super funny and made me sneeze soon after. I growl at him with my eyes illuminated. I couldn't help it. That capsule he used must have forced me to do so.

"Ahh, I see that *is* him. Damien Nichols, it's nice to finally put a name to that mug you call a face," he smiles viciously. "It's a shame that the cameras were destroyed that day, we lost all of your faces, but this time I got you."

I've had enough of both of them, "Deshawna, you betrayed your own kind, your pack. Why?"

"Simple," she responds. "I'm an omega like I told you that day, I tried to overthrow my mother because she's a fool. I lost my fight against her and rather than killing me like a *real werewolf* would, she banned me. Then the Tailors found me and I've been helping them ever since."

Before I could respond Timothy interrupts me, "Just shut it you dogs! I still can't believe he killed Bruce. You're nothing more than a kid," Timothy directs at me.

"Well he is, you saw his eyes," Deshawna points out.

Timothy sucks his teeth and says he's had enough. He twists the knife deeper in my stomach. He demands to know who my pack is and where he can find them. Again I just glare at him, barely showing that I'm in pain.

He stares into my eyes and I back into his. Since I don't give him anything, he pulls the knife out and spits on my shirt before he and Deshawna leave the cell. I hear the door slam and Timothy curse as they walk away. They're going to leave me here to see if I rot. I'm not going to give them the satisfaction. I inspect the cell, hoping I could find a way to get out of my chains. I spot a window, but it's barred and nowhere near big enough for a person to fit through. I try howling through it.

"Don't even try it, that glass is soundproof," Timothy says over the intercom.

There's only one way in and one way out. Suddenly, someone came in to give me some water to drink. It tastes funny, but I'm so thirsty that I drink it anyway. Then I feel my strength start to fade and my throat burning. The water is laced with wolfsbane, they're trying to keep me weak. When the person leaves all I can do is watch them. I don't know where I am, how long I was out nor what they have planned.

If not for the window outside, I'd have no concept of time. Hours later, Timothy returns asking me the same questions he asked before. Who my pack members are and their location. I remain silent. It's the same thing day after day, he comes in asking questions and when I don't answer them, he stabs me. Even with the laced food and water I'm given, keeping me human, my resolve doesn't change. No matter how much damage he inflicts on me, I'll still heal. I don't care how slowly.

Days go by and each one is the same. Timothy tortures me after questioning me and when I don't give him what he wants, he leaves me alone in my cell. I never noticed before, but I can feel the phases of the moon, and the full moon is coming. It could be the power of the Tremauré, but the wolfsbane starts losing its effect on me. I was barely able to make the chains move before, now I'm able to stretch them, nearly breaking them.

I start hatching a plan. I want to change into my crinos form and break free, but I still have the collar to worry about. If I can't get it off, I can't turn. Glabro may not be enough to break out. Maybe I can signal the others through the window, but my throat is so sore and with the soundproof glass I can't. I'm only given enough water to be able to speak, but the wolfbane still prevents me from howling.

Since I'm slowly building a resistance to this specific type of wolfbane, all I have to do is bide my time. Those days quickly turn into two weeks. It's the same thing over and over. Timothy thinks I'll lose my will to live and give in, but I won't. He's sent Deshawna to try to reason with me.

She turned on her own kind and started working with Tailors. I barely look her in the eyes whenever she speaks. No matter how badly she wants me to. All I have to do was wait for the others to break me free. I know they have something in mind.

Two days before the full moon, Timothy comes into the cell alone, "You've been in this cell for almost a month. This has to be grueling right? This can all go away if you just tell me where the rest of your pack is."

"Too bad," I respond. "I was just starting to like it here."

"You called them your family, yet they let you stay here for weeks on end without their alpha," he tries to bait me.

"You're pretty dumb if you think they're without an alpha," I laugh.

"Then where are they, huh?! Why would they just let you stay here all alone?" he questions.

"Oh they'll be here soon enough," I smile fiendishly.

"We'll see about that," Timothy scoffs.

Just as Timothy orders for the doors to be opened and he begins to leave, I use all the strength I've stored up and howl as loudly as I can. The window outside my cell shatters, sending a signal to everyone so they can find me. Timothy turns around frightened. The confidence he had is gone, all that remains is anger and desperation. He stabs me with his knife in my side and he leaves it there before leaving the cell.

Timothy screams at the Tailor guarding the cell," How the hell did he do that!?"

"I don't know sir, we've been giving him wolfsbane in his food and water since we brought him here," the guard responds in a panic.

I pause for a second, because I've heard that voice before. Timothy pulls the guard into the cell with me. As they enter the room, I immediately recognize the guard. It's Jakobe. I'm too stunned to speak. Before he can look me in the eye, I shift into my glabro.

"He shouldn't be able to do what he just did," Timothy shrieks. "Do you know what could happen to this facility if they realize where he is?!" Timothy screams, grabbing onto Jakobe's shirt.

"I'm sorry sir, I don't know what happened," Jakobe responds fearfully, "We'll up the dosage."

"Now! I don't know why they gave me you kids to protect this mutt. This isn't just any werewolf we're dealing with. This is the werewolf that killed Bruce, we can't be overrun."

"I'm sorry sir, this won't happen again," Jakobe says, timidly.

"It better not. We're now on high alert. His pack definitely heard that and they will be coming for him soon enough, "Timothy lets go of Jakobe's shirt who runs outside of the cell and calls on his radio for everyone to be on guard.

Timothy takes another knife and stabs it into my other side. Having the second knife in my side hurt, but not as much after seeing him lose it. Timothy punches me in the face and then leaves the cell, locking it tightly.

I sigh in relief, after he leaves the room. So many questions start running through my mind. Why is Jakobe here? Last time I talked to him, he was overseas with Jamal, Davion and Terrence in the military. He's a Tailor and I'm a werewolf. We grew up together, I can't believe that we've become enemies. I hope Davion, Jamal and Terrance aren't in on this. I question all of my next moves.

A few hours later, I hear Catalina's howl in the distance. Right behind hers, I hear everyone else's. Hearing all of them gives me relief that I'll be able to get out of here. I just hope it's before I come face to face with Jakobe. I knew they'd find me sooner or later, but I must be closer to home than I thought.

I know Timothy can't hear the howling, but Deshawna did. I howl again attempting to tell them that they can't attack yet. I tell them to wait for the full moon. I can't explain it, but lately we've been getting better at communicating through howls. Other times it's like we can read each other's minds. Everyone acknowledges and agrees to hold off. Since Deshawna isn't officially a part of our pack, I figure that she can only hear our howls. Timothy bursts into the room with Deshanwa, Jakobe and one other Tailor. I can't recognize him because he's wearing a mask. I'm glad I stayed in my glabro, so Jakobe doesn't see me.

"I don't know what you're doing, but if it's trying to scare me, it's not going to work," Timothy says aggressively. "She told me you've been talking to your pack. They won't be able to save you this time."

I know he doesn't scare easily, but I know I'm getting to him. He may be on the fence that I'm the same werewolf that killed Bruce, so I have to use this to my advantage.

"You still don't believe I'm the Tremauré do you?" I ask with a smirk.

"No, of course not," he replies. "That werewolf was stronger, more ferocious. You're too young to have been the one that ended one of the most skilled werewolf hunters this world has ever seen."

"Sir, since the commander doesn't know about this mission, should we try calling Shadowcat for reinforcements?" the Tailor in the mask asks. I look at him as he also seems very familiar.

"Why would I do that?" Timothy asks.

"Just in case sir, I'm sure she can make this one talk," Jakobe adds. "She trained us, we know her personally."

"He's right sir, Jakobe, Jamal, Terrance and I were her students," the masked Tailor says. "I know she doesn't work with us anymore, but she's still a consultant. Maybe she can tell us how to break this one."

"Absolutely not, I got this one right where I want him," Timothy says proudly. This kill belongs to me and me alone. Get someone to fix that damn window now!"

It isn't until the masked Tailor spoke, but I'm sure he's Davion. Timothy pulls the knives from my side and places them back on the table. They each leave the cell once more. I'm dumbfounded after I realize this. All of my childhood friends are werewolf hunters.

250

Who were they talking about as their teacher? Is it Mom? It couldn't be that big of a coincidence? Were they ever in the military? Did Mom or their parents get them into this? Why was I kept out of the loop? What the hell is going on?

I have the rest of the night to think about everything. My best friends are werewolves hunters, and possibly even my mom. I don't think my mom is a Tailor, I know she's a consultant for the military, maybe they were picked from the military. That seems to be the most likely since they are highly trained. I manage to calm myself down from my mini freak out, when they let me down to sleep I took the chance. I need peace of mind, but it never comes.

The next day Jakobe guards me while Tailors fix the window outside my cell. I listen to them, since Timothy didn't question me today. The most boring day I've spent here. I have to stick this out one more day, and wait for my chance. That's exactly what I'll do. Even with them feeding me though that laced food, and increasing the amount of wolfsbane they put in it, it only slows my recovery by a small margin. When the full moon rises, there'll be nothing they can do.

That day passes and the night rises. I feel the rising of the moon as I watch the moonlight hit the inside of the cell. The light eventually touches my feet and rises up my body. I feel the moon filling me with its power. I start gaining some of my strength back. This is one of the few times I feel like I should let the wolf free. He's been caged and waiting. The moon starts to reach its peak. Just before it does, Timothy comes into my cell to question me again.

I'll show him why he should be afraid of me, my pack and every other werewolf. Pretty soon I start sensing that they're getting close. Since the window is fixed, I don't know what their plan is, but it can't be like before. They'll be prepared for that.

I don't know what to expect, but I know they're going to be creative. Fifteen minutes later, I hear alarms going off and everyone scrambling. Timothy rushes out of the room, telling the guards to watch me. I feel Braheem, Darius, Omar, Chantelle, Kiara, and Nichole closing in. All of them are terrorizing the building and spreading chaos. Where's Jasmine and Catalina? I can feel them, but I don't know where they are.

I hear the sound of fighting, shouting and shooting. I anxiously wait with anticipation. Less than five minutes later, the door opens and two guards with helmets come rushing into my cell. I stare at them intensely as they close the door behind them.

After they close the door, I growl at them, "What do you want?"

They take off their helmets and I see Catalina's smiling face. She and Jasmine dressed like guards to get into my cell.

"Damien, oh my god," Catalina cries out. "Are you ok?" she asks as she wraps her arms around me.

I chuckle a little, "Yea I'm ok, don't worry about me. Just get me out of here."

"No problem," she says.

Catalina and Jasmine start to untie me, I hear Timothy's footsteps coming closer to the cell with a few other Tailors. After they untie me, I tell them to hide in the shadows until their guard is down, then knock them out and we'll get out of the room. I'm not as strong as I thought I was, so standing on my own is rough.

When Timothy enters the room with his soldiers, Jasmine and Catalina get the drop on them and knock them all out. I lean on Catalina as we make our escape from the cell and through the facility. We moved cautiously through each hallway.

They increased their security compared to last time, and the halls are small. They think they have the advantage, however, close quarters work for us. Timothy calls on the radio to have everyone in the facility corner us so we can't leave. This team isn't like the last one, they have more lethal weapons. We may have to kill in order to get out of here.

Catalina and Jasmine do what they can in taking down their soldiers. While we are moving forward, Catalina and Jasmine fight like I've never seen them do before. However long they spent planning this out is working flawlessly.

Since I'm still barely able to walk, they have to maneuver around me and it's spectacular. Leaning on them is my best option and I have complete faith in them. It's like there's no ending in sight. This place is bigger than the last one, every turn we make was met with a hailstorm of bullets. Some of them just wing us, while others barely missed us. With the alarm blaring and the building on lockdown, we'll die trying to escape. Even the windows are blocked, barred or fake. Time is not on our outside.

Without Kahlil, I'm not sure how they know the way out. After ten minutes, we finally manage to not only meet up with everyone else, but also find the main door to the exit. Catalina explains that they infiltrated the compound a few days ago and knew the way out this time. Everyone is pretty banged up and bleeding, but alive nonetheless. The main entrance didn't have anyone blocking it, but there is a metal door closing, attempting to keep us all inside.

"Y'all we gotta move faster!" announces Omar.

"He's right," Jasmine acknowledges. "The door is closing in on us and I don't think we can keep fighting like this."

"Then let's go!" I shout.

I've gained some of my strength to walk back and lead the charge for us to start sprinting directly toward the door. Everything around us starts slowing down. Every breath and change in motion that comes our way I feel. The doors are closing, and we're almost out of time. At risk of being kept prisoner with the Tailors. Who knows what they'll do to us if they trap us?

It's no use, we're all too wounded to get to the door before it closes. Just before the door hits the floor, Darius, Nichole and Chantelle grab the door, stopping it before it closes. They caught it with only enough room for them to get their hands under it, using their strength to lift it open.

"They stopped the blast door, don't let them escape!" Timothy commands over the intercom. "Shoot to wound them only. We need the Tremauré and his pack alive. Tranqs and tasers only."

We hear them get into position to fire at us, but it's too late. The three of them are able to get the door open just enough for all of us to slip under it by crawling under it. Then we were on the outside, Braheem, Kiara, and Jasmine hold open the door so Darius, Nichole, and Chantelle can slip through.

Finally, we're outside and everyone starts cheering, but that was short-lived when everyone's injuries caught up with them and we all collapse. I struggle for a second, but when I feel the moonlight against my skin I let the moon empower me. Which in turn restores everyone else, healing them slightly when I touch them. Being outside again is amazing. As I gain my strength back, I clench my fist. Being able to experience the world like a wolf again is great.

After basking in the moonlight, I open my eyes to look at everyone and they're looking at me as if they didn't recognize me, "What, what's wrong?"

"D, you ight?" Braheem asks.

"Yea I'm good, why?" I answer.

"Because, your eyes are glowing," Catalina says.

"Are they…?" I ask confused.

Everyone nods, "Oh my fault I didn't realize. I guess I got a little excited."

I take another deep breath and my royal blue color recedes and my natural brown eyes returns.

"Damien, we have to get out of here before they open that door and come after us again," Darius says.

"No," I respond. "I have to end this."

"Why does it have to be you?" Catalina questions in a worried tone.

"Cuz this started with me killing Bruce and Timothy wants revenge," I respond. "He worked with one of our own, and plotted against us. That plan got Kahlil and Tevin killed. I can't let the slide" I say sternly.

"You can't, you're not healed yet and he could kill you," Catalina cries out.

I put my hand on her cheek, "I've already died once, I won't do it again."

"I'm not leaving without you," she cries.

"Neither are we," Jasmine steps up with everyone else.

"Alright then," I say smiling. "We'll wait for them out here. Also, everyone, no matter what stay in your glabro, especially you," I say looking at her.

She must have sensed the uneasiness in my voice, "What's wrong?" she ponders.

I sigh, "Because both Davion and Jakobe are here, they're Tailors."

Catalina covers her mouth in shock, "Are you serious?"

"Yes," I say somberly, "I saw both of them myself. I still don't know all the facts yet, but what I do know is that they didn't recognize me in glabro. So stay in the back, understand?"

"Damn, I'm sorry," Omar says, scratching his head.

With tears in her eyes, Catalina agrees to stay in glabro and everyone else follows. I know that no matter what we do, Timothy and his soldiers won't stop. It's better that we fight, even if it's against friends. The plan is the same as it always is, we fight, but we don't kill unless provoked.

Time was on our side, since we held the door open, it locked the mechanism and stopped it from opening for ten minutes. That's all we need to properly heal and prepare for a fight. We aren't 100% yet, but whatever we have left in the tank is going to have to be good enough. When the door opens, we instantly turn into our glabro and slowly back away from the door. Timothy is the first one through the door along with two dozen soldiers.

He smirks and says, "What's all this? I thought you'd be across state lines by now."

"Nah, we're going to end this tonight," I reply. "One final fight between your side and mine. No fangs, no claws, no knives. No werewolf."

"Honorable challenge, the same one that Bruce offered you," Timothy ponders. "I accept. and if I win, I want to see the rest of your pack's faces."

"Fine, if I win, you'll stop hunting me and my pack and you'll rule Bruce's death as an...occupational hazard," I offer.

Timothy chuckles and agrees to the terms of the battle. He tells his men to drop their guns, and no matter what happens they're not to use any weapons. I spread out my arms and start backing up, having everyone else pull back as well. I spot Jakobe and Davion. Catalina sees them too. The judgment in their eyes is like nothing we've ever seen from either of them. I whisper to her to not let it get to her, they don't know it's us they're fighting.

Timothy drops all of his weapons from his belt and holsters. We have enough space between us to fight. My instincts tell me to kill Timothy for what he did to Tevin and Kahlil, but I have to keep it together and not kill him. I can't give him what he wants because if I do, we'll lose.

He and I stare into each other's eyes. I retract my claws and teeth, but keep my abridged nose, forehead and elongated ears. My eyes remain glowing so I won't be seen by Jakobe and Davion. I sense that he wants me to pay for what I did to Bruce, even though I was only defending myself. He isn't as calm and hard to read as Bruce was.

Just like his mentor, if Timothy had it his way, only one of us would walk away from this fight. However, I sense he values his own life. I won't kill him if he doesn't make me. Both sides start approaching each other. We stand a few paces apart. This is an ongoing war, I may not be able to end it, but we'll win this battle. I charge toward him and throw the first punch, he blocks and counters. The fight is on and everyone starts exchanging blows.

This is unlike my fight with Bruce. Timothy isn't as good of a fighter, but he definitely has the determination. With each punch or kick, neither of us breaks eye contact. if things were different, he may have the upper hand against me. My eyes shifted to Jakobe and Davion, hoping they wouldn't recognize me. In that split second, Timothy manages to catch me off guard with a punch and puts me in a choke hold.

"Hey kid, you're pretty good," Timothy whispers in my ear. "I see why Bruce had such a problem with you. I also see there's quite a few ladies in your pack. After I kill you, I'm going to take them and make them my bitches."

After he says that I lose it. I remember Jasmine, Kiara and Nichole telling us about their shared pasts and I'm not going to let that happen to them again. Especially not to Chantelle and Catalina, the glow of my eyes grows brighter.

"You aren't going to do a thing to either of them!" I scream.

The leverage I gave him, melts away. It's time to get serious. I break his chokehold and throw him off of me. When we get back on our feet again, my strikes are stronger and faster than before. Every time I swing at him, he tries to block it, but can't. Each punch lands right after the last. Timothy can't keep up with my combos. I'm not hitting him as hard as I really want to, but comments like that will never slide.

Timothy fights to stay on his feet, although it's obvious that he can't. When he finally falls to the ground, everyone stops. I get on top of him and put my hand around his throat, squeezing tightly. I growl at him as my hand squeezes. I hear him coughing as he tries to fight me off. I don't care, I could end this just by a flick of my wrist.

"Stop!!" Jasmine screams as I'm about to crush his windpipe. "It's not worth it. We heard what he said, we know you'd never let that happen."

"Just let him go so we can go home!" Kiara shouts.

I look at them then back at Timothy. I lean down to his ear and whisper, "They just saved your life."

I let go of his throat and he coughed, he's barely able to speak, but in a hoarse voice he says, "I believe you now. I can see you're the same werewolf. I doubted you and that won't happen again."

"Good I'm going to let you go now and I'm going to let you walk away with your life. Just know you're living because I allow it. If I see you hunting us or anywhere near any of my people again, I won't hesitate to kill you. Now pack up your men and get out of my city." I say, sternly.

Timothy spits blood from his mouth. He wipes his lips and starts walking toward his men. I ask him about Tevin and he says he doesn't know where Tevin is. When they broke into the house, I was the only one in there. I accuse him of lying, but he says he isn't. I'm the only one they captured.

No matter how I persist, Timothy insists he doesn't know where Tevin is. Since he's human, they don't have a need for him. Timothy then limps back to his soldiers who all go back into their building. As the doors closed, I watch as two of my best friends follow him. I wonder how long they've been Tailors and how they got associated with them in the first place. Maybe I'll get an answer to that question, but it won't be today.

We all get back home safely. I still felt bad that Kahlil isn't coming home with us. It's time for us to mourn his loss and find a way to continue with our lives without him. I have to see if we can find out what happened to Tevin, I'll never stop looking for him.

Chapter 16

After my fight with Timothy, things finally died down. There's been peace for the last year and a half. We haven't had any problems with Tailors or other werewolves. I'm glad I haven't seen Deshawna because I'd probably kill her for not only tricking me, but for turning against her own kind. Working with the Tailors is disgraceful. I don't know if it's good or not, but no one has heard from her, nor can anyone find her, including the Werewolf's Council.

I went to the Werewolf's Council attempting to find out what happened to Kahlil's body and to find out where Tevin is. Unfortunately, everyone I spoke to informs me that Kahlil is dead, but they didn't know where Kahlil's body or where Tevin is. Even though I can't find any information on them, I won't want to give up searching.

After six months of searching, and coming up empty, we give them a service at the Den. The hardest part was figuring out a way to tell Kahlil's parents. His mother is inconsolable. We lit a candle for both of them every time we're at the Den. We shed tears and love for each of them. They're a part of our family. Kahlil had so much potential and it was cut short. Even though Tevin is human, he's the only person I could turn to for advice when it came to being a werewolf. I hold his and everyone else's teachings in high regard because they tell me how to move in this world.

Things have been pretty quiet between the 9 of us for the last three months since we held their vigils. We've always been together and now that one of our pack members is gone, it's hard being not seeing him there. Sometimes we try talking to him, but the moment we realize he isn't there, we become quiet. We all grieve in our own way, but after those somber three months, we came back one by one. We are a family and it's best if we stick together.

I start thinking back to everything that's happened up until now. The werewolf that attacked me, my first change, and everything I've learned. Getting together with Catalina, meeting Braheem, Darius, Omar, Chantelle, Jasmine, Kiara, Nichole, Kahlil, and Tevin. All the battles we've fought, getting captured and finally learning that my childhood best friends are werewolf hunters.

I remember when Tailors held me captive, and the pendant I saw many of them wearing have the same symbol I've seen my mom wear. The fact that all of my friends have become Tailors worries me. For a long time, I've debated talking to my mom about it. I'm almost 24 now and in the last seven years, I've never told my mom a single thing about my life outside of going to school, work and Catalina.

In coming to terms with Kahlil's death, I figure that it's time I tell her. If anything happens to me, I want her to know the truth. Hopefully it opens up the conversation as a way to find out if my suspicions about her are true. Honestly, I'm afraid to bring it up, but I need this. It's the only way for me to see if mom has anything to do with the Tailors and if she helped Jakobe, Davion, Jamal and Terrance become Tailors themselves.

Since Mom is home and will be a little while, I figure that this was as good of a chance as any. I see her sitting down on the couch, watching TV. I walk over and sit next to her, talking and watching with her for a few hours. It's been so long since we've spent some time together that I don't want it to ruin it. When I finally gain the nerve to talk to her, I take a deep breath and start speaking.

"Mom, I have something to tell you," I begin to say. "I don't know how to tell you, but..."

She interrupts me before I can say anything further, "Is something wrong with you and Catalina? Is... is she pregnant? Did something happen?"

"What? No. Mom, stop, nothing happened," I reassure her. "What I have to tell you is..."

"Damien, you can tell me anything," she says in an affectionate tone.

I sigh, "Okay Mom, what I want to tell you is that I'm a werewolf. I've been one since I was attacked as a kid. I don't know why it took so long to manifest, but I had my first change at 17. I'm sorry I didn't say anything before now, but I didn't want to keep lying to you."

Mom stares at me quietly for a few moments. I somewhat expect her to either look at me like I'm crazy or to laugh, but I'm prepared to show her if it comes to that.

"What do you mean you are a werewolf?" Mom asks in a mild, yet serious tone.

"I mean you know the whole transforms under the full moon, hair growing everywhere, fangs, claws and super strength. You know the whole 9-foot tall monster. Half man half wolf."

My heart starts racing, I'm so nervous that she won't believe me. If she really is a Tailor then she might blow my head off. I'm not sure what to say next. Sweat starts pouring from my face. This is so different from what happened with Catalina. Her lack of response confuses me.

When I stare at Mom, she's sitting still on the edge of the couch, with her face in her hands. I kneel down next to her, "Mom? Mom, are you ok?" I ask, concerned.

Mom shakes her head before moving her black curly hair from her face. She looks up at me with a face I've never seen and speaks in a tone I've never heard, "Damien... I was hoping that it skipped you."

"What do you mean?" I ask puzzled.

"Damien, c'mon sit back on the couch," she says as she pats the cushion a few times. I did and she continues, "Damien," Mom says with a sigh. "You weren't bitten by a werewolf, you were born one. The werewolf that attacked you was from another pack, either trying to kill you or turn before you had your first shift, so you would be loyal to them."

A question pops into my head to ask her, "How do you know that?"

"I know because the night you went camping, your father came to the door to warn me that there could be an attack," she responds.

"What do you mean my father?" I ask. "Why didn't you tell me?!"

"What was I supposed to tell you? You were eight," she exclaims.

Before she continues, I jump from the couch and begin pacing through the living room. I walk back and forth with my hands on the back of my head, trying to figure out a way to process everything. This entire time I thought I was bitten and now, she's telling me I was born a werewolf?

"I thought he only showed up to try to scare me," she explains. "Then you were attacked and I watched you closely, giving you wolfsbane to counteract the bite. But I see now that I couldn't prevent the inevitable. I hoped that you weren't a werewolf and this wasn't going to be your life."

"Meaning?" I ask, confused.

She then stands up and walks into the dining room and lifts a vase, which reveals an orange button. When she presses it, all the plants, tables and furniture shift. My eyes widen as I watch my childhood home turn into an armory. I'm speechless, as I notice how many of them have Tailor emblems on them. The same emblem my mom wears whenever she leaves on her business trips. I slowly approach one of the walls.

Then I back away slowly as I catch a lump in my throat. I clear it before speaking, "Mom...why do you have Tailor weapons?"

"Because I used to be one," she responds.

In disbelief of what I just heard, I plop hard onto the couch. Nearly sinking in it as everything I thought I knew about myself is turned on its head. My mom, my friends and the life I knew are all in question now. So many thoughts are rushing in my head and I can't find the right words.

I decide to ask the simplest question I can muster, "Does this mean if not for my father, I would have been a Tailor too?"

With a remorseful gaze mom answers, "Yes, we come from a long line of Tailors. When you went camping, I asked you to be taken to one of our wolfsbane farms. In a foolish belief that if a werewolf did come after you, they'd at least be deterred from trying anything. But... I was wrong."

I start breathing calmly, "Ok so...you were a Tailor and my father's a werewolf." I state.

"Yes," The expression on her face is much more affectionate than any other time we've spoken about him.

"How exactly did that happen, when Tailors hunt and kill werewolves?" I question.

Mom nods softly, "And that was my mission. I was assigned to kill your father by going undercover and getting him to trust me. Then kill him when we wouldn't see me coming," Mom explains. "It took seven months of planning, and two of execution. But... after a year... I fell in love with your father. After three years, I told my superiors that I needed more time, but in reality I only wanted to spend more time with him. After 5 years, finally I came clean about what I was sent to do. Rather than killing me like I thought he would, we continued our relationship in secret after I told my commander that the mission was a failure and my cover had been blown. Eventually I got pregnant with you and I took the job as a consultant."

The irony that I'm the product of a Romeo and Juliette story. I pause for a moment soaking everything in. I stare at the ceiling trying to think of the right words.

"I'm sorry if this isn't what you wanted to hear, but he was just so charming and loving that I couldn't kill him," Mom says, softly.

"Mom, that's unbelievable," I finally respond. "But I have to ask what would you have done if you were around for my first change?"

"I would have called your father, he was so happy when you were born," Mom admits. "We agreed that if you turned by the time you hit puberty, that I'd let him take care of you," tears start rolling down her face. "I couldn't bear the thought of losing you. I was thankful that I didn't see you change. That's also why I never told you about anything having to do with Tailors or werewolves. I didn't want you in either world, having to constantly question which side you belong to."

"It's ok Mom, I don't blame you," I say in a soft voice. "It looks like the universe chose the world I belong to."

"No it's not, but thank you for saying so," Mom replies. "I've been going back and forth about whether to tell you since you were born."

She presses the button once more and everything goes back to normal. After grabbing a few tissues, she sits at the dining room table. I walk up behind her and hug her, "I'll never leave you no matter who my father is. He left and you've been taking care of me. Nothing could ever change that."

"Awe, that's sweet Dae Dae, but there's one other thing you need to know," she says, sniffling.

"What?" I ask.

"Your father isn't just any other werewolf. He's ranked as the most dangerous werewolf on the planet," Mom reveals.

My heart skips a beat when those words hit my ears, "Really?! You mean the one no one's seen in years?"

"Yes, so don't think that you can just go picking a fight with him," she warns. "That's also why he stepped away. For both our sake."

I start laughing, out of everything I heard from my mom, learning that's who my father is insane. When I manage to stop laughing, I tell her what I find so funny.

"I'm not worried about that at all," I say proudly.

"Why is that?" she asks.

"Two reasons, I guess you can call me a chip off the o' block because I'm also on the list since I'm an alpha."

Mom stands up and takes a few steps back, looking me up and down to examine me. She then hugs me tightly.

"What? What's wrong?" I ask frantically.

"Nothing, I just want to get a good look at you," Mom sighs, "We're the reason no one hasn't seen him in years."

"How so?" I question.

"He's always lived a secluded life and when we separated he kind of went back to his old ways," Mom answers. "Every now and again, I'll see him and we'll catch up. He asks about you and if you're a werewolf. Until now, I've been able to tell him no, but I can't say that anymore."

"W…why not?" I ask confused.

"Well, he's been at the top of both the Tailor's and the Council's list since he was about your age," she explains.

Wait, wait, wait, wait, since he was my age? There's no way that's true," I exclaim.

"It's true, No other purebred has held the title as long as he has, which is why I was sent to kill him," she explains. "There is a theory that he'll change the course of the world if he takes a more present role in the world."

Then my mother's light brown skin becomes red. I'm not sure why, but before I can ask what's wrong, there's a sudden knock at the door. It nearly makes us jump and we both are on guard. The aura of this person is unknown, but feels familiar at the same time. Whoever this is, they didn't want to hurt either of us. I walk over to the door and open it. In the doorway stands a tall, muscular, dark skin man, with a full beard on our porch.

"Hello Jamila, hello Damien," he says in a deep voice.

"Hello D'Marcus," mom replies in a soft, high tone.

"Damien, I'm your father, it's nice to meet you," he says with a smile.

I look at him in amazement. I know that I look like my mother, but seeing this man standing in front of me, I could be looking at my future self.

He also looks very young as if he isn't aging. I expect a man to be around my mom's age, not one looking a few years older than myself. The longer I stare at him, the more I see myself in him. The confidence and self-assurance he gives off is nothing like I've ever felt before.

"Aren't you going to invite me in?" he asks.

"Sure, come in," Mom replies, as we step aside, letting him in the house.

I stand dumbfounded. After 24 years, I finally meet my father and I don't know what to say to him. I have so many questions and I don't know where to start. Finding out my mom was a Tailor and I'm also a purebred all in the same day is a lot to grasp. He walks into the house, looks around before stopping once his eyes meet mine.

"Damien, I know you have a lot of questions, so feel free to ask," he says as he sits down in the reclining chair.

"I'm going to start with this one," I begin to say. "Why do you look like you're a few years older than me? You look more like we could be brothers, not father and son."

He chuckles, "That's an easy one, we're werewolves. Once we reach a certain age, we just stop aging."

"What do you mean?" I ask puzzled.

"You didn't think we had the same lifespan as humans did you?" he asks smugly.

"Well kinda..." I say, slightly embarrassed.

"You need to stop watching all those movies Son, we live longer, a lot longer," D'marcus smirks.

"How much longer?" I inquire.

"No one knows," he answers. "The longest ever recorded is 523 years, a record set by your great-grandmother."

272

"Great grandmother?!" That's a long time. What happened to her?" I ask.

"She was killed by a rival, but hopefully, there will be one of us that will live longer," he smiles at me.

I don't sure how he means that, but I feel like he has high hopes for me. I don't think I should feel any praise from the man that abandoned me. I turn away to look out the side window, so he can't read my expressions.

"Did you also know that when we have a strong enough bond with another werewolf, we could speak with each other telepathically?" he asks.

I look back at him, "I figured something like that was true. I noticed something like that a while ago. Sometimes it feels like we can read each other's minds."

I notice that Mom is no longer around. I try listening for her heartbeat in an attempt to find her, but she isn't in the house. Where did she go?

"Your mother isn't here," D'Marcus says. That's when I realized he wasn't speaking with his mouth, I'm hearing him in my head. It's clearer than any conversation I've ever had with another person, "Your mother left because she knows that it's time for me to train you."

"Train me?" I question.

"Of course, train you. Your mother's the reason I'm here," he explains. "I heard your mother tell you what would happen if you became a werewolf. It's time I take you under my paw and train you. Forgive the pun," he laughs to himself. "I hoped that I'd have more time to train, but since you're the Tremauré of all things, I might not have much to teach you."

"How'd you know I'm the Tremauré?" I ask.

"I've been keeping my eye on you," he answers.

D'Marcus changes the subject by asking if I know about the bond between a werewolf and the one they love. When I tell him no, he tells me that when the connection is strong the wolf gives their loved one of their fangs. It's through that connection that the wolf will always know that their lover needs them. He says that he gave one to Mom after she told him the truth about herself. Once the person accepts the fang they are bound together forever.

I wonder if I should give one of my fangs to Catalina. I thought about a chain she gave me a while ago. It has so such sentimental value that I always wear it. D'marcus then comments that he's just happy that our fangs grow back because if it didn't, he never would have done it.

"A werewolf's fangs are some of our pride and joy," he remarks.

While trapped in my own thoughts, I almost completely forgot about my father. He's still sitting on the couch staring at me when I turn back around. He has this look in his eyes that makes me think he knows what I'm thinking.

"You have a question," he grins.

"Yes... Why did it take me so long for me to have my first change?" I ask.

"It happens sometimes," he says in a low voice. "And the suppressors your mother had you take didn't help, but every family goes through this. Some have their first turn around the time they hit puberty. While others have their first turn on or before their 18th birthday."

"What happens if they don't turn by their 18th?" I ask worried.

"Then they're the rare occasions when it skips a generation," he answers. "Just as human as everyone else. Although, they can still pass along the family tradition."

"I didn't think that was possible," I ponder. "What happens to them?"

"Some go on to live normal lives, others stay in the family and teach the next generation. But it also depends on the family."

"Huh, I never thought about it like that," I respond.

"I would have like to be there for your first change, but I'm glad you did," he says in a warm tone. He suddenly stands up quickly, "I'm short on time, I have to leave, but I'll be back. Before I go, I must ask you to show me the eyes of our progenitor."

Since he answered my questions, I figure it was the least I could do, so I show him. When my eyes illuminate, he reacts almost instantly, like I'm the one who bit him. His eyes glow red and he let's out a small growl. I see him fighting to stay on his feet. He's almost kneeling right in front of me. It's strange that an alpha, even one as strong as him, can't resist the power of the Tremauré.

When the glow recedes, he stands tall once more and with a smirk, he holds out his closed fist and tells me to hold out my hand. When I hold out my hand, he drops a ring into my palm. When I inspect it, I see a symbol on the ring. It's the insignia for one of the purebred families. It's a gold ring with a wolf's head in the center of it and the full moon behind it. Five gemstones surround its head. I recognize this symbol from my training with Tevin.

I'm not from just any purebred family, I belong to one of the twelve oldest werewolf families. He laughs when he sees me recognizing the symbol. Each of the twelve houses has a name behind them. The first 8 represent the phases of the moon and the other 4 represent the colors the moon takes. Our family was chosen to represent the full moon, named The House of Luna. For it's, no our immense strength, power, and resilience.

D'Maurcus then shows me that he was wearing a pendant around his neck with the same symbol. Today is not turning out the way I initially intended for it to. I thought I'd be telling my mother a secret that I've kept from her for so long. However, I found out that she's been keeping an even bigger secret from me.

"This is incredible," I say excited.

He puts his hands on my shoulder, "I have to take my leave now, but whenever you're ready call me when you want to begin."

With that, he leaves me alone with the ring he gave me and my thoughts. Not knowing what else to do, I sit at the dining room table with the ring in front of me. Never in my wildest dreams did I think I'd find this out about my family. I don't know who I am anymore. Is all of this just some elaborate prank or have all of my moves been preplanned. Am I exactly where they want me to be? Everything is upside down.

Tonight is the night of our run, I can run along with everyone else and just think for a while. My life has gotten so complicated. First, losing Kahlil and Tevin, then finding out my mom used to be a Tailor. And now learning that I'm from the House of Luna.

Should I tell them? What would they say about me? Would they still see me the same as they saw me before? This is simultaneously amazing and frightening all at the same time. While thinking to myself, I don't notice Mom walking in the door. She snuck up behind me and tries to get the drop on me. My instinct kicks in and grab her arm before she has a chance to attack.

"Wow look at the reflexes on you," she says, impressed. "I'd expect nothing less from my son."

"Haha, well seeing as how sickly I was as a kid, just be happy my lycanthropy kicked in when it did," I reply.

Suddenly, the liveliness from Mom's face fades. She apologizes to me for leaving, but says she had to. The conversation I had with my father wasn't one she needed to be a part of. There's an awkward silence for a brief moment. I show her the ring like a little kid trying to show off a new toy. She says she knew about the ring and that's the reason she had to leave. Telling me about my father's side of the family is his job not hers and that's why she called him.

I now understand why she didn't tell me, she was only trying to protect me the same way I was trying to protect her. I apologize for not telling her sooner. Today came as a surprise to the both of us.

Mom then asks me a question I didn't expect from her. She asks me if I had any recent problems with Tailors. I tell her that for the last year or so I've been able to focus on work and my normal life. I start going over what happened with Timothy, his soldiers and how they captured me before trying to kill me.

"How are you still alive?" she asks frantically. "I looked at the reports of that incident and saw it was an unsanctioned mission going after the werewolf who killed Bruce, the Tremauré. Bruce captured an alpha and his beta, but they escaped when the Tremauré appeared, who helped them escape. Timothy was on a vendetta looking for the Tremauré and found him," Mom says worried. "Then the most recent incident mentioned that Timothy found the Tremauré and tried to go after him and his pack, but that went sideways as well. Other than myself and

Bruce, Timothy was next in line as the greatest hunters in the world. I can't believe they were defeated."

Mom stops once more for a second, she blinks twice before clearing her throat, "Were you a part of those attacks?" she asks in a calm voice.

I look her in her eyes as I answer, "Yes I was."

"How'd you get mixed up in all of that?" she asks, almost panicked.

I take a deep calming breath, "Not only was I a part of that attack, but... I'm the alpha and that was my beta. The Tremauré didn't show up, I...became the Tremauré," I reveal to her.

Mom's eyes widen, unsure of what to say next. It's as if she's frozen in time. I give her the full rundown of what happened with Bruce. How I found Kahlil after the show and he was captured. How we escaped before I was shot, killed and then being revived. I tell her about Deshawna and how she was working with Timothy. How she begged her way into my pack, so she could get us to trust her all the while telling them about our plans. That attack then led to the killing of not only Kahlil, but also Tevin. And even though I wanted them both dead, I let Timothy live and told them to go. Something I wish I could have gotten Bruce to do.

"I can't believe it," Mom says, breathing heavily. Her eyes rapidly move back and forth before she speaks again, "Th...that month you were away with all your friends, you were the one in the cell?!"

"Yes," I respond hesitantly. "They tried to get me to tell them about my pack, but I didn't. As their alpha, it's my job to protect them."

She's again at a loss for words. Then in a more serious tone she asks, "Are you sure that you're the Tremauré?"

"Unless there's another werewolf with blue eyes, that was given the same power I have that I don't know about then yes it's me," I answer.

"You know what that means right?" she asks.

"I didn't at first, but now I think I do," I reply, in a serious voice.

"Show me your eyes..." Mom demands.

"...What?" I ask.

"Show... me... your... eyes. I want to see them for myself," Mom says in a serious tone.

My eyes slowly illuminate, showing her that I am in fact the Tremauré. The blue light radiating from my eyes reflect off of a few surfaces around us.

"Damien this means that they know who you are and your name, they'll never stop hunting you," she warns. "Bruce was one of the most respected hunters and trainers of new hunters in the country. They also know that you're the Tremauré."

"They only know my name. For some reason, they can't find me in the database," I say proudly. "Timothy says when I was caught the first time, I was wiped from their cameras. I've been very careful. Even when they had me for the second time, I never said my full name. Jakobe or Davion never saw my face, I was using my glabro and they couldn't tell it was me."

"That's because I did everything I could to keep your face, prints and DNA from the main database," Mom explains.

"That must be why they thought I was working with someone," I muttered.

"Exactly right, I put a virus in the system to wipe you every time you appear, so you couldn't be traced back to me," Mom explains. "I see that's going to be even harder now."

"I'm sorry that I added so much more work for you mom," I apologize, hanging my head low.

"Don't sweat it, I'll make sure that it's all settled. I'll just need to run a little more interference," she says with a confident smile.

"Now you sound like a secret agent," I laugh.

"Look who's talking, one of us can transform," Mom remarks.

I ask her how she'll be able to run the interference and she says that her code name is Shadowcat and she has high level security clearance. Upon hearing her code-name, I remember when they mentioned Shadowcat and how she'd make me talk. They asked her to help with the alpha, but she turned them down each time and I'm happy she did. Even when Timothy repeatedly asked for her help in hunting me after killing Bruce, she declined. Instead, she sent Davion, and Jakobe.

We talk for a few more hours going over some things my pack and I have gone through. I tell her how I bit Catalina and how I met each member. I can tell she's a little uncomfortable, but she genuinely loves that we can talk openly. After hearing the entire story, she tells me how proud of me she is and how she's glad she is that I didn't turn out like other werewolves.

We sit, talk, eat and share some more between us. Which is nice because I haven't gotten a real chance to sit and talk with her this openly. As the night goes on, she tells me that she's heading to bed. I tell her I'm going to meet up with everyone else. As I watch my mom walk up the stairs she tells me proud of me once more. A huge grin appears on my face.

I tell her that I love her and I'm sorry that she couldn't get her wish. She tells me that I was always going to be a werewolf whether she wanted me to be one or not. She heads up the stairs and goes to bed. Before I leave to meet everyone, I see the ring and decide to take it with me.

"They're not going to believe this," I say, as I close the door.

Chapter 17

As I was walk to my car, I can't decide what to do with the ring. I want to just put it in my pocket, but I don't think that'd be respectful. Instead, I put it on my finger. The strange thing is that it didn't fit on any other finger other than my middle one. That's strange, his hands are a little bigger than mine. Did he have it made for me?

It's nice to be meeting at the Den again, no other place feels as homey. We spent the last few weeks scouting the area, making sure that it wasn't being watched and looking out for any traps lying in wait for us. Once we were sure that it was safe for us to return, we cleaned up and set everything back the way it was. Afterward, I told everyone we'd come back on the next full moon and go for our run. Tonight is that night and I couldn't be happier.

I pick up Catalina before driving to the Den. She must have seen that there's something on my mind, and asks me about it. I tell her that I'll tell her with everyone. Catalina says she's very curious since I can't keep anything from her.

We're the first to arrive, and I think about everything that happened today. I'm a purebred, from the House of Luna and my mom used to be a Tailor. I know that they aren't going to believe me, hell I experienced it a few hours ago and still I don't believe it. Pretty soon, everyone arrives, first, Chantelle and Omar, then Nichole and Kiara and finally, Braheem, Darius and Jasmine.

After waiting for a few seconds, I ask, "Has anyone heard from Kah..." I instantly stop as I look over at his headstone.

"D, it's fine bro, we don't have to meet tonight," Omar says.

"Nah, it's good. I'm just still not used to him being gone I guess," I reply.

"Yea I know," Braheem added. "Usually we play online on Thursdays and I waited for over an hour before remembering he wasn't coming."

"It's ok, we'll get through this," I say to everyone. "Okay first order of business, I have to tell you all something."

"What?" Nichole asks.

"Huh, is Catalina pregnant?" Kiara asks gleefully.

"N... n... no, she's not pregnant," I stutter, laughing nervously as Catalina and I look at each other. "Why does that seem to be the theme today?"

"Theme?" Catalina inquires.

"Never mind, listen. Y'all know how I was going to tell my mom about us?" everyone nods. "Well I did and she apparently had some news of her own."

Their anticipation has them hanging on my every word. I begin telling them the story of everything that happened when I opened up to mom about being a werewolf. I tell them how I prepared to tell her everything. But before I could, she told me something I wasn't prepared for. Mom confessed to me that I wasn't bitten, I was born.

Not only was I born a werewolf, but she used to be a hunter who was sent to kill my father and they fell in love. Soon after, my father knocked on the door and revealed that I belong to one of the twelve families. I try my best to keep everything concise, but I began to ramble from that point forward. There's no stopping me, I tell them everything. After I was done telling my story, I feel my heart racing and everyone's eyes on me.

I pause for a moment trying to read their expressions. All I see are empty stares that don't tell me anything. I end up shifting my eyes to the ground in pitied defeat. Maybe they don't see me the same because I'm not like them.

Before I could stumble onto my next words, I hear Braheem speak, "I can't believe it."

"Neither can I," exclaims Kiara.

"I wonder about my parents," Darius says jokingly, as he pats me on the back.

"I've been wondering how you've been so *strong*," Omar mocks. "I thought only a purebred could have the power you had when you fought Darnell."

"Yea I guess so," I say nervously.

"See, I told you that you have a similar smell to Darnell," Chantelle points out.

Catalina steps closer to me and puts my hands in her own, "It doesn't matter if you're a purebred or a mutt, cuz you're still my whittle fuzzy wuzzy."

I growl at her because she knows how annoyed I get when she calls me that. I tickle her then backflip away. She lunges at me and we start wrestling as we roll all over the dirt. Everyone starts laughing at us. Catalina eventually gets the better of me and pins me down. Kiara, Jasmine, Nichole, and Chantelle all cheer her on.

"You go girl, show him who's the real boss," Jasmine says excitedly, before helping her up.

I stand up and dust myself off, "I let her win."

"Suuurre you did," Nichole says, sarcastically.

Everyone walks over and tells me that no matter where I come from or who my parents are, that won't change how they see me. I am so thankful to have friends like them. I don't know what I'd do without them. As I finish dusting myself off, I look down at my hand and see the ring on my finger.

I stare at it for a second. This ring is another sign that who I think I am and who I'm meant to be are two different people. Catalina asks me if everything is ok after she notices an intense look on my face. I show everyone the ring my father gave me. Everyone is amazed to see the ring.

Jasmine comments on how expensive the ring looks and jokes about selling it for a fortune. She is the only one who wants to touch it. When I give it to her, she pockets it and tries to act like she knows nothing about it. After a few minutes, she gives it back and says that even though she doesn't like purebreds, she's glad I'm not like the ones she met.

I share one other piece of information with everyone. I tell them how my father told me that after a certain amount of time werewolves no longer age. And apparently two werewolves who share a strong enough bond can speak telepathically with one another.

"That makes sense, I used to wonder why it seemed like we could hear each other's thoughts," Kiara comments.

"I thought it was just our good teamwork, but that does explain a few things," Omar adds.

"Will he teach us how to use it?" Chantelle asks.

"He did tell me that he wants to start my training so…maybe," I admit.

"And…did you say we no longer age?" Nichole questions. "So…are we immortal?"

"I guess it's something like that," I answer. "He told me that the longest someone has lived was over 500 years."

"What happened to them?" Catalina asks.

"Same thing that always happens, she was killed," everyone grows quiet. "The only thing that really makes me wonder is what brought him to start my training now? And for what reason?"

"You're going to have to figure that out, but no matter what happens, we're going to be right beside you," Catalina says, as she smiles brightly.

I stare deeply into her eyes for a few moments. Then my gaze meets everyone else's. Her words speak for everyone. Jasmine, Braheem, Darius, Omar, Chantelle, Nichole and Kiara all have the same reassuring expression.

Soon after, I tell everyone to take off their clothes, so we can run in crinos. Seconds later everyone excitedly awaits for the full moon to reach its peak. An hour later, we are using the woods as our personal playground. There's nothing to worry about, no battles to be fought, just fun with my friends and the love of my life.

For the last few days, I've been thinking about my father, my family and what this all means. I wonder what my purpose is. The Alpha of the house of Luna and the Tremauré. How am I going to live up to both titles? So many questions and nowhere to go. I figure it's time to reach out to D'marcus and take him up on his offer.

I have no idea how to call him. He didn't give me a cell number, an address, or anything I could use. I sit down in the middle of my bedroom attempting to find out if I can contact him telepathically. He said that two werewolves with a strong enough bond can speak to each other. What could be stronger than a bond between parent and their child?

I meditate and try to remember the same feeling I had when he talked to me through telepathy. After about an hour and a half of trying, I find the connection. I call out to him and to my surprise, he answers me, saying he'll be over shortly. I can't explain it, but I got kind of excited when I hear him walking toward the house.

"Hey Son, I didn't think that you would've called for me so early," he says smiling.

"Why not?" I ask.

"Without knowing it, you've completed the first step in your training," I look at him puzzled. He laughs and says, "The first thing to master is telepathy. It took me months to be able to contact your grandfather."

"Well I guess I'm better at this than I thought," I say confidently.

"Maybe you are," my father smirks.

At first, we stand there observing one another. He walks around me in a circle, sizing me up. After circling me a few more times, he stops right in front of me and takes off his jacket. He asks me to follow him to somewhere more open. Confused, I ask where we are going, but he doesn't tell me. Interested. I follow him outside.

Initially, I thought we're going to take his car. Instead, he takes off running in another direction. Without hesitating, I follow behind him. I've never seen anyone take off with so much speed. Normally we have to pick up speed over a short time, but that isn't what he does. My father is running at sixty miles an hour like it's a morning jog. He increases his speed and I'm determined to keep up with him. We run for about thirty minutes before he suddenly stops. We stopped at a random, open grassy field. I look around realizing that I haven't been here before. I was so focused on keeping up that I wasn't watching where we were going.

He stands in the middle of the field about six feet away from me, "I'm glad you could keep up, your grandfather left me in the dust the first time I chased him. I want you to come at me with everything you got," he says calmly.

I stand there with my eyes trained on him, unsure of what my next move will be, but I accept his offer and loosen myself up, "Ight are you ready?" I ask confidently.

"Whenever you are," he acknowledges.

I rush toward him and punch trying to determine if he was serious about me coming at him with everything I have. I stop short just before I could connect. The next I know I'm on the ground.

"I told you to come at me with everything you have," he says, taking a few steps back.

"I heard you, but I thought you were talking about sparing," I groan.

"No I wasn't, this is your third test," he says sternly. "Show me what you can do."

I get up off the dirt to go after him again. I don't have the intent to kill him, but I won't take it as easy as I did before. A few minutes later, I'm on the ground once more.

"That was better, but I want you to come at me like you did when you fought Darnell," he demands.

"You know about that?" I ask curiously.

"Of course I do," he answers. "I've known you were a werewolf for a while now."

"But mom…" I say in a low voice.

"She knew too, she just couldn't accept it until now," he says in a strong tone. "Now fight me!."

This time when I attack him, I use combos that I've learned from Chantelle and Omar. Also, a fighting style I learned from Tevin. A back and forth tactic of trying to claw at him followed up with a punch. This takes a lot of skill to master, I've been able to integrate this into my own style.

Unfortunately, just like last time, I start doing better, but I can't land a hit on him. I get close a few times, but nothing connects. At this point, I start getting angry. I can only get knocked on my ass so many times before it's no longer funny.

He sees me getting angry and says, "A son of mine would fight with more viciousness, something you lack."

Three rounds later, I still can't successfully hit him. He isn't attacking me back, only staying on the defensive, evading and dodging. The more we fight, the wilder I become. I start to only go off of instinct. After about ten rounds or so, I'm tired of losing.

He stands there towering over me, exerting his skill over mine, "Okay *Dad,* let me show you what you really want to see," I say threatening him.

"Hmph, well this is getting interesting," he says, smiling with anticipation. "I was wondering when you'd stop playing with me."

We go for a few more rounds and I keep getting closer to hitting him. When I finally do, I celebrate a little in my head. He punches me for the first time and I fall straight onto my back. He laughs at me, but when my gaze meets his, it tells me I failed.

"I've had enough of this!" I shout.

I handspring back to my feet, figuring that this'll be the last time. I'm kicking this up a notch to really show him what I can do. I remove my shoes and my shirt before shifting into my glabro form and I roar at him. He chuckles and changes into his. Without thinking I go for another attack. We're going blow for blow like this was our last fight. In a short time, I manage to land a few decisive strikes, causing him to stumble. Then I clip him before forcing him onto his back and roaring in his face. Suddenly, I stop and look at him. I want him to acknowledge that I won, even if this is the first time.

"Haha, that's my boy!" he exclaims excitedly as he changes back. "I can't believe you have so much power. I thought for sure you were going for the kill."

I change back, "What do you mean?"

"You not only are a good fighter, but you have such a power inside you, *but* you only tap into it when you're angry. A family trait, the House of Luna is famous for. It's why we're one of the twelve families."

I help him back to his feet, "I don't know 'bout all that."

"Yes you do and to top it off it's being supercharged by the Tremauré," he says. "Damien, the reason we have the phase of the full moon is because we have immense strength and power. Our power usually comes out in our greatest need. Your training will allow you to harness it and control it at will. I've used that family power to become the most dangerous werewolf and I've kept that title for over one hundred years."

I pause for a moment, thinking about all the battles I've fought. About how when I was under duress, I was able to draw on that power from within. A power that I've never seen anyone else have. I've used it when I was learning to control myself under the full moon. Then again when I fought Darnell. I thought I was losing myself to the wolf, when in reality, I was using my wolf's true power.

"I guess you're right," I admit.

"Damien, my time at the top is coming to an end and now it's your turn," his voice is serious. "I've lived for over two hundred and fifty years and in that time, I've achieved great things."

"In all of that time you've never had any children?" I question.

"No, I haven't, I was waiting for a woman like your mother. Strong and able to walk with me when I require a shoulder to lean on. I didn't want to be catered to, I wanted to be cared about and respected. Qualities your mother has and then some," his eyes shining the same way I saw mom's were when she spoke about him. "It's time for me to teach you how to take my place, just like my father taught me."

"What happened to my grandfather?" I ask.

My father looks at the sky, "He died a while back," I hear the solemnness in his voice as he spoke.

I stare intently at him, "Am I ready to take that on?" I ask,

"I'd say so," he says confidently.

"Then I guess I have no choice do I?" I say nervously.

"Great, then we'll start bright and early tomorrow morning," he begins to say. "Right here in this field. I'll show you everything. You've already taken the first steps in accepting the legacy of our family."

We run back to my house and this time, I take great care in watching where we are coming from. On the way back he says that every family has their secrets and every family has their tricks. Whatever he teaches me, should only be shared within the pack.

Later that night, I lay in my bed thinking about the events of today. Catalina asks how things are and I tell her. I feel like being a part of the House of Luna is a great honor, one that I'm not sure if I'm supposed to have. Catalina reassures me that I am ready to take on this new challenge. She tells me that she believes in me and is here to support me every step of the way. We talk late into the night before falling sleep.

The next day, I walk onto the field, thinking today is going to be a great day. A new step forward. I arrive at the field at 7 a.m. and notice that I'm alone. I wait for a few minutes but he's nowhere to be found. Thirty minutes later, my ears twitch. I hear him trying to sneak up on me while my guard is down. His footsteps aren't heavy, but I hear each one land as he moves.

Though I can't pinpoint exactly where he is, I raise my guard, trying to find him, but I can't. He's coming with an impressive amount of speed. I try to be ready for whatever he has coming my way. Before I can catch him, he sneaks up on me and I'm on the ground yet again.

"Damien, you should know by now that you have to be faster than that," he says with a slight smile.

"Yea I know, I thought I was ready," I grumble.

He helps me up and says, "Alright, today's lesson is about strength and speed, this'll help me understand how much training you'll actually need."

"Didn't I already show you that yesterday and then again just now?" I ask, puzzled.

"You showed me your fighting ability, I'm talking about your raw strength and speed."

"Okayyyy, where am I running to?" I ask.

"I want you to run from one end of the field to the other, but I want you to run on all fours from one side and then bipedal on the other side."

"Why?" I look at him confused.

"Are you not a werewolf?" he asks, ironically.

"Haha, point taken," I nod.

I'm skeptical, wondering why this is a part of my training. Especially since I've never run on all fours without being in crinos. The entire field is about three hundred yards. Going from one end to the other isn't really a problem, but switching running styles is going to be tricky. Nonetheless, I have to do it. It takes me a few seconds when running on two feet then almost twice as long running on all fours. I feel like I did pretty good for my first try.

However, when I look at my dad, he has no emotion on his face. Is he disappointed? He says I did an okay enough job, but tells me to take a few steps back. I do and he runs. I don't see him move when he take his first step. As soon as I blink it's already over and he's already on the other side. I strain to keep my eyes on him while I watch him run back toward me on all fours. It's the same incredible speed.

"Do you know how I was able to go back and forth?" he asks.

"No," I answer.

"It's because I don't believe I'm still human," he reveals. "My mind isn't limited to what I think my body can do. When you're running, you run at human speeds and then tap into the wolf speed. You should be able to tap into the wolf's speed because it's your speed. Do it again and this time, run with the wolf in your heart and in your mind."

"But won't that allow the wolf to take over?" I ask.

"How so?" Dad contends. "You already have control under a full moon and you can change whenever you want. You're in control. The wolf is you and you are the wolf."

It feels like I'm learning the same lessons all over again. I close my eyes and take a heavy breath. I know what he means and he's right. I concentrate, letting the feeling of me and the wolf be one and the same. A small pulse emanates from inside of my body, similar to when I first learned to control the wolf. That feeling resonates throughout my entire being.

"That's it son, hold on to it. Feel it and use it," he encourages.

When I open my eyes, I notice my vision isn't my homid's, it's in fact my wolf eyes. He smiles when he sees me. He tells me to keep that feeling, but stop myself from fully turning. It's growing hard to balance and soon after I lose it.

He tells me to try again. I find the same feeling as before. The wolf resonates inside me, but I can't keep hold of it for long. I thought I knew what it meant to be one with the wolf, but this is on another level. I try and fail a few more times, but after the tenth time, I'm finally able to find the middle point between us. Usually I only feel this way when I use my glabro form.

He tells me to run to the other side of the field and back. I've never taken off as fast as I did at that moment. Instead of picking up speed, I bolt at a much faster rate. Normally when I run, I can go from 0-60 in seconds, but now, I'm well past that. When I run back toward my father, he looks at me with a huge grin.

"You're a natural, my boy!" he exclaims. "I know wolves who are well into their 70s who can't successfully pull that off."

"Thank you, but I have to thank Tevin for that," I say in an appreciative tone. "He's been the best mentor I could have wished for," Tevin's face forces its way to the front of my mind and I realize that he's no longer with us.

He must have seen my face change, "Yes I heard about him, I'll just have to do as good of a job as he did.

I ask him what's next since I'm pumped for the next test. He tells me that since I did pretty well with speed, it's time for the overall strength trial. We walk over to some trees and he tells me to rip one with its roots. I explain that I have no problem knocking over a tree. He says it's not the same thing, any werewolf can knock over a tree, but very few have the ability to pull it directly with the roots intact.

I have a strong sense that they are the same thing. He tells me that not only are they two different types of muscle groups, but it's also a test of true strength in both technique and control. I watch him as he digs his claws into it and pulls it with the roots intact with little effort. I ask him how he did that and he says it takes practice.

The first time I try, I don't do it. I lift the tree, but leave the stump in the ground. Some roots were showing, but that wasn't what I was tasked to do. This isn't like the speed test, I have to focus. For the next week, I try and fail to get the tree from the ground with its roots. He watches and each day I get closer.

298

Finally, after three weeks of trying, I'm finally able to find the right technique that allows me to pull the tree from the ground with the roots attached. I feel sweet relief as I look at the tree. Dad gives me a dap and a quick hug, praising me for being a step closer to completing my training.

He tells me that the next thing we're going to focus on is self-defense, but before he teaches me self-defense he wants to meet my pack. It's been a little while since we've been together, so I ask everyone meet me at the Den. Everyone's happy to meet up that I think they left work in the middle of the day. Since tonight was a new moon, it's a great sign of a new beginning for all of us. I have to admit that I'm excited to see everyone. It sort of feels like I'm missing a part of myself, since we haven't been together this entire time.

I arrive at the Den with my dad in tow. Before anyone says anything, I jump on the highest rock with him standing behind me in the shadows. I look down at everyone else as they look up with curiosity. It's weird because they're looking at me as if they don't recognize me.

"I know it's been a few weeks since we've met and I take full responsibility," I begin to say. "I've missed y'all. Baby please join me up here," I say reaching out for Catalina. "That's part of the reason I've called you all here. The other reason is to introduce my father, D'Marcus Moon, The Alpha of the House of Luna."

There's a brief pause when he walks up behind Catalina and me, "Thank you, Damien," he acknowledges. "One thing I want to clear up, my last name is Carter. Luna is more of an official name. Second, I came here to train my son Damien, so he can take my place as Alpha of the House of Luna. Before we continue his training, I wanted to see what type of pack he has."

He suddenly whistles and then eleven people come toward us from all directions. Three of whom are wearing hoods. A remarkable feeling comes over me as I sense something familiar about a few of them. Have I met them before?

"I will tell you all this," he speaks again. "From watching how all of you reacted when you saw your alpha step up here and how all of you hung onto his words, I get a similar feeling from each of you that I get from my own pack. I can tell that all of you will continue to help and support him in the future."

All of us are captivated by his presence, I want to be so much like him when I take over. I have so much to learn and I'm excited. As I look at each one of their faces, I swear I can see Braheem, Darius, Omar, Chantelle, Kiara, Jasmine and Nichole reflected in my father's pack. I can't explain it, but it feels like Kahlil's with us.

Then my father says something that snaps me out of my train of thought, "There's someone missing."

"Yea, one of our other pack members was killed by Tailors a year ago," Braheem says solemnly.

300

"I see, I brought my pack here to train each of you while I'm training my son. However, I do have some good news. Will the two of you please step up and take off your hoods?"

As he requests, two of the hooded people step closer and remove their hoods. Underneath the hoods we see Tevin and Kahlil. Upon seeing both of them, I jump from the rock and run over to give them a hug. Everyone follows close behind.

"Wha… what. How are you still alive?!" Kiara asks with tears in her eyes.

None of us can believe what we're seeing. Tevin pretty much disappears from the planet and we all were so sure that Kahlil was dead. We don't want to let go in fear that they'll disappear again.

"I can answer your question since it seems it's going to be hard for them to answer at the moment," My father says laughing. "Damien, as you know, I've been watching you for some time now. Tevin has been keeping tabs on all of you since the first day you met him. We all need a mentor and when I found out you defeated Darnell, I asked my dear friend to take care of you until it was time to reveal myself. Everything he's taught you up 'til now has also been through me."

He then explains that Tevin comes from a long line of humans who have worked on taking care of and mentoring young werewolves, both pureblood and mutt. He says that Tevin had no knowledge of me being his son, but he knew I was someone with a lot of potential. It wasn't until the night the Tailors came to his home where he learned the truth.

My father explains that Kahlil was very near death with a faint heartbeat. If the paramedics hadn't gotten there at the right time and if he wasn't a werewolf, then he definitely would have died. Kahlil was in a coma for four months and then there were another three months of additional healing, since they had to purge the wolfbane and silver shrapnel from his body. He spent the last 6 months recovering and gaining his strength. Then after Kahlil was fully healed my father decided it was time to start my training with my pack at full strength.

Tevin on the other hand was a little different. He has a secret compartment in his house that he hid in. He used the cover of the smoke bomb to get as far away as possible. He says he tried to get to me when everything happened, but he couldn't. Tevin ran to my father who explained everything to him. Since Deshawna was a purebred, they didn't want to take any chances of any other werewolves knowing where he and Kahlil were.

We can't stop crying and hugging each other that our pack is finally back together. We spend the next half an hour going over everything that has happened since Kahlil's been away. We show him his gravestone and even talk about how we tried our best to find another place like the Basement, but we have been unsuccessful. Kahlil laughs and says that after some time he'll get to looking for another place that the Tailors won't find. After all the tears, we finally settle down and got back to the meeting.

My father tells us that he still has something else to go over, "As the old saying goes, a wolf is only as strong as its pack. Over the next year, I want all of you to train with my pack individually. Catalina, I have a special teacher for you."

The final person takes their hood off and when they lift their head, I see that it's my mom. Before I can process my mom being here among all of us werewolves, he speaks again, "Catalina, your teacher as you can see, will be Damien's mother.

Everyone is speechless, attempting to figure out why my mother, a previous Tailor, is Catalina's mentor. For the next twenty minutes, they talk to get further acquainted with their teachers. It's pretty odd that Catalina is going to be taught by my mom. They don't really know what to say to each other.

In an attempt to build a connection, he asks for all of us to go on a run together as one big pack. This among other things will bring us together in the year to come. My dad then changes into crinos and his pack does the same. When he looks at me, the crimson of his eyes are something I've never seen. The muscle tone of his crinos is unbelievable.

I turn into my crinos and everyone else turns as well. I notice my mom standing there and wonder what she's going to do because she hasn't turned. She says she's going to wait for us all while we're running as a pack. My father asks for everyone to stand together. He says that I'm going to be the alpha on this run. Wherever I move, they all will follow. It's strange, I can hear him in my head, but I don't need to relay anything he's saying to everyone else. What started as growls and reading body language, is now open speech between us all.

Our run goes fantastically, for the first time we have a huge pack made up of 19 people. Something I've never thought about. I was a little nervous at first about ordering everyone, but I grow into it. In all honesty, it's like everyone has a twin. Everyone has their position and we're on the same page. Even my father is following along like everyone else. After running for a few hours we eventually come back to the Den and put our clothes back on.

"That was very well done everyone," my father says proudly. "Thank you for going along with my little stunt. I wanted to see how you all moved as one especially when there is more of you. Now with that said, everyone go stand with your students. From this point forward, you will be training with these strong men and women. Everything they teach you will help you in the long run in keeping this pack and the House of Luna together. You can of course still keep your meetings, but that'll only be if Damien or Catalina calls for it. Everything else will be dictated by your mentors."

My father starts to leave with his pack and my mom, but before he goes he stops and tells us. That we'll need to quit our jobs. The House of Luna will supply us with all the financing we'll need moving forward. None of us will have to work another day in our lives if we don't want to. The main reason we have to quit our jobs is so we can focus on our teachings. He tells us to take as much time as we need to decide.

Once they leave, we sit to talk about what the next steps could be like. We talk about what our training could consist of and what an experience this'll be. The entire time we're using telepathy, going over if we can really quit our jobs. Everyone sees the bright side, thinking that we won't need to worry about bills ever again. That's more than any reason to go along.

We play around for a few hours, but eventually all go home, eagerly awaiting to begin our training. Before we leave I ask if everyone is ready. I stare into the eyes of everyone. Catalina, Braheem, Darius, Chantelle, Omar, Kiara, Jasmine, Nichole and Kahlil, all have assured looks on their faces. We accept that this is going to be a great next step for all of us. We're finally whole again and we can go above and beyond our current limits. Even if it gets hard none of us will quit.

We all leave to go home and prepare for our training. I tell them that my dad will continue my training and they'll hear from their mentors soon enough. I drop Catalina back at her home before going back myself. Though I'm in bed, I'm too excited to sleep, but I try my best to do so anyway.

<u>Chapter 18</u>

We spend the next few days thinking about my dad's offer. Are we going to quit our jobs to learn how to be better werewolves? It didn't take much thought, and the short answer is yes, we have nothing to worry about. I think Catalina is more excited about her mentor than any of us. Spending more time with my mother has always been a goal of hers and now she has the perfect excuse. We decide to meet the morning before our training to wish each other good luck. Quitting my job feels awkward with student loans and other bills, but hearing my father say he'll take care of all of us, I trust him.

"Ight everyone, today is the day," I begin to say. "I will see you all soon enough. I want everyone to work hard and absorb everything."

"Easy," Nichole comments.

"Dame, you already know we don't back down from a challenge," Braheem adds.

"Don't worry about anything," Darius says proudly. "It's us, the pack of the Tremauré."

"Uhh, are we ready to call ourselves that?" Kiara asks.

"Honestly, at this point, I think we are," I say confidently. "We can't run from it anymore. I'm the Tremauré and it's time we move forward with it."

"I'm with you," Omar declares.

"So are we!" Chantelle cheers as she has her arms around Kiara and Nichole.

The smiles on their faces makes me realize that I'm an alpha, because of them, they choose to follow me. I still may have doubts here and there and seven years ago, I was just some regular guy, that I became a werewolf. Then I became an alpha and now I'm supposed to save the nation of werewolves as the Tremauré. Catalina and I break away from the others so we can speak alone.

"Baby, I know I seem really confident, but I dunno, am really ready to take on the family legacy?" I ask.

"How could you not be?" she responds. "All that you've done since you've become a werewolf and you still don't know? Listen to me Abucheo, you got this, no question."

"But how could I? Up until now I've been winging it at every turn. They follow me, but I honestly feel I only survived through dumb luck," I admit.

"It wasn't dumb luck," Catalina says sternly. "It's because they all see the leader you are. You're their alpha because you follow your heart. You don't lead by ferocity or cruelty like others do. You worked hard to control the wolf and use that power to protect those around you."

"I…I guess so," I mumble.

"Listen to me, you have me and you always will," Catalina stares into my eyes. "Wherever or whenever you need me, I'll be there in ten minutes."

"Five if you run," I smile softly.

"Yea, yea. I love you, Abucheo," she chuckles.

"I love you too Baby," I say softly.

We hug and kiss each other before going back to the others who were patiently waiting. With my confidence somewhat restored, I call my father and tell him that we are ready to start. He texts me several locations, each one has a name attached to it, telling them where to meet their mentors. We briefly say our goodbyes and go our separate ways.

I meet my father at the same field we've been using to train. When sees me walking onto the field, he smiles and asks if I'm ready. I nod optimistically and then explains that the next part of my training is going to involve fighting. I tell him that I already know how to fight. He says that while my skills are great, I still have room to improve. He says he's going to show me our family's fighting style.

He tells me that I need to be able to fight like the alpha of the House of Luna. All the alphas in the council, especially the main 12 have their own styles. In order to be taken seriously, I'll need to learn it as well, just being the Tremauré isn't enough to stop a more skilled opponent from knocking me down or killing me.

He holds out his hand, "Listen Damien, I don't doubt your skills, but I ask that you try fighting my way at least for a month," he offers. "Try using what I teach you in addition to what you already know. Then see how you fair. Deal?"

I stare at him for a few seconds, thinking about his offer. Seconds later, I take his hand and dap him, "Deal."

Just as our hands part, he attacks me. I wasn't prepared, and just like our last fight, I end up in the dirt, "Rule number one, always keep your guard up *and* don't expect that just because you're my son I'll go easy on you."

I jump up and smirk, "I wouldn't have it any other way."

And that's how it is for the next month. Day after day, we spar with one another. I thought I knew how he fought, but I learn early on that he only showed me the tip of the iceberg. Even when it rains, it's here we stand, trading blows with one another.

I start to learn his combos and now I'm able to anticipate his movements. Slowly predicting them and copying them to use against him. His technique is just like what he showed me before, but there's also something different about it. He fights very meticulously and powerful at the same time. I can't explain it, but using what I've learned so far feels more natural. After two weeks, I'm able to keep up with his speed, power, and precision of his combinations. Now at the end of the month, I can match him.

I feel like I can win against him if we were to fight seriously. Now it's the end of the month, I approach him, "Ight dad, I see what you taught me has improved my overall technique."

"That's what I like to hear," he says, self assuredly. "Now I want you to show me that my teaching you wasn't a waste of time."

"No problem," I put my guard up.

For the next seven days, he and I fight harder than we ever have. We tirelessly fight for six days and I barely beat him. At the end of the sixth day, I'm so sore that I can barely walk. But I still want to challenge him. We've already gone 120 rounds against one another and my win/loss ratio has shifted in my favor.

That night I'm left thinking about what he told me the first day on the field. I still think of myself as human, not as a werewolf. I have to use my strength as a werewolf. My body hasn't been the same since my first turn. My bones, my muscles, my skin, my blood, all of it is beyond what any human can achieve. I can't hide behind it anymore. The human limiter is the problem, that limiter is all mental and it can be broken.

The next morning, when I walk onto the field, I don't see him. I laugh to myself remembering he's done this before. My father knows how to hide his presence, and his scent. I have to find out where he'll come from. immediately, I hear a slight swaying of the grass a small distance away. He's coming for me and just like before, I have to anticipate his moves. I won't let him get the best of me this time.

Seconds later, I hear the sounds of his footsteps approaching. I close my eyes trying to pinpoint his location before he strikes. I feel his presence as he throws his first punch. I block his hand with my arm with my eyes still closed.

"Haha, I'm impressed," he laughs excitedly.

"I learned from the best," I say as I turn around.

"Now we can get started," he says as he throws another punch.

I manage to block the second punch and just like that, we start our first round of the day. I lose the first one, but win the second. It goes on like this for the rest of the day, he wins one and then I win one. I thought he was letting me win, but he isn't. I'm actually drawing blood when I hit him. By the end of the day we're tied at ten wins. He tells me since I'm able to fight him to a standstill, I'm ready to move on to the next lesson.

"Why can't we continue until I win?" I ask. "We're tied, I know I can win the next one."

"The goal was never for you to beat me, it was for you to try to," he answers.

"Why not just tell me that?" I question him.

"Because then you wouldn't have worked as hard," he answers.

"Huh, you're right, but I'm sure I can beat you," I say proudly.

"Your time will come," he says in an ominous tone.

After we leave the field and clean ourselves up, he tells me what the next two months of my training will consist of. It's going to focus on increasing my raw speed and strength. I initially thought it was going to be like the first day when he had me run a suicides, but it's not.

He starts me off by running 150 miles a day at 70 mph, calling it high endurance training. I thought ripping a tree at its roots was tough, but I'm almost dying by the end of the first day. In the following few weeks, I'm running further each time. Just when I think I'm good, he increases his speed from 70 to 85 mph. In an effort to help me stay light on my feet, he has me use parachutes and weights on my wrists and ankles. Telling me it's good for a wolf to be a feather or a boulder at their choice.

On some runs, he forgoes the weights and tells me to run with a boulder over my head. It was difficult at first, but eventually, I feel myself not only getting stronger, but unlocking more of my potential. Most days I'm so exhausted that I sleep for the rest of the day. My father tells me that I've been doing so well that I could rival alphas in the Council. I like hearing I'm closer to my goal.

During the second month, I can move faster than I thought possible. I can keep up with him, whether it's fighting, raw speed or strength. I can outpace him by a larger margin. Dad seems genuinely happy after I beat him the last time. My time for running 150 miles is cut in half compared to how we started and now that I can stay running at 85 for longer periods of time without breaking a sweat.

Upon completing this challenge, my father tells me that the next two months of my training will consist of learning what it means to be a wolf. I ask him what he means. He tells me that we're going to live amongst wolves.

"I don't know about this. It sort of feels useless," I say to him.

"It's not useless, it's an important part of your training," he retorts. "This is to show you the beauty of wolves in nature," his face became serious. "Damien, you let your wolf free twice a month and let it run free, but have you ever looked at its memories and gone through the experience?"

"N…no, not at first, but I did start to when I learned to control it. At first when I used to get flashes they scared me," I respond. "Since learning control, I never really thought about it to be honest. I know he has fun and I let him and that's it."

"I understand, we're supposed to be human, more civilized right? But humans are the same as all mammals on this planet. We literally have the ability to turn into a werewolf, walk in two worlds. It's time you learn the wolf's side of things." he says sternly. "At most, you only stay in your crinos form for a few hours right?"

"Yea, pretty much," I admit.

"It's great that you can, but that shouldn't be the extent of it," he explains. "For this part of your training, we're going to stay in crinos."

"Wh…why?" I question.

"Your crinos and homid are two halves of the same coin. We cannot ignore the other half. We'll go to a place that is known to have other wolves and we'll live amongst them."

"Wolves, like wolves, wolves?" I ask.

"Yes, wolves, wolves. We'll shift back and forth until you can stay in crinos. How do you expect us to live like wolves without being wolves?" Dad asks.

"How long do I have to stay in my crinos form?"

"At least 24 hours…" My father reveals.

"24 hours?!" I exclaim. "What about the size difference or the Tailors?" I ask frantically. "Won't people notice?"

"You think that anyone is crazy enough to go after the Alpha of the House of Luna and the Tremauré at the same time?" Dad asks.

"Honestly, no, I just think that this is extreme," I mutter.

"Exactly, that's the point. This is how our family has become the strongest in the world," he declares. I know this is a lot to take in, so take a few days and think about it. Come to me when you make your decision."

Am I really going to live out the next two months of my life as a werewolf? No electricity, no phones, no bathrooms, just me and him in the wilderness amongst other wolves. I've never stayed in crinos for that long. I debate, but I don't need a few days. I come to the conclusion that I submitted to this training one hundred percent and I can't back out now.

"No need, I'm with you," I say confidently.

He tells me that it's going to take us two days to get to where we're going. I suggested taking a car, but he tells me wolves don't have the luxury of cars, so we're running.

"The speed and endurance training was for this part wasn't it?" I ask, smiling.

"Yes it was," he admits.

"Well played," I chuckle.

A few days later, we take off running toward what will be our home for the next two months. On the way there, he explains that we aren't going to live amongst any wolves, we'll be living amongst what are known as dire wolves. I've never seen a dire wolf before, but I know they're supposed to be huge. I share my reservations about being around dire wolves, but he tells me not to worry.

It's a long run, but I can honestly say that I'm not as tired as I thought I'd be. We spend most of the time talking while running and only stop to eat or sleep a few hours before going back to it.

When we arrive, I half expect the wolves to see and then attack us, but they don't. Upon seeing my father, most of them ran up and hug him. This pack is at least 40 or 50 strong. It's shocking to see so many at once. These large wolves stop and stare at me, trying to figure me out. A few of them walk towards me, and I stand my ground.

These wolves are huge. Many standing as tall as I am and I'm 5ft 9. My father tells me not to show fear, and to show them who I am. The blue glow of my eyes grows slowly, yet intensely. A few of the wolves take a step back while the majority bow at my feet.

"W...what's going on?" I ask.

"They are acknowledging you not only as an alpha, but as the Tremauré," he responds. "They sensed it from you the moment we arrived, but weren't sure until now. Most have only heard rumors of the Tremauré and many don't believe he ever existed, but seeing that blue glow, they know that not only did he exist, but he's come back. They know that you're here to learn and are happy to teach you."

"How could they know I'm the Tremauré?" I ask, confused.

"All will be revealed in due time," he responds softly.

"Okayyy... what would they have done, if I was a beta?" I ask.

"Your status would be lower, but coming as an alpha and the Tremauré, you're nothing short of a king."

I ask him about this place and he explains that the House of Luna owns 75 acres of this land as a private reserve to keep wolves safe. It enables them to live and hunt without the worry of poachers. There are places like this all over the world that keep the wolf population from ever dying out. Wolves are great for the environment, just like anything else and as werewolves we can help keep them alive.

We strip naked and transform into our crinos. I stay in my crinos for 14 hours before I get overwhelmed. My father tells me that I stayed longer than he anticipated. My body aches like I was just born. I can't explain it, something inside forced me to go back to my homid. I take an hour break before I transform once more. I struggle to transform back, but he tells me to take it easy since it's the first day.

In the weeks that follow I practice staying in my crinos until I can last for 24 hours. Now it's been a month and I notice that my hands, feet and muscles are stronger than ever. I feel my body changing, further merging the wolf and I together, melding us into the same being. I thought we were close before, but this is something new.

Living amongst the dire wolves has been interesting. Learning to track and hunt like them is like seeing true nature. Seeing how wolves interact with nature and the ecosystem. I'm being taught how powerful my bite, and my claws can truly be, and instead of using them for just fighting, I'm using them for survival.

It's been a month and I've learned so much from living like a wolf. Unfortunately, I'm still having trouble staying in crinos the entire time. My father suggests that I meditate while human and in crinos. There are some tough times, but just like everything else, staying in my crinos becomes natural. I'm now able to stay in wolf form for over 18 hours. Now at the second month, I don't feel like I'm done with this part of my training. I tell my father that he was right about us being here and I ask if we can stay with the wolves a little longer. I have a lot to learn from them. He happily obliges, saying that being here for 4 months was always a part of the plan.

The next two months are like living a dream, I see the world differently, in a way that I never thought possible. My sense of smell is keener and my hearing is elevated. It's been almost seven months since I started training with my father and I didn't imagine it being this freeing. Free expression to be a werewolf, when I always have to hide amongst many others.

I thought I'd miss all the amenities of the modern world, but now, I barely think about it. I love feeling the wind in my fur, and only living off the bounty that the forest supplies. We don't eat more than we need to nor do we take from our own. I'd live like this for the rest of my life if I could.

Now it's the end of the fourth month, I walk over to my father while still in my crinos. I want to ask him what we were going to do next, hoping can maybe extend our stay a little longer. I see him kneeling in his human form, pulling clothes out of his duffle bag. I'm curious about what he's doing since he hasn't told me why he's back to his homid.

Before I can ask, he stands up and speaks to me telepathically, "Damien my Son, it's time for us to go."

"Already?" I ask, telepathically.

"You've completed this trial two months ago, as much fun as it is to live here, we shouldn't stay here much longer. You're starting to want to stay here aren't you?" he asks in a strong tone.

I transform back into my homid, "H...how did you know?" I stammer.

"It's this place, this...training. It can cause you to lose your humanity and influence you to stay in your crinos forever. If you do, your body will forget the difference between crinos and homid soon you'll be locked." There's a seriousness in his eyes.

"What do you mean locked?" I ask him.

"My brother, your uncle, locked himself after 5 months of being out here, like any werewolf who stays in crinos for more than 5 full moons."

"What happened to him?" I ask concerned.

he sighs, "Did you ever wonder why these wolves are so big?"

"Honestly, I never thought about it," I answer.

"This is what happens," he says as a wolf approaches us. "Your body forces the two beings together, fusing them into one."

"Are you saying that all of these wolves..." I stop as I come to the realization.

"Correct...all these wolves were once werewolves, that are now stuck as dire wolves and can never turn back," he says, softly.

"H...how long!?" I exclaim.

"Some fifty years, some longer, but one commonality about them is that if any werewolf stays in their crinos for more than 5 full moons, you become one. It's why this training isn't used anymore."

I look at him puzzled, "is that why the myth of dire wolves are similar to werewolves?"

he nods his head, that's exactly right."

"…w…wow," I stammer looking at the ground.

"Now it's not all bad, some choose this life," he adds.

"Why would anyone ever choose to live as a wolf?" I ask.

"The reasons differ from person to person," he replies. "But some are here to become free. To be one with nature the only way they know how. Others were sent here as punishment by the council."

I observe all the surrounding wolves. For the first time I see it, behind each of their eyes, I can identify the person they once were. I have a new respect for the power I was born with, and the pride of being a werewolf. It almost makes me cry thinking about it. I hug each of them tightly, thanking them for letting me be with them.

Soon after, I grab my clothes and get dressed. He's right, it's time for us to go. Just before we leave, I stand in the middle of the entire pack, illuminating my eyes as I meet their gaze. This time everyone takes a bow. Before I take my first step to leave, I hear all of their voices in my head.

They start telling me to take care of myself and to do all that I can to protect our race. They have so much faith in me, many of them sound like family saying goodbye while you're trying to leave a family reunion. I sense the love that this pack shares and I'm grateful that they've shared it with me. Hearing their voices fill my heart.

In order to protect our race I have to become the Alpha of the House of Luna, it's the only way I can really make a change. My father and I start making our way back home. I hear their voices fade the further we get. I'll never forget any of them.

On the way home, Dad tells me to call my pack. He says it's time we meet up with everyone. It's been 4 months since I saw them and I'm anxious to get back to my pack, my girlfriend, and civilization. At first, I thought to text our group chat, but I call them using telepathy instead.

"Everyone meet me at the Den in two days," I say, telepathically.

"Roger," Braheem responds.

"Look what the wolf blew in, I'll be there," acknowledges Jasmine.

"Abucheo, I'm so happy you're coming home!" Catalina squeals.

"Can't wait," Darius answers.

"Bout time," Omar mocks. "I was getting restless.

"We're getting the band back together," Chantelle celebrates.

"I'm so happy to be seeing everyone!" Kiara says, joyfully.

"I guess if everyone's going, I'll go," Nichole laughs.

Suddenly, there's a long pause. I wait, but I don't hear Kahlil's voice, "Has anyone heard from Kahlil?" I ask. "Where is he?"

"Damien…Kahlil's dead," Chantelle says somberly. "He's…been dead for a few years…you know this."

"N…n…no that's not right, I know he's alive!" I stutter.

"Relax bro, I'm here," Kahlil laughs. "I just wanted to mess with you since you ditched us for months. I'll be there Captain."

"Y'all suck," I laugh.

"Next time don't stay so long on those nature hikes," Kahlil mocks.

For the next few hours, we talk as my father and I run back to the city. It's such a relaxing feeling hearing us all talking together. Once we finally get back home, I thought that I'd be tired and that I'd want to sleep, but that isn't the case. I'm still wide awake, I want to go over Catalina's, but my father tells me that I should rest. I can't, I have the energy of a kid at an amusement park. 30 minutes later, I'm so tired that I fall asleep as soon as I feel the warmth of my bed.

When I wake up, I lay in my bed, unable to stop reflecting on everything I've lived through. I know I'm lucky to be alive. Me being attacked at a young age, my first change, Catalina finding out, fighting Darnell, dying to save Kahlil, the mercenary, Monique's assault and getting captured by Timothy. In any of those situations, it could have been my last day of my life. I have a lot to live up to in two different ways, but as long as I have my family behind me, I know I can tackle anything. I'm excited to see what else my father has in store for me. Knowing he'll be with me in the future to guide me gives me hope.

Without realizing it, I have to be at the Den in twenty minutes. I check my phone and see a few missed calls and texts from everyone. I respond, telling them that I'll be there soon. I get up, change my clothes and leave my house. I see my father standing in the front yard smiling. We race to the Den, zipping through traffic attempting to avoid being caught by traffic cameras.

One by one everyone shows up with their mentors. We are so excited to see each other that we hug in a huge circle. After we were done reminiscing and playing a few games, my father stood on the high rock.

"Welcome everyone, I've heard great things about your training and I am very pleased with the results. You've learned everything in record time and have exceeded our, no, my expectations. And now it's time to start the next part of your training," A grin appears on his face. "Up 'till now, you've been learning separately. Now, it's time to see how what you've learned works within the pack."

He proceeds to tell us that we have the night to ourselves. He also tells us that we won't hear from him or his pack for the next three months. We are to continue together from here on out. Whatever we have to work on, we have to rely on each other to help. They won't teach us any further. Whatever we do from here on out is up to us.

We have many questions, but none are answered. We say our awkward goodbyes and they take their leave. I give mom and dad one last hug before walking over to Catalina to give her a long awaited kiss. I haven't seen her in months and I'm not wasting any time. Seeing her face is always the best part of my day.

"I'm sorry I was gone so long," I begin to say. "I love you so much."

"I love you too, Abucheo," she smiles with tears in her eyes.

I see the tears forming in her eyes and I wipe them away as I pull her in close, letting her head rest on my chest. We step away from the others and share a nice walk under the night sky. We talk about how we've missed one another and what we can do for the next three months. It's great to hear her voice, smell her perfume and feel her touch. I bask in all of it as much as I can.

After an hour or so, we rejoin the others. I step up to my high point to speak to everyone, "Okay now that we're all reacquainted, it's time to get back to business," I announce. "It's almost 10 and there's no full moon tonight. That's not going to stop me from asking if we should run as wolves or as humans?"

"Wolves!" Everyone shouts in unison.

"Of course, let's not let night go to waste, let's run!" I shout.

I look up to the sky and take one deep breath. Focusing my senses, smelling the grass, the trees, the leaves, and the other animals in the forest alongside us. I can hear and smell everything around me. I can feel all the changes in the air pressure. Even the gentlest breeze against my skin. I have never felt this powerful before.

When I open my eyes, I see everyone staring at me. I try to figure out why, but I can't. I look down at myself and notice that without trying, I turned into my crinos. I didn't feel myself do it. I thought I was still human. My clothes are torn and all over the place. I laugh as Catalina comes next to me and turns, ripping her clothes as well.

Shortly after I raise my hand and Braheem, Darius, Omar and Kahlil all turn bursting through their clothes as they laugh. Catalina raises her hand and Jasmine, Chantelle, Kiara and Nichole turn ripping straight through their clothes. We'll be naked after this, but it's worth it.

"D, I don't know what training you've been doing, but you look just like your father," Braheem says, telepathically.

"I agree with Braheem," Omar confirms. "You also have the same presence you had when you fought that Tailor."

"Which time?" I ask.

"When you became the Tremauré, you're emanating a strong aura that reaches for miles," Omar explains.

"I have to say it is a really good look for you," Catalina says as she bumps my shoulder.

"I guess I ought to if I'm going to take on the family legacy right?" I admit. "I might as well look the part. Let's go everyone."

I lead us all into the forest, running faster than ever before. I hear their thoughts in my head as we play through the night. It's honestly like we were never apart. Being with everyone makes me appreciate every moment we've had together. All the growth and all the tears we've shed. Honestly, I don't know where I would be if it wasn't for them.

Chapter 19

It's been a month since I've heard from my father and I'm not sure what to do. Every day for months we've been side by side training and things were going well, so why do we have free rein after all this time? He had very strict rules that we needed to follow, but now he tells us to work on the rest of our training ourselves.

I am enjoying the new free time, but I'm left wondering what's next. What's the purpose of not contacting any of us for three months? I try not to think about it, because I know it's for something important. I tried talking to my mom about it, but she tells me that she can't tell me anything. Her words are short, yet haunting, it gets me thinking that something big is happening.

2 months have now gone by and I still can't figure it out. We've been training together and it's been fun seeing what everyone has learned. Catalina calls and says she wants to throw me a party to celebrate my 25th, but I'm not sure if I want a party. My birthday is a month away and she asks me about cake, presents and where I'd want to go, but I haven't given it much thought. I give her a few ideas and tell her to keep it a

surprise. After I get off the phone with her, I finally hear from my father, who texts me to meet him.

The message he sent includes an address. When I search it on maps, I see that it's the same location as the Basement. The Basement burned down, why is he requesting I meet him there? I text him back, but he doesn't reply. Curious, I go to the Basement's location. Once I arrive at the warehouse, I expect to see a vacant lot, but that's not what I find. I see him standing in front of a newly erected building.

"W... wait what's going on?" I ask.

"I had this building rebuilt after it burned down and had it converted into a training area for all of you," he says, smiling. "Now this place can be used as a *real* base of operations."

He pulls a remote from his pocket and presses a button and the doors open. The building looks the same on the outside, but when we enter I see that it's not.

"Kahlil, my design team and I worked on this place after he recovered," he explains. "He told me how much this place meant to all of you so we worked on getting this place ready for all of you."

He shows me around, the main floor has many uses, like for meetings and even has separate offices for all of us. There's a fully functional kitchen and three bathrooms. Sitting in the far corner, there's a large meeting table with enough seats for everyone that sits in front of an 85 IN TV. My eyes widen as I look around the room. Never in my wildest dreams did

I think the Basement place could look like this. He shows me an entertainment center that's filled with surround sound and gaming systems.

He tells me that we can use this place to our heart's content. Everything has been paid for and is state of the art. He sits me down at the meeting table to show me that there are sublevels below designed for each of us. Sort of like a dungeon and my level is at the very bottom. We can decorate it however we choose. There's a security room linked to cameras, monitors and motion sensors just in case anyone tries to break in.

I honestly don't know what to say. I was sure that the Basement was gone forever and I had Kahlil looking for another location. Who knew he had this in his back pocket? I ask him why he did all this, he simply says that it's a final gift before my final test. Suddenly his mood changes. The expression on his face is something I can't place. It's ominous if I'm being honest.

"Damien, there's something I didn't tell you," he says solemnly.

I stare at him intensely, "What is it?"

"As you know I'm training you to take my place as Alpha for the House of Luna," he reminds me.

"Of course that's the whole point," I respond.

"That's not all," he pauses. "In order for you to take over for me, you'll have to kill me and absorb my power to take as your own."

"Y...you're joking right?" I chuckle.

"No...I'm not," he says in a serious tone. His gaze doesn't break for a moment.

"I'm already an alpha, why do I need to kill you?" I exclaim.

"It's not the same," he sighs. "You killed an alpha and took his power. He comes from a lower status than us and same goes for when you killed Monique. It's not the same as if you killed me or any alpha from one of the Council."

I'm at a loss for words, "But...D...Dad, I don't want to kill you. I mean I want to carry on the family legacy, but I don't want to do it that way."

"It is your time and you are ready," he proclaims. "I've lived on this earth for two hundred years and I've done all I can when it comes to protecting our way of life. It's time for me to pass the torch. I couldn't have wished for a better son. Unfortunately, anything I teach you from this point forward would impede your growth."

"You can't be serious!" I shout as I jump up from my chair.

"I had the same reaction when your grandfather came to me with this," he admits. "The difference is he told me this, years before he started my training. If I told you back then you never would have wanted to start."

"You're damn right!" I exclaim. "I just can't believe that out of all the things werewolves can do and this is the only way I can succeed you," I blurt out. "I've never killed anyone without a reason and I don't have a reason to kill you."

I want everything he's telling me to be a test of my resolve. He's trying to see if I can kill him to become alpha. That has to be the case right? Unfortunately, he has the same intense stare in his eyes. Is this really the only way for me to succeed him? I only met him a year ago. The only other person who's answered so many of my questions about myself. The person I aspire to be. There's so much I want to ask him, so much more I want to learn.

Before I can utter my next statement, he tells me to leave it for the night and to go home. I feel so awkward about the entire thing that I'm not sure who to talk to. I'm not sure how to bring it up. Can I really kill my own father? For the next few days, I can't focus on anything, basic duties take me twice as long to do. There's no way I can kill my father after only knowing him for a year.

Two weeks have gone by and my mind is still in a fog. The days blend together. I've been keeping this to myself. I think it's best I talk to mom, hopefully she can talk some sense into him. She's home today, I'll help her do some yard work and find a way to bring it up.

The entire time we're working I'm trying to work up the nerve to talk to her about it. Just before I can, she goes inside to get some water. Two minutes later, I hear her scream my name. I turn around and run inside. Now in the kitchen, I see the fridge is wide open and the faucet is running and she's nowhere to be found.

"Damien, help me!" I hear her scream.

Her voice doesn't sound like she's too far, so I run in the direction of her voice. I run to the front yard and down the block. I can't hear her voice anymore, so I try to follow her scent, but it stops after a few blocks. I go back to the house to investigate, hoping to find any clues left behind. I'm seriously worried, but I try to remain calm.

I sense fear when I'm searching the house. There's a faint scent of a few others, not just Mom's. It's a very familiar scent, I've been around them before. They're members of my father's pack! I spot a note left on the counter that I missed when I initially rushed in.

It reads, *'Damien, we have your mother, if you want her back, come to the Basement with your pack. We'll be waiting with your father.'*

"I have to get her back!" I shout. I put two fingers to my forehead and call out, "Everyone, I don't have time to explain, meet me at the Basement."

Seconds later, everyone hears my request and rushes over. I take off running, rather than staying in my homid, I shift into my glabro to sprint at 100 MPH. I have to make it to the Basement, Mom's life could be in danger. I arrive at the same time everyone else does. As soon as the last person appears, I immediately start explaining.

"My father had the Basement rebuilt after it exploded. Not only that, but he reinforced it. I don't know all the specifics, but I do know that he had my mom captured and they brought her here. I can't exactly tell you what will be waiting for us once we get in there, but I'm going in."

Without blinking, everyone steps up. As a way of saying I didn't need to ask. I thank them as we slowly enter the front door. The lights on the inside are on, and we see the large, open floor. It looks the same as when I was here two weeks ago. There's no one in sight. We stay in formation as we cautiously walk through the room. I see a sign that points us to an elevator. We get on it and it only goes down one floor. When the doors open we see an empty space with a door on the other side. As we proceed forward, we're stopped by Isaiah, one of my father's pack members.

"Isaiah, what are you doing?" Darius asks. "You have to let us pass."

"There's only one way to continue from this point and get to master Damien's mother, and that's through this door, we talked about this." he says as he points behind him.

"Isaiah, you taught me a lot, so I'll ask you nicely to get out of our way," Darius insists.

"Nah, I won't be doing that," Isaiah smirks.

"I'll move you if I have to," Darius threatens.

"Good luck with that," Isaiah says with a grizzly smile.

He pushes a button on the wall behind him as Darius charges. The room starts to change. The floor is replaced with balance beams in the middle of it. Darius screams for us to continue while he handles Isaiah. I feel kind of bad leaving him, but I know I have to trust in his ability to handle this. We continue to the next chamber, where we're stopped by Catherine, another one of my father's pack members. Now she's standing in our way.

"Ooh, good job getting past Isaiah," she begins to say. "But you know Nichole is the one who has to fight me, so the rest of you can continue."

Nichole steps up, "I'm ready, let's get this over with so I can kick your ass!"

"Are you sure about this?" I ask.

"Yes I'm sure, I got this," I've never seen such a determined look from her before, she's usually such a laid back person. "Go get your mom," Nichole cheers.

"Right," I nod. "Let's go."

Then as if on cue, both of them start fighting one another. Katherine pushes a button on the wall and suddenly heavy boulders and logs start swinging back and forth. Nichole isn't bothered by the change of the room. She tells us to get on the elevator and continue going down.

One by one, chamber after chamber, there's a challenger for everyone. It's just like he said, there was a special room designed for each of us. One stays behind, while the others proceed. It goes on like this until it's just Catalina and me. As we step into the second to last room, we see that it's completely empty. It's nothing like the other chambers.

We cautiously walk through the large, empty space, with our guards up. Every step feels like we're moving closer to our own undoing.

"Both of you stop!" We hear a voice echo throughout the area.

Suddenly, my mom comes from beneath the floor, peering directly at us. It then dawns on me that this would be the room where Catalina will be the one fighting.

"You were never in any real danger were you?" I ask, sternly.

"Very good, my bright boy," Mom responds. "We had to find a way to get you all here and one by one. Each person fights and kills their mentor. Just like you will your father."

"You knew all of this from the very beginning?" Catalina cries out.

"Of course I did, at first I didn't think you'd all go for it, but when a mother's in danger, her child would stop at nothing to protect her," My mom says, proudly. "Catalina, Hija, I'm sure as you know it's your turn to fight me while Damien goes to fight his father."

I was about to say something, but Catalina stops me, "Damien...you know she's right don't you?"

"But that can't be, you're about to fight to the death...with my mother," I say, worriedly.

"I know that, it's not like any of us want this, but it's what needs to happen," Catalina says in a soft and caring tone. "I'll do everything I can to not kill her, but I may not have a choice."

"Why would I let the two of you fight?" I say as my eyes well up.

"Dae Dae, it's part of your training, just like it's a part of hers," Mom answers. "Neither of us want this, but it's the way it has to be."

"Why does it have to be this way? Why can't it be different!?" I question.

"It can be different, but not until after you take your father's place and use your power as the Tremuaré to change things. Now go!!" My mom screams as she points to the door.

Hearing my mother's words and seeing the determination on both of their faces, I know there's no turning back. I have to press on by myself to confront him. I just hope that by leaving the two of them, I'm not abandoning either of them. I run forward, and get on the elevator. As I'm making my way down the hall, I hear the fighting between them begin.

The doors open and the light on the other end of the hall turns on. This my father's doing, if anyone can stop this, he can. Just as I enter the final chamber, I see him sitting at the far end of the room, in a very large chair.

"Damien, are you ready for your final trial?" he asks in an ominous tone. "From this point forward, I will not be holding back, so prepare yourself for the fight of your life, Son."

He pushes a button on the wall and just like every other room, it changes. Rather than something balance based or something that made fighting completely difficult all together, the ceiling opens up. The smell of fresh pine, wood and grass enters the entire chamber. I look and see a beautiful starlit night sky.

"I'm here aren't I?" I ask. "I don't think I would be able to be here if I wasn't. You made sure of that."

"The apple doesn't fall far from the tree," he smirks.

"I also don't expect you to take it easy on me," I proclaim.

My father stands from the chair and we each take a step toward one another. I take off my shirt and he does the same. I shift into my glabro and he follows suit.

"Are you ready?" he asks menacingly.

"There's nothing between us but air and opportunity," I say confidently. "And I have more than enough air, so let's go."

He charges at me and throws the first punch when I come into his range. The fight is on, we're going blow for blow, matching with one another. I'm getting hit here and there, but I hold my own. It's almost like I'm fighting myself. I know I can defeat him, but can I kill him? He sees my conflict and catches me off guard by sweeping my leg, and knocking me to the ground.

From that point forward, he leads with a ground and pound. All I can do is guard myself against his onslaught of punches. I have to escape his attack or I'll lose and he'll kill me. I have to stop thinking about not hurting him and start fighting back. I block one punch and counter with another before throwing him off of me.

I jump to my feet while my father looks at me and wipes his face. My punch rattles him, but only for a second. We start going back at it, this time no matter what I do, his moves are faster, more precise, and stronger. He punches me in the face, claws at my chest and punches me in the abdomen. Before taking a few steps back, I drop to the floor coughing.

"C'mon Damien, I taught you better than this," he says, harshly. "Fight me without mercy, or it'll be you who dies tonight."

I'm hunched over on the floor coughing. Just as he says that, Darius appears in the chamber gasping for breath and covered in blood. He's already defeated Isaiah...killed Isaiah.

"Damien, don't worry, I'm here for you bro!" Darius screams across the room. "We're in this together and nothing is going to stop us! You're going to die if you don't fight at full strength. Trust me."

Upon hearing his words, I cough once more, wipe my mouth and get back to my feet. He's right, I do have to stop holding back. All the training and fighting

338

I've done up to this point means nothing if I don't fight for those who'll fight for me. I thank him for his words of encouragement.

I go at him this time without holding back. I still don't want to kill him, so I'll subdue him. My strikes become cleaner, exact and controlled. I can win, I've done so, so many times before. I start overpowering him, catching him with a left hook and then a right, finally ending my combo with a spartan kick to his chest that throws him back a few feet.

My father catches himself, and smiles back at me, "Good, good Damien. Use your power to overwhelm your opponent. Your power is yours, the wolf is you and you are the wolf."

Less than two seconds after he says that, he sprints toward me without warning. A barrage of punches and kicks in various combinations come my way. The only thing I can do is evade him. I barely have any wiggle room to counter or find my opening. I have to step up my game even more.

Though I'm trying, I can't stop him. Every punch that connects feels like I'm getting hit by a brick. Even if I'm able to find an opening and throw a punch, he counters and hits me even harder. I'm on the verge of losing. I thought I was gaining the upper hand, but I was wrong. He knocks me down and I struggle to get back to my feet. While sparring, I was determined to beat him as a father/son competition, not ending his life.

"Damien, get up!" I hear Catalina scream, as I see her running into the chamber.

I didn't notice anyone else entering after Darius. They're all pretty banged up. I see that they're tired and seriously hurt. It's going to take them some time to heal since their wounds are werewolf inflicted, yet they're still here for me. This is no different from before.

"Damien look, all your friends are here and they've completed their fights, they're just waiting for you," my father says. "Don't keep them waiting."

"Yea I guess they have, haven't they?" I laugh. "I must look pretty pathetic."

I look at all of their faces, the worried, saddened expressions that they wear. I can't let all their hard work, everything they've sacrificed to be here with me go to waste. Killing people they spent the year getting to know, because they believe in me. I can beat him. I have to fight for myself the same way they fought for me. I'm they're alpha and it's time I act like it.

"Dad, I want to thank you for everything you've done for me," I begin to say. "But all of my friends beat their final test, and so will I. They've fought so hard for me and I know I need to do this to prove that I can become the Alpha of the House of Luna, but I still wish there was another way."

I brace my stance and illuminate my eyes with the power of the Tremauré. I growl and race toward him. I fight with all of my power and all of my training behind me. He tries to stop me, but he can't. I'm stronger than him, faster than him. He gave me the skills necessary to do what needs to be done and I will not waste it.

His defense is nothing to my offense and I use it to knock him onto his back. He tries to get back up, but I immediately knock him back down. I pin him down and roar in his face.

He starts laughing as he talks, "Damien, you've done a great job, now kill me so you can take your rightful place as alpha."

My father closes his eyes with a peaceful smile. As I was about to dig my claws in his chest and rip out his heart, I pause. I know what I'm supposed to do, but he's still my father.

"You're still lacking the necessary motivation, let me help you," he says, harshly. He throws me off of him and uses his claws to go for my throat, slowly trying to rip it out. I feel his claws in neck." C'mon Damien, what are you going to do?!"

I inhale sharply and react by kicking him across the room. When his back hits the wall he's too stunned to move. I take my chance and rush toward him and punch through his chest. The same familiar blood warmth of blood covers my hand. As I rip it out, he falls from his feet and I hear him gasping for air as he takes his last breath. I lay him on the ground. He wants to say something, so he holds his hand up and I take his into my own.

"Good job Son, I… I…"

That 's it, he can't get out his last words. I know he wanted to say more, but he died before he could get it all out. A surge of energy pulses through my body and I feel a connection that I didn't have before. It starts in my hands and flows through the rest of me.

As incredible as this feels, the only thing I feel is overwhelming sorrow. I just killed my father. Tears form in my eyes as Catalina walks up to me and puts her hand on my shoulder. The others follow close behind.

"Damien," Catalina says in a soft voice.

I don't move, I can't move. I'm frozen in place. They stand there behind me unsure of what to do.

"I… I killed him," I whimper, looking at my blood soaked hand.

"Damien, go ahead bro, no one's going to think any less of you if you do it," Braheem insists.

I close my eyes and take in as much air as I can, only holding it for a second before letting out the loudest roar I have ever done in my life. I'm screaming to the heavens for my parents. My roar echoes throughout the entire complex and the night sky. In a single night, I lost both my parents. One of which was killed by my own hands. The roar then turns into a loud cry. I start sobbing over my father's body.

"D c'mon, we've got to go," Omar urges.

"No, I won't leave him!" I scream.

One after one, they leave me alone in the chamber. Shortly after, I gather my mother's body and lay it next to my father's and I sit between them. They're the ones who brought me into this world and it's because of me that their lives ended at the same time. I look up upon hearing the sound of thunderclouds overhead. I walk over and press the button to close the roof. I watch as the cover slowly closes over my head. Before the sky is completely covered, I look at my parents' bodies, wishing that they find peace.

As the final piece of the cover seals shut, I feel it also shutting on my soul. Would I be able to carry on without their guidance? The complete darkness of the room is just right. I want to be alone in the darkness, I deserve to be.

Chapter 20

It's been a few months since the death of my parents and after everything that's happened, I wasn't into celebrating my birthday or doing anything with anyone. I just shut down and shut myself off from the outside world. I haven't spoken to anyone in weeks and I've barely left the house. Most days I just sit on the couch for hours on end, contemplating life.

A few hours after everything was over, some people from both the werewolves Council and the House of Luna came to pick up all the bodies. There was barely anything said other than them saying that they were sorry for my loss and that the Council should be in contact with me about taking my father's place. I don't want anything to do with them, I just want to bury my parents without any red tape.

Council members and wolves from House of Luna all attend my father's funeral. There are also others who claim that they're business partners. It's my first time seeing his body since that night and I'm frozen when I see him in the casket. When I see Tevin, I'm not sure what to say to him, so after the service, Catalina and I go home.

The service that we hold for my mother includes a lot of her close friends. Some of whom I can tell are Tailors. Jakobe, Davion, Jamal and Terrance all attend as well. When I spot them they're accompanied by their parents. During the ceremony, I don't let myself get too close to them. They don't know that it was me who defeated Timothy and killed Bruce. When they get close enough to offer their condolences, I remain quiet. Everything I say at her vigil is kept brief as I almost out myself for being responsible for her death.

After their burials, I move their bodies to a separate location, so none of their enemies try to take their body parts as trophies. The official story we tell everyone is mom was hit by a hit-and-run driver and no one has been found, though the police are still looking.

After I make sure they are in a secure location, I go into self-isolation. I'm broken, because I killed my parents just to get a title. I don't care about anything anymore. I'm unable to get the image of my parents lying dead next to me out of my head. Every time I close my eyes, it's all I see. It keeps me up at night.

Catalina and the others stop by occasionally to try their best to cheer me up and keep me company. However, I'm not the best company. I thank them for their efforts, but I want to be left alone. At first, I said that I'll be fine, although I'm not sure anymore. Eventually they stop coming around and tell me to contact them when I'm ready. The only time I can get away from the numbness is by running, so for the last few months that's all I've been going. Night after night I go on a run, saying nothing to anyone about where I'm going.

I have to stay in homid because whenever I change, something goes wrong. It hurts so bad when I transform into crinos. It's so bad that for the first time in years I'm afraid of the wolf. I feel the same enormous pain of my bones breaking, and the intense, fiery needle like hair that protrudes from my skin. I'm in searing pain every time I transform. And just like before I lose myself, not knowing where I am when I wake up in the morning.

I haven't told anyone about my issues in transforming, so I forgo transforming all together. The furthest I can do is glabro. It's the only way to prevent me from blacking out when I transform. I don't know what I'm doing. I'm in fear of what I'll do. With the power of the Tremauré, who can stop me?

Tonight, like many before, I'm running through the woods trying to find an escape from my feelings. I run through the woods as fast as I can for as long as I can. I want to keep running, it's the only time I feel free. I keep a speed of 115 MPH, making sure that no Tailors or humans can see me.

"Damien, slow down!" I suddenly hear Catalina calling out to me.

When I see it's her, I slow down. If she was anyone else, I would've kept going and eventually lost them, but I can't do that to her. I love her way too much. I've shut everyone else out. I can't do that to her.

"Abucheo, why are you three states away?" she asks. "Where are you running to?" she has a concerned look on her face.

"I...I don't know," I respond. "I didn't realize how far away I am. When I'm running, it's the only time I can think clearly."

"Why, what's wrong?" she asks.

"I don't know, maybe it's because I'm not worthy to be the next Alpha of the House of Luna, the Tremauré, or even an alpha," I blurt out.

"What are you talking about, of course you are," she asserts.

"If that's true, then why did my parents have to die?!" I scream. "They died because of me. They died so I could achieve my birthright, but so what!?"

"Abucheo stop, talk to me," she pleads.

"There's no point, no matter what I do, I seem to get someone killed, captured or hurt. You should stay away from me."

I hang my head low and I drop to my knees. She sits in front of me and takes my head in her own. She pulls me in close and rests my head on her chest. The more I think about this, the angrier I become. I feel my anger rising, about to burst through me. I want to talk, but my breathing changes and becomes erratic. I want to feel the taste of blood in my mouth. I don't care if it's human or animal. I want to feel it running all over my tongue.

"Damien!" Catalina screams.

I snap out of my trance, she must've been calling me for a while, for her to scream as loudly as she did, "What? What just happened?"

"I don't know, but I didn't like it," she says in a scared tone. "Please don't shut me out."

"I won't, I promise," I apologize.

"Also promise me that you will stop running from yourself" she requests.

I sigh softly as I caress her face, "I promise."

We head back home, crossing the multiple state lines. I didn't realize how far I actually ran. I want to tell her what I'm feeling and what's really going on with me, but where do I start? I thought I could figure it out on my own, but my control of the wolf is all over the place. I have to fix this before the wolf attempts to take me over.

Can I gain back control or is this just a small hiccup? I can't be sure. This is driving me crazy, but I have to try. I have plenty of time for me to try to figure this out. I hope I haven't alienated everyone and it's not too late to ask for forgiveness. I'm so distracted that I didn't notice when we got to the front of my house. I just stare at it, not wanting to go inside. It's so empty without my mom. Catalina pleads for me to go inside with her and I do. We fall asleep with me holding her.

The following night, Catalina goes out with some friends. I grab my hoodie and decide to go on another run. I think it's time I take her advice and try to stop running from my feelings, but what's the first step? Since running is the only time I feel free, I'll use it to stop running from my feelings. This time, I won't go three states away.

I decide to run in an area close to the Den. I start thinking about the power I've been given. Starting from becoming a werewolf then becoming an alpha and now the Tremauré who's the Alpha of the House of Luna. Why am I having issues when I transform? Is it the power that my father had? Can I learn to control this? All these questions are driving me crazy. I stop asking the questions and not getting answers. I can't deal with this right now.

I feel like fighting, I need to get some of this pent-up aggression out and a good fight will do it. I don't care about the type of fight, I just want a fight. I stop running and listen for anyone or anything that can give me what I want.

"Someone help me!" I hear a woman screaming.

My eyes shoot open, and I dart in the direction of the scream. I find a woman a short distance away who's being chased down an alleyway. I jump onto the rooftop to observe what's happening. That's when I see them, a young woman, who can't be more than 21, being chased by two guys deep into an alley. I continue to watch them, waiting for the right time to intervene. I see her attackers closing in on her.

"Oh c'mon honey, what's wrong?" One of the men asks. "All I want is a little kiss."

"Please, please leave me alone. I just want to go home," the young woman pleads.

"Hey Pete, I don't think she likes us very much," the other says.

"I think you're right, she doesn't seem too fond of us," Pete replies. "Oh well, I guess we have to see what kitty has for us under that dress, since she wants to play hard to get."

They inch toward her. I can't take it anymore, I can clearly feel their predatory intentions for her. The vile things I sense coming from them make me sick to my stomach. I throw on my hood and jump from my perch and land in between the young woman and her would be attackers.

"Who the hell are you!?" Pete screams at me.

"The question isn't who I am, but what I'm going to do if you don't leave this woman alone," I declare.

"Ha, yea right kid, you have no idea what you're getting yourself into," he insists.

"Oh really? Why don't you show me?" I coax them.

"Be Careful, I don't want you to get hurt because of me," she warns.

"Don't worry, I can handle them," I say looking back at her smiling.

The other guy tries to sneak a punch, but it's so obvious that instead of dodging, I let it connect. He smiles, thinking he got me. I spit before turning back to him and grin. This is exactly what I'm looking for. He throws another with two more following behind that first one. He's better than I thought. He's

350

obviously fought before, but his punches can't hurt me. I could fight back, but I want to savor this.

Soon after, Pete joins in and they fight me at the same time. It makes me feel a little better knowing I can let out my anger on these two. Memories of my father start flashing in my mind, reminding me of the fights we had with each other. Unfortunately, as fun as this is, I can't let this go on for too long, so when I see my opening I take it. They're light work, so I have no choice but to pull my punches.

In punching both of them, I'm letting out my feelings, but I can't use them like punching bags. Eventually I knock them out, wishing it could have lasted longer, but I'm defending someone, not fighting for myself. I call the police after I sit them on the end of the alley for the police to pick them up. I check on the woman, who's fixing herself up, trying to get all the dirt from her dress.

I turn back to her, making sure to keep my head low and staying in the shadows. I don't care if the two of them saw my face, they need to know who whooped their asses.

"Are you ok?" I ask her.

"Yes, thank you," she says softly. "Are you hurt?"

"No, no I'm fine. I've taken a punch before," I answer.

"I can't thank you enough, those guys probably would have raped me if you hadn't intervened," she says horrified.

"I'm just glad that I was able to help you," I admit. "Do you have anyone you can call to take you home?"

"Y….yea, I came here with a few of my friends and they're in the bar. I just stepped outside to take a phone call when they came at me," she responds

"Great, then let's get you back there," I gesture to her to leave the alley.

I walk with her back to the bar and watch as she enters. She turns and offers to buy me a drink, but before she finishes her question, I jump onto the roof. She searches for me for a few seconds, but eventually goes inside the bar. I listen to make sure she finds her friends. After sorting through all the conversations, I hear her speaking with her friends, so I go home.

The next morning, I awake to the smell of waffles, eggs and sausage. Someone's making breakfast. At first, I think it's Mom since it smells like her cooking and I get excited and run to the kitchen. When I get there, I spot Catalina, the smile I had, slightly turns into a frown.

Catalina turns to me, "Abucheo, I just wanted to come over and cook you breakfast, since I know you're not eating well."

"Thank you baby, what time is it?" I yawn as I walk over and give her a kiss.

"It's 10:30, so it's still pretty early," she responds. "The food's almost done, so go sit down. How are you feeling?"

"I'm feeling better than I was before, I guess," I answer her.

Catalina asks me what happened last night, she came by but couldn't find me. I tell her about how I went running to figure things out, but I wasn't getting anywhere. Then I wanted to let out my anger and went looking for a fight. I heard a woman being attacked and saved her before things escalated and got her back safely. Since then I've been feeling better. Something about beating those guys up was everything to me.

I tell her that I feel like myself, more so than I have in months. I liked fighting those guys. I like fighting for someone else, and for the first time since my parents' deaths, I don't have a weight in my chest. Catalina places the plates on the table and takes my hand in hers. She stares deeply into my eyes.

"It's ok, you've been through a lot and you've been put under more pressure than any person could really handle," Catalina says in a heartfelt tone.

"No it's not, it's nowhere near acceptable the way I have been treating you, Darius, Braheem, Chantelle, Omar, Kahlil, Jasmine, Kiara, or Nichole," I proclaim. "I have to get a grip because If I don't..."

Before I can utter another word, Catalina pulls me in close for a kiss to stop my rambling.

"What happens if I keep blacking out every time I turn?" I ask. "I don't want to hurt anyone."

"Damien, I think you're going through the five stages of grief," Catalina says softly.

"The five stages of grief?" I ponder.

"Yes, the five stages of grief, Denial, Bargaining, Depression, Anger and Acceptance."

'What makes you say that?" I ask.

"I've been doing some digging online, because of how you've been acting the last few months. You're past the depression stage and now you're in the anger stage and the wolf inside you is reacting to your feelings of doubt. Which could explain why you're having issues turning and blacking out."

After she says that, there's a long pause before either one of us speaks. It's as if someone hit pause on the world around us. I can't hear the birds chirping, dogs parking or cars driving on the road. I sigh deeply and think to myself.

Maybe she's right. The death of my parents really took its toll on me. I didn't really really know my father or my mother after finding out she's a Tailor. Their blood is on my hands, even if Catalina was the one who killed my mother, I'm the reason that they were put in that situation.

"Catalina, you're right, I do need to deal with this," I finally say. "I need to move forward so *we* can move forward. You, me and the pack."

After we eat, I stand up and tell her I need to get dressed and go out. She asks me where I'm going. I tell her that I don't know where, but I need to go. I still have things to sort out. I tell her that I'll be back soon. I start to walk up the stairs and she stops me.

Catalina grabs my hand and says she's coming with me, but I protest.

"Boo, when you go off by yourself I get so afraid that it could be the last time I see you," she says in a caring tone. "Please go back into the dining room for a second."

I pull her in close and hold her head against my chest. I kiss her once on the forehead and then on her lips, "I love you so much that there's no comparison that anything means more to me than you," I say in a soft voice.

"Are you sure?" she asks, looking at me with loving eyes.

"Yes I'm sure," I smile.

As I hold her close, she puts her arms around me. We stand there for a few minutes holding each other. I tell her that I truly need to go. It took me too long to realize that I can't keep my feelings bottled up or try to fix it all by myself. I put my head on her chest and apologize for closing her out and not coming to her earlier.

Catalina tells me that everything is going to be alright and she isn't going anywhere. She'll be with me no matter what. I then ask her what I should do when it comes to controlling my wolf. I tell her that I'm not sure if I can turn anymore since every time I try, it hurts and I lose control. I tell her that I'm afraid to try. Catalina looks at me with the most confused expression I've ever seen. She's looking at me like she has no idea who I am.

"Wh… What's wrong?" I ask her.

She says nothing, she just stares at me and takes a few steps away. Catalina then looks me up and down and walks into the dining room. I follow her, but I instantly lose her. I search around the house, but she's nowhere to be found. I walk around once more and I finally find her standing in the living room with a cloth in her hand. There's something under it, but I can't tell what it is.

She has a blank expression on her face. I'm having trouble reading it. Without a second thought, Catalina throws whatever is in her hand directly at my head. I catch it and realize that it's one of my Mom's Tailor knives. The burning sensation singes my skin and I drop it.

"Catalina what the hell?" I ask irritated, while shaking my hand, trying to cool the burn off.

"I wanted to see what would happen," she says, in a stern voice.

"What do you mean, you wanted to see what would happen?" I question.

"I wanted to make sure that you're the man, and the wolf that I know."

"Okay and that has something to do with throwing silver at me?!" I exclaim.

"It has everything to do with me throwing that knife at you. Aren't you Damien Nichols?" she asks almost instantly.

"Yes?" I answer.

"The most dangerous werewolf in the world?" she continues to question.

"Yes?" I answer her again.

"The one with the power of the Tremauré?" she asks.

"Yes…" I responded with confusion.

"The heir to the House of the Luna?" she asks.

"Yes, where are you going with this?" I ask her.

"If that's who you are then I need you to start acting like it," she asserts. "You're an alpha who started his pack, not because you needed one or even because you wanted one. You started the pack to protect one another and that is the sole reason everyone is so loyal to you."

"Yea I guess so," I say, shrugging.

"Honey, listen to me, you have the power to be the greatest werewolf in history…" Suddenly, she stops speaking. I know there's more she wants to say, but she doesn't. She just keeps staring at me. Catalina then takes a few short breaths to calm herself down before continuing, "When it came to learning how to control the wolf under the full moon. You did it so you wouldn't hurt anyone, including me. You weren't sure if you could and yet you still tried and learned to control it. You're the strongest person I know and you never let doubt control you, so don't let it happen now."

After she says that, she walks out of the living room and leaves me alone. I sit down on the couch to think. Catalina isn't mad at me, she's upset that I lost confidence in myself. She wants what's best for me. Without trying to, I lost my meaning, my purpose for doing all of this. I had a name for it, but I can't even remember what that name is anymore. There's no definition for it, nor is there a real word for it either. She's trying to get me to remember why I do the things that I do. I commend her for that, I was given the responsibility to protect my people, all werewolves current and future. To be a symbol, just like the first Tremauré.

Up until now I've been keeping all of my feelings on the inside and I can no longer do that. I have to start healing. Catalina has been with me this entire time, ever since she found out I'm a werewolf. I can't wish for a better partner.

I stand up knowing what I need to do. I run up the stairs and put on some fresh clothes. I thank Catalina for getting my head on straight and I tell her that I'm going out, and not to worry because I'll be back and we'll talk. She looks at me with a smile and tells me that she'll be here when I get back.

Chapter 21

When I walk outside, I see the sun and for the first time in a while, I feel its warmth on my skin. I smile as I take off running. There's somewhere I've been avoiding for months. In order to confront my fears and deal with my pain, I have to visit my parents' grave.

I sprint at full speed with the full power of the wolf inside of me. It doesn't feel like I'm being held back. Since it's on the way, I stop at the Den to remove Kahlil's and Tevin's headstones. There's no reason to keep them anymore, they are alive. Upon seeing the headstones, I pick them up one by one and break each one over my knee. I proceed to smash them into smaller pieces, keeping them is a reflection of the past, not a sentiment to the future.

Once they're in small enough pieces, I run to the cemetery where my parents are buried. I haven't visited once since I had them moved. I wasn't ready until now, in order to confront my fears, and deal with my emotions. This is where I should have gone all along. As soon as I spot their graves, I stop. I didn't think I'd freeze when I got here, but here I am.

I stand there frozen for a few more minutes while I gather my thoughts. It's like there's an invisible wall stopping me. Unsure of what to do next, I continue to stand there staring at their gravestones. After a few minutes pass, I feel a gentle breeze behind me, like something is pushing me forward, trying to get me to take my first step. Can I do this?

Miraculously, I'm finally able to move. As I slowly approach the headstones, the surrounding air grows quiet. The only thing I can hear is the sound of the wind rustling through the trees in the distance. I drop to my knees, as I read their names.

I sit there for a few minutes waiting, hoping for something to happen. I'm anxiously waiting for something to put me on guard or something to tell me how I can stop suffering. I close my eyes and search for an answer. Is there something I'm missing? I feel the power of the Tremauré, and the power of the Alpha of the House of Luna flow through my body, but nothing else.

When I open my eyes, I feel a still calming sense of peace. I stare at their headstones, wishing that they can tell me what I'm supposed to do. Is there something I'm supposed to say? I'm so lost.

There's so much I want to say, but nothing is coming out. I hang my head in sorrow. A few seconds later, tears form in my eyes and fall from my face. The only thing I can manage to say is, "I'm sorry, Mom, Dad, I don't know what I'm supposed to do."

I can't control it anymore, my rage wells up inside of me, I want to break everything around me. I start punching at the dirt hoping it'll give me any sign of relief, but it doesn't. With all the power I have at my disposal why couldn't I save my parents? The Tremauré brought me back to life, so why couldn't he do the same for them? I couldn't figure out a way to keep them alive.

"Isn't there something I can do to bring them back?!" I scream to the heavens.

The birds and other animals hear my screams of pain and scurry off as fast as they can. I'm hunched over crying at their graves, laying everything onto the table. I thought I could hold it back, but I can't anymore. I began balling my eyes out asking for my mother and my father to come back. Asking to see them one more time.

"Damien," I hear a voice calling my name.

My ears perk up and I start looking around, wiping the tears from my eyes. I search, but I can't find the source of the voice.

"Damien, it's okay you didn't do anything wrong," the voice says.

My eyes shoot over to my mother's grave and I see her standing before me. I'm relieved to see her, but at the same time I'm afraid that my mind is playing tricks on me, "M…m…mom?" I say softly.

"Yes, Dae Dae," she responds. "I don't blame you for what happened."

"You should blame me, because if it wasn't for me, you'd still be alive," I exclaim. "I put both of you in serious danger all because of that stupid ass test."

"No sweetheart, I knew full well what I was getting into and I knew what was coming," she explains. "I was dreading the day you became a werewolf, but that doesn't mean I wasn't prepared for it. I could have stayed out of it, but I decided not to. It's a mother's job to help her son become a young man. And look at the young black king you've become."

"But Mom, you mean more to me than that!" I cry out.

"I will always be there for you, but you also have Catalina who loves you just as much as I do. You two have a love that your father and I shared and that's all I could have wished for you."

I feel grateful hearing my mother's words. How do I respond to that? Catalina is there for me in every way I need her, "I understand that, but that doesn't mean I won't need you in my life. A man will always need his mother."

Mom then smiles as her face begins to glow. Everything about her starts to light up just from her smile. I grew up with that smile. As I'm staring at her face, I'm reminded that I've seen Catalina with the same one. Mom will always be my mom, but Catalina is the one I should focus on.

Seconds later, my Dad appears beside her, "What are you doing here?" he asks sternly. "You should be continuing your training and securing your place as Alpha of the House of Luna."

I stare at him with a blank face, unsure of what to say. Another breeze blows past me, this time it's stronger than before, it sends a small shiver up my spine. Goosebumps begin forming along my arms and legs.

"It's hard for me to do that knowing that the reason you're not here is because of me," I finally say. "After a year I had to take your life. I didn't get a chance to know you. I know there are times I'll have to kill, but I know there's more I can learn from you."

He lets out a heavy sigh, "Damien, I've trained you in almost every way my father trained me. And you're right, it's not fair that we didn't get the chance to really know each other, but that's how our world works. I can only show you so much. There are things you'll have to learn on your own."

"I guess I can understand that, but I still wish I could have known you longer," I blurt out.

"If the circumstances were different then yes we would have had more time. But the fact of the matter is I don't have anything left to teach you."

"Meaning?" I ask.

"Meaning you're your own alpha and have been for a while now. I can't be there forever. If I stayed then you would have become like me. The Tremauré has his own path and that's why your training was only a year," he explains.

"That's not true!" I scream. "I know there's more you can teach me."

"Not true Son, I was raised around violence and fighting," he says. "If I stayed, then you would have grown attuned to how I do things. By growing up with your mother you have the one thing that I didn't. Do you know what that is?"

"No," I say as I shook my head.

"You have a way of controlling your power in a way I never could. You get stronger for those around you, not just for power to please your old man like I did. Every generation gets stronger than the last and you are by far stronger than I was at your age. I felt it the day you were born. You're meant to do great things beyond me."

After he says that, he stands there smiling at me with tears forming in his eyes. He tells me that he's proud of me. I ask him how he saw so much in me and he tells me that whenever I'm fighting for the sake of others, my power is unmatched and I still have so much potential. He can't help me unlock it, but I'll find out who can.

He says he got tougher toward me at the end to show me that the Council isn't going to be as lenient as him. He tells me to remember to believe in myself and believe in my pack. He reminds me that he's been watching me from the shadows ever since my fight with Darnell. Then when I became the Tremauré, he couldn't have been happier that our king chose a member of our family to change the world.

He tells me that I was chosen because I wanted to protect, not wanting more power to control anyone else. Then the memory of what happened that day pops into my mind. The darkness that enclosed my mind vanishes and the memories of becoming the Tremauré reveal themselves. I was revived because I felt bad that I couldn't save them and that's all I thought about. The Tremauré could have let me die and asked anyone, but he saw something in me and made me his successor.

"Son, we've taught you all that we can," they say in unison. "We knew the risks in giving you all trials to make sure to guide you this far."

I stare at them smiling back at me. I guess I finally understand why things happened the way that they did. I feel both of the hands touch the top of my head. I reach up and grab both of their hands trying to savor this moment for as long as I can.

"Damien, never forget that just because we're gone, it doesn't mean we're not with you at all times," they say in unison again. "You are our son and that will never change. It's up to you to change the world. Remember that if it ever gets hard, you can rely on your friends for help."

After they say that, they slowly fade away. The warmth of their hands fades with them. I sense their spirit leaving the area and my own spirit getting lighter.

"I Damien Nichols, Son of D'Marcus Carter and Jamila Nichols," I begin to say. "Heir to the House of

Luna, the current Tremauré and the most powerful werewolf on this planet, have a duty to protect my family, my friends and the entirety of the werewolf population. I will do so until my heart stops beating," I proclaim.

I stand on my feet and gaze at the sky for a few minutes before looking back at their headstones. I take a second to inhale before howling for as long as I can. No longer in pain, and happy to take on this responsibility.

I take one more look at their graves and say, "I love you both, thank you for giving me my confidence back and setting my mind right."

Another breeze blows past me and it doesn't send a shiver up my spine. It feels like a warm hug from my parents. I feel my body pulse, starting from my spirit and spreading to my fingertips. The wolf is no longer against me, it is me. I've been fighting myself, and I finally stopped. An alpha who doubts himself is useless to everyone.

I will not doubt myself, it will only get me in more trouble. I have to be able to make those tough decisions, it's what an alpha of the council does and so will I. I'll change the werewolf society from the inside, I just have to be smart about it. Just then I sense a presence coming up from behind me. I don't react to it because there isn't any malicious intent coming from them. I laugh to myself realizing it's Catalina.

"Baby, what are you doing here?" I ask her.

"Abucheo I've been here for a while now," she states.

I turn to her, "How long?"

"Long enough to hear your speech," she giggles.

"Pretty intense if you ask me," Braheem says walking behind her.

I see everyone else approaching, "Wassup D," Omar asks.

"You didn't think that we'd abandon you did you?" Jasmine asks, smiling.

I look at everyone and then I look back at Catalina, "You brought them here?" I ask Catalina.

Catalina nods, "I called them after you left the house. I knew where you were going, so we followed and made sure you said your peace."

I grasp onto her legs, "I'm sorry I should have told you all what I was going through. I was so afraid of what I did and what I might become, so I just shut down."

Catalina lowers herself so we're at eye level and holds up my head. She smiles, as she stares into my eyes, "I don't blame you for shouldering everyone's weight, but you can't hold it all by yourself. That's what we're here for. To help you when you need it. I've been waiting for you to realize that, but after what you said earlier, I had no choice but to push you. You needed to come here and face this all your own."

"Listen to your queen bro," Kahlil says.

I chuckle as I stand up and walk over to everyone. When I approach them they all give me a hug or a dap.

"Y'all I'm sorry too, I shouldn't have closed y'all out," I say.

"Don't worry about it Damien," Jasmine responds. "Like it or not, we're your family before we're your pack."

"She's right, I can't imagine shouldering all of that and still having the ability to function," Braheem adds. "I've had your back since day one and nothing we've been through could change that," Braheem starts to say. "If it wasn't for you, I'd be all alone and probably end up dead or a part of someone else's pack who doesn't care about anyone else's life but their own."

"Like Omar and I were," Chantelle says.

"Or like Nichole and Jasmine and I were," Kiara chimes in.

"I'd probably give into my rage and would've gone on a killing spree if you hadn't talked to me that day," Darius says. "I know I asked you to leave me alone, but I'm honestly glad that you didn't."

'What about me?" I'd probably be a dead carney," Kahlil laughs.

"If anyone should be sorry, it should be us," Jasmine admits.

"Why?" I ask curiously.

"Because we let you shoulder the burden after everything went down, and left you alone when we should have stayed with you."

"It's ok, there were wrongs on both sides," I admit. "We can't let that happen again or our family will fall apart."

"Ight, enough of all this mushy stuff, let's get out of here," Braheem mocks.

I chuckle and agree as Catalina hands me a few tissues to blow my nose and wipe my eyes.

"Why don't we go out for a run and then out to dinner later?" Nichole suggests.

"Sounds like a great plan!" I exclaim.

Catalina kisses me and then we all run from the cemetery and into the nearby woods. We're going to stay together as a pack and as a family for as long as we can. I couldn't wish for anyone better. Before it's out of view, I stop and turn back once more to look at my parents' headstones. I see them waving at me from the top of the hill. All I've gained outweighs what I've lost. I smile as I watch them fade one last time before running into the woods with my pack.

About the Author

As an author I have always believed in following my dreams. By writing I've taken those steps to follow that dream. Every time I write a story for the readers' enjoyment, I put a part of myself out in the world, hoping to inspire others just like me.

If this is the first time you're reading anything from me then please check out any of his previous literary works by online social media. I hope you'll also enjoy my other works of literary work both past, present and future. When I'm not writing or editing, I'm playing video games, spending time with friends or cooking with my wife.

. Please leave me a review and share this with like minded readers, we can build a community together. Maybe one day we'll meet in person.